SCREENING THE NOVEL

INTERMEDIATE

THIS ITEM MAY BE R

D0495236

INSIGHTS

General Editor: Clive Bloom, Lecturer in English and Coordinator of American Studies, Middlesex Polytechnic

Editorial Board: Clive Bloom, Brian Docherty, Gary Day, Lesley Bloom and Hazel Day

Insights brings to academics, students and general readers the very best contemporary criticism on neglected literary and cultural areas. It consists of anthologies, each containing original contributions by advanced scholars and experts. Each contribution concentrates on a study of a particular work, author or genre in its artistic, historical and cultural context.

Published titles

Clive Bloom (*editor*)
JACOBEAN POETRY AND PROSE: Rhetoric, Representation and the Popular Imagination

Clive Bloom, Brian Docherty, Jane Gibb and Keith Shand (*editors*)
NINETEENTH-CENTURY SUSPENSE: From Poe to Conan Doyle

Gary Day and Clive Bloom (*editors*)
PERSPECTIVES ON PORNOGRAPHY: Sexuality in Film and Literature

Brian Docherty (*editor*)
AMERICAN CRIME FICTION: Studies in the Genre
AMERICAN HORROR FICTION: From Brockden Brown to Stephen King

Jeffrey Walsh and James Aulich (*editors*)
VIETNAM IMAGES: War and Representation

Further titles in preparation

Screening the Novel

The Theory and Practice of Literary Dramatization

Robert Giddings

Keith Selby

Chris Wensley

MACMILLAN

First published 1990

Published by
THE MACMILLAN PRESS LTD
Houndmills, Basingstoke, Hampshire RG21 2XS
and London
Companies and representatives
throughout the world

Printed in Hong Kong

British Library Cataloguing in Publication Data
Giddings, Robert, 1935–
Screening the novel: the theory and practice of
literary dramatization. – (Insights).
1. Cinema films and television. Use of adaptations of novels
I. Title II. Series
791.43′75
ISBN 0–333–45792–7 (hardcover)
ISBN 0–333–45793–5 (paperback)

Contents

List of Illustrations

Acknowledgements

Thanks are due to Terrance Dicks and other members of the BBC production team of *Vanity Fair* for their generous cooperation; to Joyce Hawkins for making available original costume designs; to John Adams, of the Drama Department, University of Bristol, for his advice and encouragement; Nancy Williams for her help with picture research and our editors Brian Docherty and Sarah Roberts-West, and to John M. Smith.

Introduction

In the home-light. It was a scene – glowing almost at those
evening pictures at Longfield. Those pictures, photographed on
memory by the summer of our lives, and which no paler after
sun could ever have the power to reproduce. Nothing earthly is
ever reproduced in the same form. . . .

Mrs Craik: *John Halifax, Gentleman* (1857)

The leading ideas which form the substance of this book emerged
while the three of us were involved in teaching scriptwriting
to several generations of undergraduates in the Department of
Communication and Media at the Dorset Institute. A series of quite
basic issues presented themselves when we came to examine the
practice of adapting existing literary texts to the broadcast media.
We found ourselves having to explore considerations of narrative
style and technique, and having to evaluate existing examples of
film and television adaptations of the classics in a new light and
from new perspectives.

We found, obviously, that it was not simply a matter of translating
a story from a literary medium into moving pictures of one kind
or another. We were soon engaged in analysing narrative in one
medium and another, and perceiving what could be done well in
one medium and not in others, in discovering the strengths and
weaknesses of language, sound and pictures.

Historically, the novel succeeded the drama, but absorbed some
of its qualities (character, dialogue) while adding possibilities of its
own (interior monologue, point of view, reflection, comment,
irony). Similarly, film initially followed the basic principles of
narrative prose and copied stage drama. Among the earliest
examples of film used to tell stories are those seeming contradic-
tions-in-terms, silent versions of Shakespeare – such as Forbes
Robertson's *Hamlet* (1913) and Herbert Beerbohm Tree's *Macbeth*
(1916).

The early cinema was called 'The Bioscope' because, it was
claimed, it imitated life, but it was really a synthesis of early
technology and the new electricity. Film may have been a non-

verbal experience, but it based its narrative on the Western European cultural experience of literature. Its basic syntax clearly belonged to the same civilization which produced Shakespeare, Racine, Pope, Fielding, Dickens and Balzac.[1]

There are several basic problems which face the adapter when attempting to render literature in media terms. Even though film, radio and television were quick to establish their own basic techniques and forms, which evolved to satisfy the imperatives of the market and the possibilities of the means of production, distribution and consumption, each new attempt begins afresh in its endeavour to tell in new terms what the writer intended to say.

One of the major problems is that of style. Film, and even more especially television, matured at a time when naturalism and realism were the dominant modes in Western European and North American culture. Consequently, when engaged in translating classics of the past, particularly of the last century, the tendency has been (albeit unconsciously) to translate nineteenth-century literature into a synthetic 'historical' realism in which everything must seem authentic and true to period. Obviously this attempt is bound on occasions to run seriously against the grain of artistic imagining. Dickens, for example, poses very considerable difficulties in this respect. It is easy to assert that Dickens was a 'Victorian novelist' (whatever that is) and to attempt to reconstruct his fiction in the context of some kind of authentic chronologically identifiable moment. Even this has its problems. Costume drama inevitably dresses everybody bang on-period, whereas in any living moment of the past people would have worn old, out-dated clothes, as well as the truly 'fashionable' clothes of the time. Also, the past shared neither our obsession with the crisp cleanliness of clothes, nor the chemistry and technology daily to indulge such mania. Yet our classic serials show people all dressed (seemingly) in their Sunday-best – except criminals and the lower orders, who are appropriately shabby and grubby. Then there is the matter of teeth. These were seldom very clean, and most people lost quite a few in the journey through life, and this loss began quite early. Yet our crisply dressed-in-period-costume actors and actresses grin fulsomely at us with glistening complete sets of teeth.

Then there is spoken language. For some reason or other word got around and was widely credited, that the entire population of last-century England, with the notable exception of the lower and criminal classes, had been star pupils at singularly severe elocution

Not needed when filming about fiction [handwritten marginal note]

classes. The further back we go, the more arch the pronunciation of the English language becomes, and somewhere between the Brontës and Jane Austen we definitely enter the land of prunes and prisms. As with the neurosis for clean clothes, we are only projecting on to the 'past' the assumptions of the present. It is fascinating to note that our modern class structure and the means for the distribution and consumption of culture so distort our perceptions of the past. In 1983 Donald Pleasance gave a much-praised performance in a television play in the role of our great national hero, Dr Samuel Johnson. He exhibited not a trace of a Staffordshire accent. And yet the Great Cham's accent was so thick and strong that David Garrick used to imitate him to his face, saying 'Who's for *poonch?*' and so on.[2] Yet when we do D. H. Lawrence stories and adapt those rugged 'working-class' novels of the fifties and sixties the attempt is always made to get the Nottinghamshire and 'Northern' accents right. Is it the case that our preconceptions condition us into associating certain regional accents with the 'working class'? In a society where the cultural goodies are mainly consumed by the well-to-do must all creative/cultivated persons speak 'good' standard English? If so, it must follow that if Dr Johnson was a scholar and a writer and an Oxford man, then he must speak good South-Eastern English. The media, then, are unwittingly part of an ideological conspiracy in which we are invited to look back at our past through the distortions of our present culture. Boswell himself commented that:

An intermixture of provincial peculiarities may, perhaps, have an agreeable effect, as the notes of different birds concur in the harmony of the grove, and please more than if they were exactly alike.

But no, when recreated by contemporary thespians, figures from the past must all be made to sound like well-bred direct-grant/Oxbridge educated mynah birds from the South of England.

In the case of Dickens there are very complex matters of chronology to consider. Take a recent example in the commendable attempt to bring *Little Dorrit* to the wide screen. An immense effort in decor and costume design has obviously been exerted, and what we see approximates to our conceptions of the 1850s. (The novel was written during May 1855 and June 1857, serialized by Bradbury and Evans in monthly parts between December 1855 and June

1857, when it was also published finally in volume form. The period sense is reinforced by the use of music from Verdi operas – mainly *Rigoletto*, *La Forza del Destino* and *Otello*. And yet it is demonstrably impossible to fit an exact and strict chronology on *Little Dorrit*.

Much of the satirical element – the attacks on government and civil service inefficiencies, and the Merdle scandal, may directly be associated with the conduct of the Crimean War and the swindles and eventual suicide of John Sadleir (1814–56).[3] Much of the action of *Little Dorrit* centres on the Marshalsea Prison, yet this was closed in 1842.[4] Another piece of chronological evidence is given us by John Chivery. When his amorous overtures are rejected by Amy Dorrit in Chapter 18 he goes home, composing on the way a new inscription for a tombstone in St George's Churchyard:

> Here lie the mortal remains of JOHN CHIVERY, Never anything worth mentioning, Who died about the end of the year one thousand eight hundred and twentysix, Of a broken heart, Requesting with his last breath that the word AMY might be inscribed over his ashes, Which was accordingly directed to be done, By his afflicted Parents.

In *Little Dorrit* several threads in Dickens's thinking combine. He is looking back to his own family's experiences when his father was harassed by debt-collectors and eventually imprisoned, spending time in the Marshalsea. This period was in the years 1821–4. John Dickens was imprisoned between February and May 1824. But Charles Dickens is reacting to contemporary occurrences in his private life, as well as to current affairs in the mid-1850s. Among the most important would obviously be his re-meeting Maria Winter (née Beadnall), his childhood sweetheart. She was now a plump and rather silly, scatterbrained lady. She appears as Flora. At the same time his infatuation with the young actress, Ellen Ternan, was growing to an intense passion, fanned by their appearing together in Wilkie Collins's melodrama *The Frozen Deep* which was rehearsed and performed between November and January 1856–7. He was eventually to leave his wife and set up house with Ellen Ternan. This may well be in the background of the sensitive treatment of the love story between Arthur Clennam and Amy Dorrit. He saw Gounod's *Faust* in Paris in 1855, and may well have been so deeply moved by it in recognizing the close parallels between Faust's seduction of the young and innocent Marguerite and his relationship with Ellen Ternan.[5]

The major public events were the Crimean War (January 1853 to March 1856) and the terrible incompetence in British logistics which resulted in so many deaths of servicemen from wounds, infection and disease, and a campaign of public disapproval which led to the resignation of the Prime Minister, Lord Aberdeen. Additional material from current affairs to satirize the British craze for the achievement of quick gains from investment and speculation he found to hand in the financial chicanery, collapse and failure of the Tipperary Bank and the suicide of its chief, John Sadleir, which provided him with the Merdle episodes. This thematic multiplicity, embracing several different time-sequences running concurrently, is very difficult to handle in film terms, partly because of the very specific quality of photography itself.

In moving pictures the visual precision of the image impresses a sense of immediacy, of the here-and-now, which creates a sense of the continuous present. Film is now, as you see it. The very sharpness of this sense of the present time provides for a swift but credible switch of time from past to present. It is this which makes flashback so effective an element in the vocabulary of film. It is difficult to achieve in literary text. (Few would admit it, but isn't this one of the qualities which makes Conrad's novels so difficult to read?) This is the result of the language, of the voice which tells you things. Whether first or third person, there is a narrator between you as the consumer of the text, and the material which is presented as the 'reality' you are invited to imagine. The shifting, imprecise chronology of a literary text has many strengths and possibilities which the skilled writer exploits. But it works against the tendency of moving film which is towards the exact representation of the moment. In translating literature into moving pictures, once-upon-a-time collides with here-and-now.

Two examples may demonstrate this. In *Citizen Kane* (1940) the idea of the gradual decay of John Foster Kane's marriage is conveyed in one brief sequence which is a mixture of several scenes at the breakfast table. These demonstrate film's ability to deploy the nature of time transition. Narrating the story, Kane's friend Leland says:

> She was like all the other girls I knew in dancing school. They were nice girls. Emily was a little nicer. She did her best – Charlie

did his best – well, after the first couple of months they never
saw much of each other except at breakfast. It was a marriage
just like any other marriage.

There then follows a sequence which is a montage of scenes which
cover a period of nine years, from 1901 to 1909. They are played
in the same set – at breakfast table – with only changes in lighting,
special effects outside the window, and wardrobe. The first scene
is early in the marriage. The scene mixes before our eyes and we
are at the same breakfast table a few years later. They sit a little
further apart now. There has been no abrupt shift in their
conversation which has continued over the mix from scene to
scene. But the visual images tell you what you need to know.
There is now a sense of distrust between them. There is a further
mix. Still at the same breakfast table we see Kane and Mrs Kane
further estranged, even as their conversation continues. The scene
mixes again and the couple are separated. There is no connection
between them. Kane is reading his *Enquirer* and Mrs Kane is
reading the *Chronicle*.[6]

It is the strength of that sense of location in time and place,
which is characteristic of the meaning moving film constructs with
the cooperation of its audience, which makes this easeful series of
modulations possible. This is why film is so good at exposition
(notoriously difficult in literary text.) Moving pictures take you
there, to the very place, and show you who is who and what is
what. Film is very good at conveying considerable information and
detail in a short space. As Marshall McLuhan wrote:

> In terms of other media such as the printed page, film has the
> power to store and convey a great deal of information. In an
> instant it presents a scene of landscape with figures that would
> require several pages of prose to describe. In the next instant it
> repeats, and can go on repeating, this detailed information. The
> writer, on the other hand, has no means of holding a mass of
> detail before his reader in so large a bloc or *gestalt*. . . .[7]

On the other hand, the novelist's problems in briefly indicating
the complexities of location and chronological time, free the writer
to deploy irony, *double-entendre*, depth symbolism, with a richer,
roving imagination. Think how many miles of celluloid and what

immensity of cunning in montage would be required to realize these two sentences of William Makepeace Thackeray's which conclude the Waterloo chapter of *Vanity Fair* (1848):

> No more firing was heard at Brussels – the pursuit rolled miles away. Darkness came down on the field and city: and Amelia was praying for George, who was lying on his face, dead, with a bullet through his heart. (*Vanity Fair*, Chapter 32)

There is a temptation, understandably seldom resisted, for the makers of adaptations in terms of moving pictures, to follow the inclination towards the spectacular, to concentrate on what will look good in film. Consequently the memorable moments in many films of the classics are not, as it were, the literary or poetic or dramatic ones. When we think of *Henry V* (1944), for example, what comes to mind is not one of the great soliloquies, or Henry's prayer before Agincourt:

> I Richard's body have interred anew,
> And on it have bestowed more contrite tears
> Than from it issued forced drops of blood.
> Five hundred poor I have in yearly pay,
> Who twice a day their withered hands hold up
> Toward heaven, to pardon blood: and I have built
> Two chantries, where the sad and solemn priests
> Sing still for Richard's soul. . . .
>   (*Henry V* iv, 1, 315–22)

These lines, which Shakespearian scholars and critics would consider among the most beautiful in the play, moving, mellifluous and full of power, are cut from the film version. The memorable moments in Olivier's film are the lowering of the Constable of France on to his steed, the charge of the French cavalry and the exciting 'Whoooooosh!!' as the English bowmen's arrows wing their deadly way on to the galloping French horsemen. It is significant that as a solution to the 'problem' of the Shakespearian soliloquy it was considered an effective wheeze to have the camera focus on Olivier's motionless-but-deep-thinking-face as we *hear* on the soundtrack his intoning voice:

> Upon the king! Let us our lives, our souls,
> Our debts, our careful wives,
> Our children and our sins, lay on the king:
> We must bear all. . . .
>   (*Henry V* iv, 1, 250–53)

In *Great Expectations* the noticeably Dickensian moments are very difficult to realize in cinematic terms – the slice of bread-and-butter down Pip's trouserleg and its associations with guilt, the animal way in which the convict on the marshes attacks his food, the gloomy poeticism of the prison hulks:

> By the light of the torches, we saw the black Hulk lying out a little way from the mud of the shore, like a wicked Noah's ark. Cribbed and barred and moored by massive rusty chains, the prison-ship seemed in my young eyes to be ironed like the prisoners. We saw the boat go along side, and we saw him taken up the side and disappear. Then, the ends of the torches were flung hissing into the water, and went out, as if it were all over with him. (*Great Expectations*, Chapter 5)

What we recall after seeing David Lean's film are the marvellous cinematic moments – Pip's scream as he is grabbed by the convict, the lock of hair on the forehead which identifies Herbert Pocket as the boy Pip fought in Miss Havisham's garden, the daunting figure of Jaggers (scarcely described in the novel), the superb artwork which puts Satis House before our eyes, the terrible steamer accident during which the convicts fight. These are scarcely Dickensian touches, but they are moments of which any film-maker would justly be proud. And they are the kind of things in which cinematography excels itself.

There are occasions when the effort outclasses itself. There is a fine example in the ball-before-Waterloo sequence in *Vanity Fair*. Thackeray wrote these scenes in 1847–8. He was a mid-Victorian novelist looking back on events which happened when he was scarcely four years old. The whole Wellington/Waterloo myth was still constructing. By the time *Vanity Fair* was filmed by the BBC Classic Serials department the popular memory and folk imagination had absorbed several celebrated reconstructions of the 'eve of Waterloo'. The modern mass media took over, expanded and fully realized those glamorous moments before the slaughter

as two vast armies met on 18 June 1815, which Byron had already
immortalized in 1816:

> There was a sound of revelry by night,
> And Belgium's capital had gathered then
> Her beauty and her chivalry, and bright
> The lamps shone o'er fair women and brave men.
> A thousand hearts beat happily; and when
> Music arose with its voluptuous swell,
> Soft eyes looked love to eyes which spoke again,
> And all went merry as a marriage bell;
>   But hush! hark! a deep sound strikes like a rising knell!
> Did ye not hear it? No; 'twas but the wind,
> Or the car rattling o'er the stony street;
> On with the dance! let joy be unconfined;
> No sleep till morn, when Youth and Pleasure meet
> To chase the glowing Hours with flying feet –
> But hark! – that heavy sound breaks in once more,
> As if the clouds its echo would repeat;
> And nearer, clearer, deadlier than before!
>   Arm! Arm! it is – the cannon's opening roar!
>   (*Childe Harold's Pilgrimage* Canto III: 21–2)

This refers to the Duchess of Richmond's ball, actually held on
15/16 June, the eve of the battle of Quatre Bras.[8]

Quatre Bras was an important preliminary encounter before
Waterloo. One of Napoleon's commanders, Michel Ney, duc
d'Elchingen, Marshal of France, had been ordered to halt Wellington's troops at Quatre Bras at the same time as Buonaparte himself
was to deal with the Prussian armies at Ligny, eight miles away.
The Prussians were beaten but Wellington's powerful resistance
prevented Ney's sending reinforcements or reliable intelligence
that would have made the defeat decisive – the full price for this
was paid at the final engagement of 18 June. But the legend was
born that on the evening before Waterloo the leading lights of
society danced away the hours as one by one the military commanders slipped quietly but bravely out into the night to join their
regiments as they departed to fight the battle of Waterloo. The
legend snugly accommodates itself alongside other beloved 'historical' moments in which British warriors seem laconically to respond
to threatening national enemies but then proceed to give them the

thrashing they deserve, such as Drake's 'There is plenty of time to win this game, and to thrash the Spaniards too' as the Spanish Armada approached, and Nelson's 'I have only one eye. . . . I have a right to be blind sometimes: . . . I really do not see the signal!' at the battle of Copenhagen.[9] The Waterloo Ball legend has been reinforced by several celebrated film treatments such as *The Iron Duke* (1934), *Marie Walewska* (1937), *Waterloo* (1970) (as well as the previous film version of Thackeray's novel, *Becky Sharp* (1935) which was, incidentally, the first feature film in three-colour Technicolor).

Thackeray's treatment of the Duchess of Richmond's Ball in *Vanity Fair* contributed, in its day and in its way, to the gradual construction of the popular folk memory of the 'Ball Before Waterloo'. In fact, his treatment of the Ball is extremely interesting. He asserts that it was a celebrated event:

> There never was, since the days of Darius, such a brilliant train of camp-followers as hung around the Duke of Wellington's army in the Low Countries, in 1815; and led it dancing and feasting, as it were, up to the very brink of battle. A certain ball which a noble Duchess gave at Brussels on the 15th of June in the above named year is historical. . . . (*Vanity Fair*, Chapter 29)

He goes on to sketch in the details, emphasizing the glitz of the occasion, the social glamour of the guests and the difficulty of obtaining tickets. He then places the leading figures of the novel, George, Amelia, Dobin, Rawdon and others, in this context and provides a bit of drama and dialogue about Rawdon's gambling, Amelia's social naiveté and the impression Becky makes, and leaves it at that as far as action is concerned. The main matter of importance here is the exposure of George's state of mind immediately before these final military engagements, and Thackeray goes to a lot of trouble to show us what is in George's mind. This is not the stuff of which splendid sequences in costume drama are made, and quite understandably there is the temptation to 'realize' the Duchess's Ball in terms of film, even though the treatment may fly, not only in the face of the textual evidence in the original novel supposedly in the process of being adapted for moving film, but in the face of history itself.

A great deal is actually known about this famous ball. There is an excellent and detailed account by Sir William Fraser.[10] The Ball took place in what had been a coach-house, but was then a single, low, whitewashed brick building with square pillars and low ceilings. It was far from the sumptuous, chandelier-decked, glittering mini-palace of legend. According to Fraser's account the company was splendid, with numerous aristocrats and military commanders, numbering over two hundred persons, plus servants.

Although Thackeray does not make much of all this, such scenes of high-class socializing have been the very stuff of costume drama from its earliest days. Consequently the temptation was to make a great deal of do in the BBC version. It was beautifully done and was wholly convincing. It was filmed at Waddesdon Manor, in Buckinghamshire, which was built in the style of a Loire *château*, for Baron Ferdinand de Rothschild. It was designed in the Renaissance style by Gabriel-Hippolyte Destailleur between 1874 and 1889.[11] The sequence in the BBC's 1988 version of *Vanity Fair* looks authentic and although it was only a piece of gratuitous schmalzing, it furthered the narrative and made the points Thackeray wanted to make. But what is its justification? Were the film-makers trying to be true to the novelist? Or trying historically accurately to reproduce the moment the novelist had tried to recreate? The fact is and should be admitted, that film-makers, TV classical serial makers and all the rest of them, have their own goals and imperatives, and that the cry of being 'true to the text' is not defensible, and need not be defended. We enjoy Verdi's *Macbetto*, *Luisa Miller*, *Don Carlo*, *Otello* and *Falstaff* as Italian operas, and do not judge them as 'versions' of original works by Schiller and Shakespeare. Why don't we enjoy and judge films of Dickens, Thackeray, Jane Austen and company *as films or television drama*? Is it because the novel-as-film/TV-serial is a separate *genre*? It seemed to us that these were absolutely basic questions which needed airing.

We found insufficient lecture and workshop time to cover most of these points as they came up. Hence the book. We needed to concentrate on fundamental theories and approaches to the screening of novels, to explore how novels worked as texts, and then to examine existing examples of attempts to translate narrative prose fiction into moving film and to place these endeavours in the wider cultural discourse of the media's attempts to reconstruct the past.

Robert Giddings
Keith Selby
Chris Wensley

Notes

1. See Robert Giddings, 'The Writing on the Igloo Walls' in Alan Bold (ed.), *The Quest for Le Carré* (London: Vision Press, 1988), pp. 188ff and Walter Ong, *Orality and Literacy – The Technologizing of the Word* (London: Methuen, 1982), pp. 141ff.
2. Christopher Hibbert, *The Personal History of Samuel Johnson* (London: Longman, 1971), p. 33.
3. John Butt and Kathleen Tillotson, *Dickens at Work* (London: Methuen, 1968), pp. 226–30; and Alan Bold and Robert Giddings, *Who Was Really Who in Fiction* (London: Longman, 1987), p. 214.
4. Ben Weinreb and Christopher Hibbert (eds), *The London Encyclopaedia* (London: Macmillan, 1983), pp. 499–50.
5. Edgar Johnson, *Charles Dickens – His Tragedy and Triumph* (London: Hamish Hamilton, 1952), Volume 2, pp. 1130–31.
6. William Kuhns, *The Moving Picture Book* (Dayton, Ohio: Pflaum, 1975), pp. 16–17 and Pauline Kael: *The Citizen Kane Book* (London: Paladin, 1978), pp. 183–9.
7. Marshall McLuhan: *Understanding Media* (London: Routledge & Kegan Paul, 1969), pp. 307ff.
8. David Howarth, *A Near Run Thing – The Day of Waterloo* (London: William Collins, 1968), pp. 32–4.
9. Drake's remark is quoted and authenticated in *The Dictionary of National Biography* and seems ultimately to be based on the account in William Oldys' *Life of Ralegh* which appeared in his edition of Walter Ralegh's *History of the World* published in 1736:

   The tradition goes, that Drake would needs see the game up; but was soon prevail'd on to go and play out the rubber with the Spaniards.

   William Oldys (1696–1761) was Norroy King of Arms and a distinguished antiquary and an early authority on the Elizabethan period. He amassed a considerable library. His notes for the life of Shakespeare were used by Isaac Reed, the distinguished Shakespearian scholar, in his edition of Nicholas Rowe's *Life of Shakespeare*. He would seem a reliable source for Drake's remark. Nelson's turning a blind eye is recorded first in Robert Southey's *Life of Nelson* (1813), Chapter 5.
10. Sir William Fraser, *The Waterloo Ball* (London: Harvey, 1897).
11. See Peter Furtado et al., *The Country Life Book of Castles and Houses in Britain* (London: Newnes, 1986), pp. 19 and 156.

1

The Literature/Screen Debate: an Overview

This chapter provides an overview of the critical debate concerning the transfer of novels into television and film drama. The major issues are outlined and discussed, with particular reference to the adaptation or dramatization[1] of prose fiction into the medium of film and television. The majority of the issues discussed refer equally to film and television, since the concern is generally with the 'visualization' of the prose text; however, certain differences between the two visual media will become evident.

It has become traditional in books concerned with screening the novel to open with the statements by Joseph Conrad, the novelist, and D. W. Griffith, the film-maker, which seem almost to echo one another: 'The task I'm trying to achieve above all is to make you see', Griffith is reported to have said in 1913 when outlining his aims as a film-maker.[2] Sixteen years earlier Conrad had stated: 'My task . . . is by the power of the written word, to make you hear, to make you feel – it is before all, to make you see.'[3]

To this, one might add Herbert Read's advice to writers in 1945:

If you asked me to give you the most distinctive quality of good writing, I would give it to you in this one word: VISUAL. Reduce the art of writing to its fundamentals, and you come to this single aim: to convey images by means of words. But to convey images. To make the mind see. . . . That is a definition of good literature. . . . It is also a definition of the ideal film.[4]

Morris Beja in *Film and Literature*[5] argues that written stories (novels) and filmed stories (film/TV) are but two forms of a single art: the art of narrative literature, which he defines as any work which recounts a sequence of events, a story. However, any attempt to transfer this sequence of events from one medium to another is not a simple process. As William Luhr and Peter Lehman have pointed out:

1

The narrative in a novel or a film provides only one of many
elements that cohere into the work. Abstracted from its place in
the work, the narrative remains simply an element – it carries
none of the work's value with it. . . . The reputation of a classic
novel often led film makers to assume they could reconstruct
the major events of the narrative and that the novel's 'greatness'
would carry the rest.[6]

They go on to argue that although the same 'story' may be told in
any number of ways, 'once the work is produced, the pre-existent
story becomes aesthetically irrelevant.'[7] Luhr and Lehmann support
such a view by reference to Tomashevsky's distinction between
story and plot: story is a pre-text for plot; story is logical and
chronological, whereas plot is organized by the artist into a
sequence to suit his own purposes.

Tomashevsky also describes the concept of a 'motif' as being,
'the meaning behind an irreducible part of the work', distinguishing
between 'bound motifs' which cannot be omitted without disturb-
ing the chronological chain of events, and 'free motifs' which may
be omitted in a summary.[8] A necessary corollary of this is, as Luhr
and Lehman point out, that an adaptation will usually include all
the bound motifs, but may omit the free motifs, even though these
may have been crucial to the original's impact.

Although both novel and film/TV share this storytelling function,
there are significant differences in the methods of production, and
in the consumption of their various products. Novels are produced
by individual writers and are 'consumed' by a relatively small,
literate audience. Film and television are the result of groups of
people engaged in industrial production, and are consumed by a
disparate, mass audience. George Bluestone has refined this
position a little by pointing out that the values and attitudes of the
small middle-class reading public might be incomprehensible to
the mass film public, and that the passage of time between the
production of the novel and the subsequent film will intensify
this.[9] Cinema and television production is highly costly, and to
justify this expenditure, audiences must be large; consequently,
these commercial pressures, combined with the restrictions imposed by the more overt censorship of these mass media, create
different requirements from those experienced by the novelist. It
is the manner in which the film industry attempts to manipulate
the process of adaptation that Bertolt Brecht described so precisely

in *The Threepenny Lawsuit*: 'we put ourselves in the position of a man who lets his laundry be washed in a dirty gutter, and then complains that it has been ruined'.[10]

However, in a pamphlet published by the BFI, Philip Simpson provides a necessary corrective to the romantic ideal of the novelist in sole control of his creative and aesthetic endeavours whilst the film and television-maker is engaged in factory-line, profit-driven labour. As he points out, early novelists were paid for each page produced, and Dickens's episodic serials meant strict editing for length, with the shape determined externally. Film-makers such as Jean-Luc Godard and Alfred Hitchcock, he suggests, can produce highly individual work. He discusses the production and consumption of the novel and film of *Jane Eyre* to illustrate his point.

The novel appeared in 1847, was a critical success and was circulated by the commercial libraries. But, although novels were a popular form at that time, the evidence suggests that *Jane Eyre* would be read only by a middle-class readership amongst whom a high percentage were women. *Jane Eyre*, the film, based upon an adaptation by Aldous Huxley, was made in 1944 at a time when cinema was massively popular in the United States and Great Britain, particularly among women. Novels were published in three volumes in 1847 and read by a small readership with the time for a leisured read of a morally significant text. Hollywood films in 1944 usually had to be around 90 minutes in length and were viewed by a mass audience seeking entertainment in wartime, an audience with whom melodramas were particularly popular. When we look at this book and this film today we should be aware of the differences in the contexts of production and consumption before we begin the comparison of each text.[11]

This is a view developed by Dudley Andrew, who asks:

> What conditions exist in film style and film culture to warrant or demand the use of literary prototypes? . . . The choices of the mode of adaptation and the prototypes suggest a great deal about the cinema's sense of its role and aspirations from decade to decade. Moreover, the stylistic strategies developed. . . . not only are symptomatic of a period's style, but may crucially alter that style.[12]

Eric Rentschler similarly justifies his choice of film adaptations by asking:

Why do artists adapt certain material at certain times? . . . The major impetus linking the articles has been to expand the field of adaptation study so as to include sociological, theoretical, and historical dimensions, and to bring a livelier regard for inter-textuality to the study of German film and literature . . . the ways in which film-makers in Germany have engaged – and been engaged by literary history, an exchange conditioned by a larger general history.[13]

The length of time necessary for a viewer or reader to consume the product is also a significant element in any comparison. A novel will commonly be several hundred pages long, taking a reader several hours, whereas an average feature film may only last an hour or two. Also, the reader of the novel is in control of the process: he can pause at will, check back over incidents and facts, and reflect upon the action. The viewer of the film, unlike the solitary reader, is involved in a collective experience, in which the action presses relentlessly on; there is no opportunity for pause or recap. With regard to television, the situation is somewhere between the experience of novel reading and film-viewing; a television adaptation of a novel will often devote several hours to its material, often in weekly serial form, and in addition, the availability of video cassette recordings is now giving the viewer some of the flexibility of consumption previously enjoyed exclus-ively by the reader: the ability to pause at will and to check forwards and backwards through the material. As Morris Beja points out:

> When a three-hundred-page novel is made into a two or three-hour movie, a great deal will have to be sacrificed. Less will be lost in a television serial, to be sure, which may last from eight to ten or even twelve hours. . . . In one respect the quality of the experience in watching a serial television version of a novel will undeniably be closer to reading most novels than a feature film can be: for it will be something we come back to periodically, rather than something we complete in a single sitting.[14]

The transmission of the experience from producer to consumer is also significantly different. As Martin Esslin[15] has pointed out, when we read there is a linear progression, ordered and controlled by the reader. In dramatic forms, including film and television, the words follow this structure, but the other signs come at the viewer simultaneously, and the director or designer can hardly control the order or intensity of interpretation. Jonathan Miller, however, suggests that in one sense the experiences undergone by a viewer and a reader are not dissimilar:

> In fact, although the television viewer is unaware of it, when watching the screen he undergoes an experience similar to reading narrative prose. Like sentences which automatically exclude whatever they do not refer to, movie shots eliminate what they do not show. The reader of a written narrative is just as unaware of the succession of separate sentences as the television viewer is of the alternation of discontinuous shots. In both cases, what gives the artwork its coherent textuality is the way that the reader of one and the spectator of the other can identify referential implications that cross the boundaries between consecutive but discontinuous sentences or shots.[16]

The manner in which these 'referential implications' are communicated, however, is central to any discussion of adaptation; clearly, as a sign system, the word on the page is different from the screen.

Charles Peirce and his successor Roman Jakobson identified three types of sign: icon, index and symbol. When any communication system refers to an object, person, concept and so on (the 'signified'), it employs the signs at its disposal (the 'signifier'). An icon is a sign which represents an object mainly by its similarity to it; the relationship is not an arbitrary one: a photograph of a man will resemble the man himself. An index is a sign which points to another object; in other words, it suggests an existential bond between itself and its object. An example is the 'torch of knowledge' sign formerly used to indicate a school. The third sign, the symbol, can only be understood by convention; its does not resemble its object, nor possess any bond; there is no immediate relationship with the object, other than an agreed one among users of the sign; for example, English speakers agree that the letters c-a-t are the symbol for a domestic feline pet, and such agreement has the force of linguistic law.[17]

In film and television, iconic and indexical signs predominate, with the symbolic – the codes, and 'grammar' of film and television – secondary. In prose, the symbolic sign is used exclusively. These distinctions are at the heart of the debates carried on by writers about film concerning realism and expressionism in the cinema: André Bazin, for example, stresses cinema's ability to reveal, to create a perfect aesthetic illusion of reality, whereas Christian Metz insists that the aesthetic of cinema must refer back to an agreed code to achieve its full meaning.

Clearly, however, the film or television image is predominantly iconic whereas words in a novel are symbolic; in other words, the film or television image implies a close relationship between signifier and signified, compared to the arbitrary relationship of verbal language. The image, therefore, is specifically representational: not 'a room', but a specific room; not 'a bird', but a swallow.

This apparent ability to achieve precision, exactness and 'reality' was, Philip Simpson argues, also an influence upon the initial development of the novel, just as it excited film-makers. He shows how early novels broke away from the previous traditions of fiction, focusing on individual human experience and the view of the world obtained from sense perceptions; place became stressed also, as well as time, what E. M. Forster calls 'life by time'. Language was valued less for its own qualities than as a 'referential medium' to convey facts, in other words, its realism.[18] Cinema, and by implication television, have taken over this role:

This is because of the predominantly indexical/iconic character of most films, and 'the illusion of reality' which the cinema provides. The cinema seems to fulfil the age-old dream of providing a means of communication in which the signals employed are themselves identical or near-identical with the world which is the object of thought. Reality is, so to speak, filtered and abstracted in the mind, conceptualised, and then this conceptualisation of reality is mapped on to signals which reflect the original reality itself, in a way which words, for instance, can never hope to match. . . . Hence the immense attraction of realist aesthetics for the theorists of the cinema. . . .[19]

With regard to non-iconic signs developed exclusively by film and television – in other words, the so-called 'grammar' of the screen – Martin Esslin identifies the following:

1) Signs derived from the camera:
    (a) Static shots – long, CU etc.

    (b) Panning shots
    (c) Travelling shots
    (d) Slow motion and accelerated motion.
2) Signs derived from the linking of shots:
    (a) Dissolve
    (b) Cross fade
    (c) Split screen
    (d) Sharp cut.
3) Signs derived from editing:
    (a) Montage
    (b) Rhythmic flow of images.[20]

Eisenstein, however, describes how early film-makers, particularly D. W. Griffith, found hints in Charles Dickens's novels for all their major innovations. He finds examples in Dickens's novels of montage, dissolve, superimposed shot, close-up, pan and so on:

> Let Dickens and the whole ancestral array, going back as far as the Greeks and Shakespeare, be superfluous reminders that both Griffith and our cinema prove our origins to be not solely as of Edison and his fellow inventors, but as based on an enormous cultured past. . . .[21]

Joseph Frank notes how film's ability to manipulate time through flashbacks and a narrative which develops several events simultaneously can be traced back to Flaubert's *Madame Bovary* and the County Fair scene, in which three levels of action unfold together.[22]

Others looked for other influences. Bruce Morissette points out:

> As soon as Eisenstein and his successors came to general agreement that the closest generic affiliation of film . . . was with the novel, most of the prevailing arguments for and against this rapprochement were quickly proposed and discussed. Eisenstein sought principally to find in pre-cinematic novels the formal sources for film techniques. The search for literary analogues to camera angles, analytical scene cutting, flashbacks, dissolves, and most of the other recognized film effects (even speed-up and slow motion) led some critics back into history, from the nineteenth-century novel all the way to Homer and Virgil, whose

Aeneid was studied by Paul Leglise in a book-length essay as an
'oeuvre de pré-cinéma'. Almost at once, other critics reacted
against the setting up of literary sources for film forms by arguing
instead the influence of film on the novel. This idea, still strong,
was in turn modified by the view that the true relation between
the two genres is one of convergencies, or reciprocal interchan-
ges, with film and novel sharing new ways of formalizing
fiction.[23]

For example, Beja suggests that the effects of modernism on film
and the novel have led to a move away from a linear chronological
progression in both media. As Jean-Luc Godard said, 'Films should
have a beginning, a middle and an end, but not necessarily in that
order!'
Keith Cohen sees close relationships between the very sign
systems themselves:

A basic assumption I make is that both words and images are
sets of signs that belong to systems and that, at a certain level
of abstraction, these systems bear resemblances to one another.
More specifically within each such system there are many
different codes (perceptual, referential, symbolic). What makes
possible, then, a study of the relation between two separate sign
systems, like novel and film, is the fact that the same codes may
re-appear in more than one system.[24]

And Dudley Andrew comments:

This suggests that despite their very different material character,
despite even the ways we process them at the primary level,
verbal and cinematic signs share a common fate: that of being
condemned to connotation . . . thus for example, imagery
functions equivalently in films and novels. Narrative codes
always function at the level of implication or connotation. Hence
they are potentially comparable in a novel and a film. The
story can be the same if the narrative units (character, events,
motivations, consequences, context, viewpoint, imagery and so
on) are produced equally in two works. Now this production is,
by definition, a process of connotation and implication. The
analysis of adaptation, then, must point to the achievement of

equivalent narrative units in the absolutely different semiotic systems of film and language.[25]

Even if it can be shown that the two sign systems do in fact influence and to some extent replicate one another's methods of narration, there continues to exist a constant debate between theorists from both areas as to the primacy of each particular system. Cinema with its vaudeville and fairground origins struggled in its early years for respectability, which partly explains its desire to acquire some of the novel's apparent cultural distinction by absorbing and adapting novels for the screen. Equally, television in its early years was regarded as a markedly inferior art form compared to theatre and the novel. Consequently, one frequently finds sharply polarized views, such as the following:

A well-made film requires interpretation while a well-made novel may only need understanding. . . . The cinematic world invites – even requires conceptualisation. The images presented to us . . . are narrational blueprints for a fiction that must be constructed by the viewer's narrativity.[26]

A generation nurtured on the visual is less inclined to bother with the visual of print; the photo-visual gives one a greater sense of being 'in' something; it requires much more imagination to read. Camera-vision cripples the use of the mind's eye. . . . It is all there for us to see, not to imagine.[27]

Despite such strongly-expressed polarities, however, there has nevertheless been a close relationship between the two media, in terms of material originally published in prose narrative, but subsequently adapted for the screen. There do not, however, seem to be any universally-accepted principles which may be applied when examining such transfers. Brian McFarlane stresses the 'sheer improbability that an illusion of reality created in one form (i.e. the novel) could be re-created in another (i.e. film or television) without major change'.[28] And critics frequently warn viewers or readers against expectations of close fidelity between prose source and visual drama; Luhr and Lehman note that:

Criticism of films using novels as a source will frequently centre on their 'fidelity' to the events of the novel, not on their artistic integrity. References are constantly made to what is 'left out' or 'changed', instead of what is there.[29]

George Bluestone similarly reminds his readers that it is wrong to assume:

a separable content which may be detached and reproduced . . . that incidents and characters are interchangeable or that the novel is a norm and that the film deviates at its peril . . . for changes are inevitable the moment one abandons the linguistic for the visual medium.[30]

Luhr and Lehman also stress the requirement for the finished product to have its own integrity:

The basic aesthetic imperative is to approach a work through the attributes of the work itself and not to assume it to be in any important sense derivative because it bears resemblance to a prior work. If it is derivative, if it makes no sense without recourse to a prior text . . . then it is not aesthetically realised. If it is aesthetically realised, then its use of source material is of historical, not aesthetic interest.[31]

George Linden, whilst agreeing with this, seems to see the film adapter almost as a missionary working on behalf of the novel:

A successful adaptation of a novel should not be the book. Nor should it be a substitute for the book. If it is truly successful, it should be a work of art in its own right which excites the reader to go re-experience that work in another medium: the novel.[32]

Many critics have attempted to describe and classify the types of adaptation from novel to screen which are undertaken. Morris Beja sees two main classifications:

If we may oversimplify for the sake of discussion, there are probably two basic approaches to the whole question of adaptation. The first approach asks that the integrity of the original work – the novel, say – be preserved, and therefore that it should not be tampered with and should in fact be uppermost in the adapter's mind. The second approach feels it proper and in fact necessary to adapt the original work freely, in order to create – in the different medium that is now being employed – a new, different work of art with its own integrity.[33]

Michael Klein and Gillian Parker identify three types of adaptation: first, 'most films of classic novels attempt to give the impression of being faithful, that is literal, translations'; their second category 'retains the core of the structure of the narrative while significantly re-interpreting, or in some cases de-constructing the source text'; and the third 'regards the source merely as raw material, as simply the occasion for an original work.'[34] For category one, they cite as evidence the film *Tom Jones*; for category two, *Barry Lyndon*, reinterpreted as a modern parable of class alienation; and for category three, *Apocalypse Now* broadly dramatised from Joseph Conrad's *Heart of Darkness*.

Geoffrey Wagner also points out three methods of dramatization: he defines as his first category:

Transposition – in which a novel is directly given on the screen, with the minimum of apparent interference. This has been the most dominant and most pervasive method . . . it has also been the least satisfactory . . . and typically puerile. . . . The film was envisaged as a book illustration, an effect frequently heightened by an opening in which the pages of the original are turned over.

The second category of translation he identifies as 'Commentary':

This is where an original is taken and either purposely or inadvertently altered in some respect. It could also be called a re-emphasis or re-structure. . . . This seems to represent more of an infringement on the work of another than an analogy which may simply take a fiction as a point of departure. Yet film can make authentic reconstructions in the spirit of so many cinematic footnotes to the original.

Finally, he discusses 'Analogy':

To judge whether or not a film is a successful adaptation of a novel is to evaluate the skill of its makers in striking analogous attitudes and in finding analogous rhetorical techniques . . .

analogy must represent a fairly considerable departure for the purpose of making another work of art . . . an analogy cannot be indicated as a violation of a literary original since the director has not attempted (or has only minimally attempted) to reproduce the original.[35]

Wagner provides many examples, among which are Robert Stevenson's film of *Jane Eyre* (1944) as a transposition; Mike Nichols' *Catch-22* (1970) as a commentary and Luchino Visconti's *Death in Venice* (1971) as an analogy.

Dudley Andrew also identifies three types of adaptation from prose to screen, and labels them 'Borrowing, Intersecting and Transforming'.[36] 'Borrowing' implies no question of an attempt to replicate the original work; instead, the audience calls up new or powerful aspects of a cherished work, as in the medieval Mystery plays from the Gospel, or Verdi's *Otello*. 'Intersection' he defines as a refusal to adapt: rather, an attempt to present the distinctness of the original text, and to give it its own life in the cinema, involving an interplay between the aesthetic forms of one period and the cinematic techniques of our period. His examples include filmed plays, and many of the films of Pier-Paulo Pasolini. His third category, 'Fidelity or Transformation' aims to reproduce something essential about an original text, by which the film tries to measure up to a literary work, and ultimately the skeleton of the original becomes, more or less thoroughly, the skeleton of a film.

Keith Cohen looks for a more radical response from the film-maker to his literary material: he calls for 'subversive adaptations':

Adaptation is a truly artistic feat only when the new version carries with it a hidden criticism of its model, or at least renders implicit (through a process we should call 'deconstruction') certain key contradictions implanted or glossed over in the original. . . . The adaptations must subvert its original, perform a double and paradoxical job of masking and unveiling its source, or else the pleasure it provides will be nothing more than that of seeing words changed into images. Furthermore, the specificities of the new sign system . . . require that reproduction take full cognizance of the change of sign. For it is these specificities that make possible the truly radical reproduction that exploits the semiotic transformation in order to redistribute the formative materials of the original and to set them askew.[37]

Morris Beja concludes rather lyrically, and somewhat imprecisely:

> Of course what a film takes from a book matters; but so does what it brings to a book. When it brings dedication and talent (or, if we are truly fortunate, genius), the result can be what André Bazin calls 'the novel so to speak multiplied by the cinema'. The resulting film is then not a betrayal and not a copy, not an illustration and not a departure. It is a work of art that relates to the book from which it derives, yet is also independent, an artistic achievement that is in some mysterious way the 'same' as the book but also something other: perhaps something less but perhaps something more as well.[38]

Dudley Andrew, on the other hand, widens the debate to include all representational films:

> Every representational film adapts a prior conception. Indeed, the very term 'representation' suggests the existence of a model. Adaptation delimits representation by insisting on the cultural status of the model, on its existence in the mode of the text or the already textualised. In the case of those texts explicitly termed 'adaptations', the cultural model which the cinema represents is already treasured as a representation in another sign system.[39]

Eric Rentschler comments:

> In this way, adaptation in its widest sense amounts to an act of understanding, the attempt to read one's own meaning into and out of the texted realities that surround us, to shape a personal discourse from the stories and history with which we live.[40]

Restricting the discussion, however, only to screen adaptations from literary texts, there are certain specific problems of transfer which require analysis. These include points of view, time, imagery, psychological realism, and 'selective perception'.

Point of view, the perspective from which a story is told, is clearly important in all narrative art, giving meaning, for example, to a painting or to a novel, each art-form evolving its own styles to convey point of view. Joseph Boggs[41] identifies five modes by which the novel exploits point of view: first person; omniscient author; limited third person (in which the narrator is privileged

and omniscient but only on one character; dramatic point of view
(in which the reader is not conscious of the narrator, since he does
not comment but merely describes the scene); and stream of
consciousness, interior monologue. He adds that these methods
are not all available to the camera; for example, first-person novel
point of view is not the same as seeing the action from the camera;
in the novel, the narrator tells and the reader listens, but there
is not equivalence, rather a warm intimate relationship. Bruce
Morissette[42] develops the point, showing how the first-person
narrative presents itself as reality, frequently employing devices
such as telling someone or writing a diary, often causing a close
involvement of the reader with the events and the characters; he
suggests, however, that it can also lead to alienation: we listen but
do not speak and thus fully identify, or we may object to the moral
viewpoint of the narrator.

The issue for film and television adaptations is how to convey
this subtlety of point of view. Brian McFarlane summarizes the
problem nicely: 'If the film is to have any value of its own, it will
need to have its own point of view, its own sense of the significance
of what it is presenting.'[43]

George Linden also outlines the issues without offering any
immediate practical solutions:

> For a film to be an adequate rendition of a novel, it must not
> only present the actions and events of the novel but also capture
> the attitudes and subjective tones toward those events. This the
> novelist can do quite freely by using description or point of view.
> It is much more difficult for the director, since he must either
> discover or create visual equivalents for the narrator's evalu-
> ations. . . . If the tone of a work is lost, the work is lost; but the
> tone of a novel must be rendered in an aural/visual patterning
> instead of by the use of descriptive dialogue or other narrative
> device. The author's intellectual viewpoint must become the
> director's emotional standpoint. . . . Of course, if the director
> succeeds in his effort, he will have produced not a copy of the
> novel, but a new object.[44]

Colin MacCabe argues that the narrative of the film itself conveys
the artist's voice, and shapes our responses. He argues that just
as the narrative prose surrounding the dialogue of the characters
is a 'metalanguage' which enables the writer to direct the reader's

responses to what the characters are saying, so:

> The camera shows us what happens – it tells us the truth against which we can measure the discourses. . . . This narrative of events – the knowledge which the film provides of how things really are – is the meta language in which we can talk of the various characters in the film.[45]

Bruce Morissette makes a similar point:

> The camera becomes an 'existence' that appropriates and becomes in the film a point of view outside any mental content within a character or narrator or neutral 'third observer'. The point of view passes in a way to the spectator himself, who becomes with the aid of the camera, a new kind of fictional god: one who, if not omniscient, can nevertheless move about with seemingly magic powers. . . .[46]

In fact, the point of view of the camera can change many times during a narrative; also cutting and editing can cause frequent and extreme shifts in perspective, just as depth of field, focus, and zooms can specify particular characters or objects, and montage can create mood and emotion. Film and television can pretend to show everything without authorial intervention, achieving Henry James's desire to replace the omniscient narrator, but first-person point of view is notoriously difficult to carry off successfully, although attempts have been made to suggest that the central character's eye is the camera lens.[47] Multiple points of view, however, always cause problems, as Geoffrey Wagner points out:

> We cannot in cinema play with too many points of view; the imagistic associations aroused would begin to be meaningless, would cease to contribute to structural unity and general sense.[48]

The screen's ability to convey time also deserves consideration: 'the novel has three tenses; the film has only one.'[49] Similarly, Robbe-Grillet in the introduction to his script for *Last Year at Marienbad* comments:

> The essential characteristic of the image is its presentness. Whereas literature has a whole gamut of grammatical tenses. . . .

by its nature what we see on the screen is in the act of happening, we are given the gesture itself, not an account of it.[50]

It is the 'tenselessness' of the visual image that George Linden finds of particular interest:

A novel is a remembrance of things past; a film is a remembrance of things present. . . . While the novel is a narrative that deploys past events moving towards a present, a film directly displays the present . . . the essence of film is its immediacy, and this immediacy is grounded in its tenselessness.[51]

Jonathan Miller finds prose a far more fluent medium for achieving subtle chronological relationships:

Although film has an unrivalled capacity for showing events as they happen, it has none of prose's fluent dexterity for representing the present in relationship to the past; the frequency of events of their uniqueness or how things might have been in contrast to how they turn out to be.[52]

George Bluestone discusses the novel's problems in trying to capture the flux of time, particularly the presentness of our consciousness yet also the blurring of distinction in memory between past and present: language is discrete, whereas memory is continuous; language uses one tense at a time, whereas memory can blend two. But he agrees that film image is always present tense and has priority over any attempts by dialogue or music to suggest past or memory: 'The novel renders the illusion of space by going from point to point in time; the film renders time by going from point to point in space.'[53]

All drama is, of course, distinguished from other narrative forms because it is a performance; Brecht struggled to provide theatre audiences with the objective detachment of a prose reader who might reflect upon past events instead of being gripped by present inevitability – but his theories have had little influence upon the dominant realist style of film and television.

In fact, the realist aesthetic of the screen can cause problems when there is a need for metaphor or symbolism. Geoffrey Wagner argues that: 'The written image, the metaphor on the printed page, is altogether distinct from the physical existence conferred by throwing a picture on a screen.'[54]

Because of the iconic nature of the screen image and the symbolic nature of the prose narrative, the two systems work differently upon the consumer: 'where the moving picture comes to us directly through perception, language must be filtered through the screen of conceptual apprehension'.[55] The writer, however, can exploit the mind's desire to see resemblances in order to classify, by suggesting resemblances between many quite disparate objects through metaphor. Jonathan Miller clearly regards the use of metaphor as one of the most distinctive, precise, and exclusive qualities of prose:

> It is only in language that one can state an explicit comparison between one thing and another – between lips and peonies, mouths and letter-boxes. Although a picture can be viewed with the knowledge that a metaphorical implication is intended, there are no communicative resources within the pictorial format for making such implications explicit.[56]

George Bluestone sees 'packed symbolic thinking' as being 'peculiar to imaginative rather than to visual activity', suggesting that 'the film metaphor must be predicated upon a clear suspension of realistic demands'.[57] Virginia Woolf, on the other hand, suggested something of the nature of the written image and the impossibility of visualizing it fully:

> Even the simplest image: 'My love's like a red, red rose, that's newly sprung in June' presents us with impressions of moisture and warmth and the flow of crimson and the softness of petals inextricably mixed and strung upon the lift of a rhythm which is itself the voice of the passion and the hesitation of the love. All this, which is accessible to words, and to words alone, the cinema must avoid.[58]

However, the television and film-maker can achieve a form of metaphor through editing. Disparate images can be linked to suggest connections, but the exact precision of the verbal image can rarely be transferred.

Clearly relevant to this discussion is the nature of perception, as George Bluestone points out: 'Between the percept of the visual image and the concept of the mental image lies the root difference between the two media.'[59] Likewise, Jonathan Miller argues forcefully that the differences cannot be reconciled: 'the experience of visualising something, as the result of reading a description of it, is altogether different from seeing it in the form of an actual picture'.[60] He quotes Richard Wollheim's essay[61] attached to *Art and Its Object* which contends that there is a fundamental difference between representational objects (pictures, photographs, TV and cinema images) in which we see both the medium and the object – for example, the brush strokes and the frame as well as the subject of the painting – and the mental image, which has no such awareness of a medium; it is not like a photographic image, but somehow is the object itself. Miller develops this point by arguing that where the novelist can refer to those details in a description which are significant or relevant, the screen image is forced to introduce a whole array of background information:

> In some mysterious way, the description of a scene [in a novel] appears to be fully occupied by what it describes and never appears to lack what it fails to mention. In a film, 'each frame would find itself inescapably loaded with unnecessary detail'.[62]

There is clearly much still to discover about this relationship between the mental and the photographic image. Book illustrations of characters described therein were the subject of controversy well before the screen/literature debate. Gustave Flaubert, for example, stated:

> Never, as long as I live, shall I allow anyone to illustrate me, because the most beautiful literary description is eaten up by the most wretched drawing . . . the idea is closed, complete, and every sentence becomes useless.[63]

And Thomas Craven wrote in 1926:

> I doubt if the most astute and sympathetic reader ever visualises a character; he responds to that part of a created figure which is also himself, but he does not actually see his hero. . . . For this reason all illustrations are disappointing.[64]

Virginia Woolf in an early response to cinema adaptations of novels commented:

> The results are disastrous to both. The alliance is unnatural. . . .
> The eye says 'Here is Anna Karenina', a voluptuous lady in
> black velvet wearing pearls comes before us. But the brain says
> 'That is no more Anna Karenina than it is Queen Victoria'. For
> the brain knows Anna almost entirely by the inside of her mind –
> her charm, her passion, her despair. All the emphasis is laid by
> the cinema upon her teeth, her pearls, and her velvet.[65]

George Bluestone has written that 'literary characters are insep-
arable from the language which forms them',[66] a sentiment which
Jonathan Miller echoes:

> The fact that someone is in a novel . . . does not mean that they
> are in the novel in the same way that someone else might be in
> Birmingham or in a cubicle. They cannot be taken out of the
> novel and put in a film of it. . . . (they) are made out of the same
> material as the novels in which they occur, and they cannot be
> liberated in order to make a personal appearance in another
> medium.[67]

Virginia Woolf's comment that we know Anna Karenina 'almost
entirely by the inside of her mind' points to another quality of
prose fiction which may cause problems for a screen adaptation,
namely the ease with which a writer can deal with psychological
states, memory, and abstract concepts: 'We cannot see what we
cannot see; in fiction we can.'[68]

George Bluestone describes the problems:

> The rendition of mental states – memory, dream, imagination –
> cannot be as adequately represented by film as by language. If
> the film has difficulty presenting streams of consciousness it has
> even more difficulty presenting states of mind which are defined
> precisely by the absence in them of the visible world. . . . The
> film having only arrangements of space to work with, cannot
> render thought, for the moment thought is externalised it is no
> longer thought. The film, by arranging external signs for our
> visual perception, or by presenting us with dialogue can lead us
> to infer thought. But it cannot show us thought directly.[69]

The camera can reveal external truths, it can show us the appearance, it can probe the surface, but it cannot deal with abstract concepts: as Morris Beja says, it can show someone in pain, but not 'pain'; it can show a woman and a child, but cannot convey the word 'mother'.

Jonathan Miller argues that in a novel, description, narrative, and explanation are interlinked, whereas in a dramatization, the element of explanation is a fragile attachment, subject to the ability of the spectator to infer what is suggested:

> The difference between a play and a novel is that the actions in the latter are often explained in the very process of representing them, whereas in a play, the performance may be guided and directed by such an interpretation in the hope that the spectator will glean such a conclusion by hindsight . . . it is misleading to think of description and depiction as interchangeable modes of representation. What the novel offers us is a transcription of thought and although the thoughts of an author necessarily take objects, people, and scenes as their arguments, as soon as these are rendered into a dramatic form, where the visible representations of actions replace the descriptions of them, the essential subject of fiction disperses into thin air.[70]

There are, of course, many reasons why screen adaptations of novels are undertaken, despite the problems discussed above. A film or television dramatization can develop or release the narrative through the creative utilization of its own distinctive signs and structures. George Bluestone notes that:

> With the abandonment of language as its sole and primary element, the film necessarily leaves behind those characteristic contents of thought which only language can approximate: tropes, dreams, memories, conceptual consciousness. In their stead the film supplies endless spatial variations, photographic images of physical reality, and the principles of montage and editing.[71]

The screen image can establish diverse relationships between a variety of characters and objects which enable the viewer to make simultaneous judgements on the action and relationships shown; in addition, a great deal of information can be conveyed almost instantaneously by presenting a character or event against a background which can establish a complex of secondary information. The close shot of a character's face, by which meaning can be conveyed by the slightest movement, and the use of sound to emphasize, prepare, or undercut the screen images are also features which can greatly enhance the narrative. William Jinks in *The Celluloid Literature* provides many examples of how film had developed its own 'figurative language of images and sounds'.[72]

Without doubt, however, analysing the use of novels as source material for film and television scripts reveals a steady and significant popularity. Lester Asheim has calculated that between 1935 and 1945, 17 per cent of films released by major studios were adapted from novels – this represents approximately one thousand films.[73] Morris Beja puts the percentage of American films derived from novels as between 20 and 30 per cent of the total released each year, adding that three-quarters of the best awards at the Academy have gone to adaptations, and that of the top twenty money-earning films of all time reported by *Variety* in 1977, fourteen were based on novels.[74] This popularity leads Beja to suggest that the oral traditions of narrative gave way to the written form, the novel, which is now giving way to the visual, namely film and television; certainly, it reflects the screen's insatiable appetite for script material, which happily supplements original scripts with borrowing from sources as diverse as comic strips and opera. As Geoffrey Wagner comments: 'when the source of a film is a prior work of art, perhaps a well-known novel, there is an extra-curricular meaning to start with'.[75]

John Ellis makes a similar point, suggesting that the screen seeks a cultural respectability when adapting a novel: 'the adaptation trades upon the memory of the novel, a memory that can derive from actual reading, or . . . a generally circulated cultural memory. The adaptation consumes this memory, aiming to efface it with the presence of its own images.'[76] But there is no general agreement upon what types of novel transfer most successfully to the screen. Some have argued that novels in which the portrayal of inner states of mind predominate produce unsatisfactory films; others argue that the better the novel, the less successful will be the film adaptation: Anthony Burgess claims that 'brilliant adaptations are nearly always of fiction of the second or third class', and François Truffaut that 'a masterpiece is something that has already found its perfection of form, its definitive form'.[77] Stanley Kubrick,

however, considers that success depends not upon the quality or
otherwise of the original novel, but upon the film's ability to find
its own style:

> To take 'the prose' style as any more than just part of a great
> book is simply misunderstanding just what a great book is . . .
> style is what the artist uses to fascinate the beholder in order to
> convey to him his feelings and emotions and thoughts. These
> are what have to be dramatised not the style. The dramatising
> has to find a style of its own, as it will do if it really grasps the
> content . . . it may or may not be as good as the novel; sometimes
> in certain ways it may even be better.[78]

Certainly, there is clear evidence that a film adaptation of a novel
leads to a renewal of interest in the book itself:[79] sales increase, as
do borrowings from libraries; films based on original scripts will
often have simultaneous publication of a 'novelization', the book
of the film. Nevertheless, it remains the case that the majority of
viewers of a typical film adaptation will not be familiar with the
original novel. Stanley Kaufman comments acidly:

> An editorial in the current *Esquire* [March 1959] suggests a double
> standard for criticising films made from novels: that reviewers
> should treat such films as complete in themselves because most
> people haven't read the originals and a review that points out
> divergences is only spoiling their fun. It is a stirring little crusade
> for the sacredness of ignorance, and if only our culture can keep
> most people from reading books, it may prevail.[80]

In fact, the IBA Research Department has carried out several
surveys into the effects of television dramatization of novels upon
reading habits. The research was carried out by Dr J. M. Wober in
1985, as part of the regular IBA Audience Reaction Surveys.[81] A
weighted sample of 3000 respondents completed a questionnaire
relating to the effect of television adaptations upon their reading
habits. Of these, 46% indicated that they had bought or borrowed
a book directly as a result of seeing a television programme, with
the proportion somewhat smaller amongst older people (40%) and
markedly greater amongst upper socioeconomic groups (56%).
When the question was restricted to the past year, 36% of the
sample reported that they had bought or borrowed a book as a

result of a television programme; and when the question was further restricted to fifteen popular drama serials, the proportion fell to about 25%. However, in response to a subsequent question, one-quarter of the sample who said they had obtained a book as a result of a television programme admitted to reading half or less than half of it. Although a significant number of respondents preferred the television version to the book, especially among lower socioeconomic groups, there was a clear tendency for more people more often to prefer the book. A previous survey by Dr Wober with regard to fifteen dramatised novels,[82] revealed that television reaches three times as many people as those who claim to have encountered the literature directly – with the distributive power noticeably more for men than women, young than old, and particularly for lower social-class than higher social-class respondents. For example, well over half the sample had read none of the fifteen titles listed, whereas a similar number had seen five or more of the fifteen adaptations listed.[83]

It may be useful at this stage to summarize some of the questions raised by the adaptation of prose fiction into film and television. The major problems are summarized by Morris Beja, who asks:

> How should a film-maker go about the process of adapting a work of written literature? Are there guiding principles that we can discover or devise? What relationship should a film have to the original source? Should it be faithful? Can it be? To what? Which should be uppermost in a film-maker's mind: the integrity of the original work, or the integrity of the film to be based on that work? Is there a necessary conflict? What types of changes are permissible? Desirable? Inevitable? Are some types of work more adaptable than others?[84]

There are, however, as this chapter has demonstrated, far more specific problems, such as: the question of objective and subjective viewpoints; the presence or absence of a narrator; time – past, present and future; verbal and visual descriptions; and literary and visual imagery. In addition, sociological issues such as the methods of production, distribution, and consumption of the novel and the film are relevant, as well as consideration of the effects of film and television adaptation upon the understanding and appreciation of the original novel: does the adaptation add to the body of

interpretation, criticism and analysis of the text, or does it in some
way damage or replace the experience of reading?

These are clearly issues worthy of discussion. There can be no
definitive answers, since adaptations are quite obviously undertaken for a variety of reasons, ranging from the attempt to
reproduce a novel as faithfully as possible, through to the use of
the source merely as a stimulus to original work; sometimes the
adaptation is undertaken with the aim of bringing a literary
work to a wider audience, sometimes to trade off its cultural
respectability, sometimes to cash in on its popularity, sometimes
to comment upon or develop an aspect of the original text, and
sometimes because of a paucity of good original scripts. And
certainly, there has never been a shortage of voices arguing for the
merits of the novel, its scope and human variety, and warning
against the dangers of what we might lose in forgetting the power
of the original text. Jane Austen, writing nearly two hundred years
ago in *Northanger Abbey*, seems to foreshadow the whole debate:

> 'Oh! it is only a novel!' replies the young lady; while she
> lays down her book with affected indifference or momentary
> shame.—'It is only *Cecilia*, or *Camilla*, or *Belinda*;' or, in short,
> only some work in which the greatest powers of the mind are
> displayed, in which the most thorough knowledge of human
> nature, the happiest delineation of its varieties, the liveliest
> effusions of wit and humour, are conveyed to the world in the
> best-chosen language.[85]

Notes

1. Within the BBC, a clear distinction is made between 'adaptation' and
   'dramatization'. An 'adaptation' is the preparation of a television
   version of a work which is already in dramatic form, for example a
   stage play. A 'dramatization' is the preparation of a television drama
   from a work which was not previously in dramatic form, for example
   a prose narrative.
2. Lewis Jacobs, *The Rise of the American Film* (New York: Harcourt, Brace
   & Co., 1939), p. 119.
3. Joseph Conrad, Preface to *The Nigger of the 'Narcissus'* (London: Dent,
   1897).
4. Herbert Read, *A Coat of Many Colours* (London: Routledge, 1945),
   pp. 230–31.
5. Morris Beja, *Film and Literature* (New York: Longman, 1976).

6. William Luhr and Peter Lehman, *Authorship and Narrative in the Cinema* (New York: Putnam, 1977), p. 291.
7. Ibid., p. 174.
8. Boris Tomashevsky, 'Thematics', in *Russian Formalist Criticism: Four Essays*, trans. Lemon and Reis (Lincoln, Nebraska: University of Nebraska Press, 1965), p. 68.
9. George Bluestone, *Novel into Film* (Berkeley: University of California Press, 1957), p. 2.
10. Bertolt Brecht, 'The Film, the Novel and the Epic Theatre', in *Brecht on Theatre*, trans. John Willett (London: Eyre Methuen, 1978), p. 47.
11. Philip Simpson, *Film and Literature*, BFI Film Year Education Pamphlet, pp. 1–2.
12. J. Dudley Andrew, *Concepts in Film Theory* (New York/Oxford: Oxford University Press, 1984), p. 104.
13. Eric Rentschler (ed.), *German Film and Literature* (London: Methuen, 1986), p. 5.
14. Morris Beja, *Film and Literature*, op. cit., p. 84.
15. Martin Esslin, *The Field of Drama* (London: Methuen, 1987), p. 36.
16. Jonathan Miller, *Subsequent Performances* (London: Faber, 1986), p. 66.
17. For more detailed analysis, see Martin Esslin, *The Field of Drama*, op. cit., and Peter Wollen, *Signs and Meaning in the Cinema* (London: Secker and Warburg, 1972).
18. Philip Simpson, *Film and Literature*, op. cit., p. 4.
19. Peter Wollen, *Signs and Meaning in the Cinema*, op. cit., p. 165.
20. Martin Esslin, *The Field of Drama*, op. cit., pp. 104–5.
21. Sergei Eisenstein, 'Dickens, Griffith and the Film Today', in *Film Form*, trans. Jay Leyda (New. York, 1949; London: Dobson, 1951), pp. 195–255.
22. Joseph Frank, *The Widening Gyre* (New Brunswick: Rutgers University Press, 1963), pp. 14–16.
23. Bruce Morissette, *Novel and Film* (Chicago: University of Chicago Press, 1985), p. 15.
24. Keith Cohen, *Film and Literature: the Dynamics of Exchange* (New Haven: Yale University Press, 1979), p. 4.
25. Andrew, *Concepts in Film Theory*, op. cit., p. 103.
26. Robert Scholes, 'Narration and Narrativity in Film', in *Quarterly Review of Film Studies*, 1:111 (August 1976), p. 291.
27. Leon Edel, 'Novel and Camera', in J. Halperin (ed.), *The Theory of the Novel* (London: Oxford University Press, 1974), p. 182.
28. Brian McFarlane, *Words and Images* (London: Secker, 1987), p. 2.
29. Luhr and Lehman, *Authorship and Narrative*, op. cit., p. 192.
30. Bluestone, *Novel into Film*, op. cit., p. 5.
31. Luhr and Lehman, *Authorship and Narrative*, op. cit., p. 223.
32. George Linden, 'The Storied World', in Fred H. Marcus (ed.), *Film and Literature: Contrasts in Media* (New York: Chandler, 1971), p. 169.
33. Beja, *Film and Literature*, op. cit., p. 82.
34. Michael Klein and Gillian Parker (eds), *The English Novel and the Movies* (New York: Ungar, 1981), pp. 9–10.
35. Geoffrey Wagner, *The Novel and the Cinema* (Rutherford, New Jersey:

Farleigh Dickinson University Press, 1975), pp. 222–31.
36. Andrew, *Concepts in Film Theory*, op. cit., pp. 98–104.
37. Keith Cohen, 'Eisenstein's Subversive Adaptation', in G. Peary and R. Shatzkin (eds), *The Classic American Novel and the Movies* (New York: Ungar, 1977), pp. 245 and 255.
38. Beja, *Film and Literature*, op. cit., p. 88.
39. Andrew, *Concepts in Film Theory*, op. cit., p. 97.
40. Rentschler (ed.), *German Film and Literature*, op. cit., p. 3.
41. Joseph Boggs, *The Art of Watching Films* (Mountain View, California: Mayfield Publishers, 1985).
42. Morissette, *Novel and Film*, op. cit., p. 93.
43. McFarlane, *Words and Images*, op. cit., p. 2.
44. George Linden, 'The Storied World', op. cit., pp. 158 and 163.
45. Colin MacCabe, 'Realism and the Cinema: Notes on Some Brechtian Theses', in *Screen*, Summer 1974, Vol. 15, Pt 2, pp. 10–11.
46. Morissette, *Novel and Film*, op. cit., p. 37.
47. See Robert Montgomery's film *Lady in the Lake* (1946) – in which the hero is never seen except in mirrors.
48. Wagner, *The Novel and the Cinema*, op. cit., p. 199.
49. Bluestone, *Novel into Film*, op. cit., p. 48.
50. Alain Robbe-Grillet, quoted in Beja, *Film and Literature*, op. cit., p. 75.
51. George Linden, 'The Storied World', in J. Harrington (ed.) *Film And/As Literature* (Englewood Cliffs, NJ: Prentice-Hall, 1977).
52. Miller, *Subsequent Performances*, op. cit., p. 233.
53. Bluestone, *Novel into Film*, op. cit., p. 61. See also discussion, pp. 54–61.
54. Wagner, *The Novel and the Cinema*, op. cit., p. 11.
55. Bluestone, *Novel into Film*, op. cit., p. 20.
56. Miller, *Subsequent Performances*, op. cit., p. 226.
57. Bluestone, *Novel into Film*, op. cit., pp. 22–3.
58. Virginia Woolf, 'The Movies and Reality', in *New Republic*, XLVII (4 August 1926), p. 309.
59. Bluestone, *Novel into Film*, op. cit., p. 1.
60. Miller, *Subsequent Performances*, op. cit., p. 214.
61. Miller, ibid., see pp. 214–16.
62. Miller, ibid., p. 229.
63. Gustave Flaubert, quoted in Miller, ibid., p. 213.
64. Thomas Craven, 'The Great American Art', in *Dial*, LXXXI (December 1926), pp. 489–90.
65. Woolf, 'The Movies and Reality', op. cit., p. 309.
66. Bluestone, *Novel into Film*, op. cit., p. 23.
67. Miller, *Subsequent Performances*, op. cit.
68. Wagner, *The Novel and the Cinema*, op. cit., p. 183.
69. Bluestone, *Novel into Film*, op. cit., pp. 47–8.
70. Miller, *Subsequent Performances*, op. cit., pp. 238 and 240.
71. Bluestone, *Novel into Film*, op. cit., pp. viii–ix.
72. See William Jinks, *The Celluloid Literature* (London: Glencoe Press, 1971), pp. 116–34.
73. Lester Asheim, *From Book to Film*, PhD Dissertation, University of Chicago, 1949.

74. Beja, *Film and Literature*, op. cit., p. 78.
75. Wagner, *The Novel and the Cinema*, op. cit., p. 203.
76. John Ellis, 'The Literary Adaptation', in *Screen*, Vol. 23, May/June, 1982, p. 3.
77. Both quoted in Beja, *Film and Literature*, op. cit., p. 85.
78. Stanley Kubrick, quoted in Beja, ibid., p. 80.
79. See *Vanity Fair* analysis (Chapters 6–8), Bluestone, *Novel into Film*, op. cit., pp. 4–5, and Beja, *Film and Literature*, op. cit., pp. 87–8.
80. Stanley Kaufman, 'Signifying Nothing', in Peary and Shatzkin (eds) *The Classic American Novel and the Movies*, op. cit., p. 306.
81. J. M. Wober, *Television and Reading* (London: IBA, 1985).
82. J. M. Wober, *Fiction and Depiction* (London: IBA, April 1980). Titles used were *Wuthering Heights; Rebecca; Nicholas Nickleby; The Stars Look Down; The Forsyte Saga; From Here to Eternity; The Prime of Miss Jean Brodie; I, Claudius; Rich Man, Poor Man; War and Peace; Anna Karenina; The Mayor of Casterbridge; Clayhanger; Murder Most English; People Like Us.*
83. J. M. Wober, ibid., Table of results:

Number of Titles	Books read before seeing TV adaptation by %	TV adaptations seen by %
0	58	1
1	11	5
2	13	10
3	6	16
4	6	13
5	3	12
6	0	10
7	3	12
8	1	8
9	1	5
10	0	4
11–15	0	5

This means, for example, that 3% of the sample had read 5 of the books listed, whereas 12% had watched 5 of the adaptations.

84. Beja, *Film and Literature*, op. cit., p. 81.
85. Jane Austen, *Northanger Abbey* (1818), 1983 edition (London: Macmillan Education) p. 22.

2

The Re-creation of the Past

It has been said that although God cannot alter the past, historians can; it is perhaps because they can be useful to Him in this respect that He tolerates their existence.

Samuel Butler, *Erewhon Revisited* (1901)

So far we have seen something of the various theoretical approaches taken toward the notion of literary dramatization. One of the major ideas to come out of this discussion was the question of the audience's historical relationship to the text. This is something which becomes increasingly important as we move further from theory into practice, for, of the many thousands of novels available to the programme- and film-maker, the nineteenth-century novel appears perennially attractive. Indeed, the nineteenth-century novel (Dickens, Thackeray, Eliot, et al.) forms the core of the BBC Classic Serial output. As such, it is the novel in this form which provides the imaginative locale in which much of our sense of the past is created. This recreation of the past is a palpable forgery, as we are all aware; but it is not unique either to the media, or to the twentieth century.

George Chalmers (1742–1825) was a distinguished lawyer and outstanding antiquary. He published biographies of Daniel Defoe and Tom Paine, edited Scottish poets and wrote numerous Scottish biographies. Joseph Warton (1722–1800) was an MA and DD of Oriel College, Oxford, and a scholar of some considerable distinction, contributed to Johnson's *Adventurer*, made a notable translation of Virgil and made classic editions of Pope and Dryden. Richard Valpy (1754–1836) was a brilliant headmaster of Reading School, a DD of Pembroke College, Oxford and one of the most outstanding scholars of his day. Herbert Croft (1751–1816) was a reputable barrister and author of some merit – he had contributed to Johnson's *Lives of the Poets* and projected a new edition of Johnson's *Dictionary*. Samuel Parr (1747–1825) was a learned pedagogue, headmaster of several schools and prebendary of St Paul's – he was regarded as the Whig Doctor Johnson. James Boswell (1740–95), whose biography of Johnson is one of the enduring masterpieces of our literature, was educated at Edinburgh and Glasgow and a well-qualified lawyer who became secretary of foreign correspondence to the Royal Academy late in life. This panel of outstanding intellectuals all testified to the authenticity of works by William Shakespeare which had been found in manuscript by William Henry Ireland (1777–1825).

In 1796, Ireland published, in folio, *Miscellaneous Papers and Instruments, under the hand and seal of William Shakespeare*, including the tragedy of *King Lear* and a small fragment of *Hamlet*, from the original. Ireland produced manuscripts, which he claimed to be in Shakespeare's handwriting, and to these was added, in April 1796, the drama *Vortigern and Rowena* 'from the pen of Shakespeare', which was announced for production at Drury Lane, with a professional cast including John Kemble and Dorothy Jordan in the title roles. Richard Brinsley Sheridan (1751–1816), the manager of Drury Lane at the time, had been completely pursuaded of the play's authenticity. It played to a capacity house but was detected as a fake by Edmund Malone (1741–1812), whose superb edition of Shakespeare had been published in 1790. This was something of a setback, as young Ireland (a mere 19 years old at this time) was already well advanced on other plays by Shakespeare, including *Henry II* and *William the Conqueror*.

All Ireland's forgeries were published by his father, a dealer in prints and antiquarian bookseller, who loyally supported his son's claims. It was his opinion that his son was too stupid to have been capable of such invention.[1] But Ireland's exposure was merciless and those who had supported his claims with their expertise shared some of the boy's shame. What is interesting here is that Ireland should have fooled the professional academics, intellectuals and scholars so completely. But we of the twentieth century who have so recently witnessed the discomfiture of Lord Dacre over the Hitler diaries have little cause to feel all that superior. Van Meegeren's case in 1948 demonstrated how the willing can be convinced they are looking at Vermeers and de Hoochs, just as more recently Tom Keating has fooled many an expert with his own forgeries.

But the real skill of the forger does not lie solely in the ability to put together something which looks like the work of another identifiable creator; the nature of the appetite to be satisfied is as important a consideration as the object which satisfies it. It is this which makes the contemporary interest in the past so interesting. Exploring the shape, texture and construction of the kind of past we seem to crave will help us identify what it is in contemporary culture of which this need is a symptom.

The attempt to recreate classic novels from the past in terms of moving film, a process which accelerated with the advent of television, should be seen as part of the much larger efforts made by the media to reconstruct the past in which it is possible to discern the film and broadcasting industries assuming the role of historiographers.

The arrival of colour television in British households from July 1967 has intensified the concentration of the past as basic source material for the television industry to exploit. As George Brandt comments:

> Soon enough broadcasting companies felt the urge to exploit to the full an innovation for the sake of which viewers were being asked to buy new sets and pay higher licence fees. Years before, the introduction of Technicolor and other colour systems in the cinema had been an invitation to lavish spectacle; history was to repeat itself in television. Colour is a designer's dream. True, the first of the high-class costume dramas, the BBC's *Forsyte Saga*, was a black and white affair. (Immensely successful, with splendid performances and high production values, this serial proved a blockbuster for the export market; it was shown in the United States, Portugal, Hungary – even in the Soviet Union, where it was transmitted in a dubbed Russian version; by 1970 the BBC reported that some 160,000,000 viewers in forty-five countries had seen this instant classic.) But colour was a major feature, appealing to domestic viewer and overseas buyer alike, in such costume serials as the BBC's *The Six Wives of Henry VIII*, ATV's *Edward VII*, Thames Television's *Edward and Mrs Simpson* and *Jenny* (the story of Churchill's mother) and – last but not least – London Weekend's fictitious evocation of an Edwardian upper-middle-class household, *Upstairs Downstairs*. . . .[2]

In the face of such comment it seems almost ironic that no previous age in history has had better means with which to reconstruct the past than ours. Not only do we inherit a vast storehouse of objects – statuary, paintings, ornaments and artefacts – but we have photography, film and sound recording which enable us to see and hear what our ancestors actually looked and sounded like. It can be no accident that the 'past' with which our media seems particularly concerned, certainly as far as classic novels are concerned, is the nineteenth century – a major warehouse of historical commodities and evidence, and a period still almost within living memory in which culture we feel we have strong roots. When media people talk about 'classic novels' they usually mean mid-Victorian novels. It is significant that many masterpieces of eighteenth-century narrative prose fiction which, on the face of it would make superb costume drama, remain still unravished brides of quietness as far as radio and television are concerned.

And yet the past constructed by the media is a forgery, even though (like all good forgeries) it is produced only after a lengthy immersion in old documents and a thorough acquaintance with the old masters. It was in Foyle's second-hand bookshop that Noel Coward came across some bound copies of the *Illustrated London News*:

> The first fell open at the picture of a troopship leaving for the Boer War; he bought the lot and on the way home his mind filled with the music-hall songs of the period and of his early childhood – 'Goodbye My Bluebell', 'Goodbye Dolly Gray' and 'We're Soldiers of the Queen, My Lads'. They rang a bell in his head and he somehow knew that he'd found what he wanted for his spectacular. . . .[3]

The spectacular was *Cavalcade* which opened in 1931. It told the story of the generations of a British family from the Boer War to the First World War in terms of a musical pageant. Its timing was perfect. At a time of considerable national crisis, *Cavalcade* played out the theme of national strength, unity and pride. It was exactly what the public wanted at the time. Its success is out of all proportions to its merits – it won an Academy Award for the best film of 1932, its stars won Oscars, and its supporting actress an Academy nomination.

The historical validity of such performances is not really the issue. The past constructed by the media is a forgery, but like all forgeries it has considerable fascination. We may cite a few obvious examples – photography is an important element in the way media practitioners seek to recreate what the past looked like. One very serious consequence of this is the fact that because portrait photography for many years was done on long exposure we have gained the impression that the Victorians were solemn people, because the camera required them to sit still and straightfaced while having their pictures taken. Such is the influence of the visual image.

Another source frequently (and understandably) resorted to is the illustrations in contemporary editions. As far as Dickens is concerned, most of these are by Hablot Browne (1815–82), who also illustrated works by Lever and Ainsworth. Although Dickens used other illustrators, including Cruikshank and Cattermole, a very useful and harmonious association existed between Dickens and Browne (or 'Phiz' as he was called). Browne illustrated all Dickens's novels except *Hard Times* and was dropped in favour of Marcus Stone when *Great Expectations* appeared in book form. The impact of 'Phiz' on our conception of what Dickens's fictional world looks like is considerable, yet it is important to remember that Browne was very prone to caricature and grotesque exaggerations. This is all very well, and indeed, all very Dickensian, but in terms of recreating the Dickens world in cinematography it does pose several significant problems. Not the least of these is the fact that in film-making there is always a tendency towards realism and naturalism, which is part of the received tradition so well established in photography. Film-makers invariably work on the assumption that they are doing Dickens a service in attempting to make their movies look as much like 'Phiz' illustrations as possible. But this, in fact, can lead to some severe distortion. The cultural *coup d'état* achieved by television as the major source of cultural production and distribution is vital here: most people's historical imagination is made up of the timescale passively acquired from learning the kings and queens of England at school, some input from historical fiction, with a constantly reapplied top dressing of period colour, pointing and detail supplied by the small screen.

This is not helped by the general thrust of western European thinking toward the idea of 'progress' – that whatever the course of history is, or whatever byways it might take, it is inevitably forwards in its ultimate direction, and that consequently our age is a better one than all preceding ages. Modern Times, as an historiographical construction, seem to have been put together in the mid-seventeenth century, to a very considerable extent the result of the English Revolution. Dr Robert Birley asserted: 'On the 5th of July 1641 the England which we know today was born.'[4] On this date the Privy Council, Star Chamber and High Commission were overthrown. The remedial legislation enacted by the Parliament which met in November 1640 laid the political foundations of modern Britain.[5] Unwittingly, we are all Macaulayans, unless we consciously strive against the stream. The inevitability of the Whig view of history is not only intoxicating; it provides such a convenient standpoint from which to view the past, and such a clear set of assumptions through which to look at the past:

> I purpose to write a History of England from the accession of King James II down to a time which is within the memory of men still living. . . . I shall relate how the new settlement was . . . successfully defended against foreign and domestic enemies . . . how, from the auspicious union of order and freedom, sprang a prosperity of which the annals of human affairs had furnished no example; how our country, from a state of ignominious vassalage, rapidly rose to the place of umpire among European powers; how her opulence and her martial glory grew together; how, by wise and resolute good faith, was gradually established a public credit fruitful of marvels which to the statesmen of any former age would have seemed incredible; how a gigantic commerce gave birth to a maritime power, compared with which every other maritime power, ancient or modern, sinks into insignificance. . . .[6]

Macaulay's *History* was greatly esteemed in its day, and it may subsequently have suffered in estimation as professional academic historians have tempered and readjusted the concept of our past, but it is important to realize that Macaulay's rabid nationalism and optimism have permanently affected our thinking, certainly at a deeper, populist level. And let it not pass unrecorded that his noble and heroic example was imitated at a humbler level by such journeymen as John Richard Green, whose *A Short History of the English People*, first published in 1874, has had immense influence on several generations of readers, and that the work of popular historians such as Sir Arthur Bryant (1899–1986) continues to reinforce, seemingly supported by the evidence of history, the myth of the forward march of Britain along that never-ending road of greatness, power and progress towards a state of perfection whose achievement and full realization is an essential part of God's Plan for the World.

The great divide between ancient and modern times, medieval and industrial Britain, seems to have occurred during the English Revolution. As Christopher Hill writes:

> 'The civil wars have left in this nation scarcely any trace of more ancient history', reflected Dr Johnson, and if any turning point between medieval and modern ways of thought can be found it was undoubtedly the rude intellectual shock of civil war, regicide, and republic. Evidence of an increasing historical sense is to be found in the appearance of the word 'anachronism' about 1646.[7]

A work such as Thomas Fuller's *The Worthies of England* (1662) is shot through with this new historical sense. Fuller was trying to describe the present, which he knew was new and exciting and changing, at the same time as he tried to preserve an English past which was in danger of disappearing forever unless he wrote down as much about it as he could lay his hands on. This new perspective, so typical initially of the seventeenth century, has significant consequences for us in the late twentieth century and affects the way we attempt to see the past, and, in fact, conditions the very nature of the 'past' we construct. It leads us easily into the temptation of viewing the past through the distortions of the present. We look back to the past as travellers on a journey look back to the way they have come. If we modernize those staging-posts along our journey to our own way of thinking, it is in a sense a way of admitting they are no longer appropriate or relevant in their original form to speak to us of the twentieth century. If we slavishly endeavour to recreate them as we think they might have appeared in their own time we produce a fake antique. Consider the hidden agenda of Laurence Olivier's celebrated film version of *Henry V*. It opens in Elizabethan London at a performance of Shakespeare's play. We start as spectators in the Globe and gradually, almost imperceptibly we move out of the restrictions of the theatre into the real make-believe world of costume drama, with real horses, real grass, real armour and real blood and arrows which whistle through the air as they descend on the French cavalry. In effect we move from a noticeably bad production of Shakespeare's great play into a very good film production. The film argues for its own historical accuracy, rather than for what seem by contrast the crude Elizabethan attempts at staging.

Of course, we are all well aware of the vast ideological import Olivier's film carried in 1944.[8] But over and above that, the film carries a typically modern message: our age is better than the past. Although Olivier might have got the fledging on the French arrows historically perfect, most would probably argue that Shakespeare's genius is to be found in his transcending of historical accuracy, rather than any slavish adherence to it. Many of Shakespeare's plays are, in fact, notoriously anachronistic.

There is, however, an interesting irony to be discovered here. Our class structure and the means for the distribution and consumption of culture seriously distort our perceptions of the past. For example, in May 1983 Donald Pleasance appeared in a television drama as Samuel Johnson. Yet there was not the trace of a Staffordshire accent – which we might have expected, if only for the sake of historical accuracy. Johnson's strong Staffordshire accent was frequently remarked. David Garrick, the actor, who knew Johnson of old, used to imitate him to his face, bawling: 'Who's for poonsh?'. The Revd Henry Hervey noted that Johnson said 'woonse' for 'once' and pronounced 'there' as if it rhymed with 'mere'.[9] But our twentieth-century preconceptions condition us into associating certain regional accents with the professional classes and others with the working classes. In a society whose culture is metropolitan-dominated, it seems part of the natural order that all creative/cultivated persons should speak 'good' standard English. It must follow from this that if Samuel Johnson was an intellectual and a scholar and had been to the University of Oxford, then he must speak English with a south-eastern accent.

The media invite us to look back at our past through the refractions, flaws and distortions of our present. Dr Johnson himself believed that languages were the pedigrees of nations;[10] but far from respecting these pedigrees, the modern media cast the conversations of figures from our past in terms of the accepted tones of the present. Even Shakespeare himself must have had a regional accent to make his noble King Henry v talk like a rustic. Consider, for example, the concluding couplet of the famous 'Once more unto the breach' speech:

> Follow your spirit; and on this charge,
> Cry God for England, Harry and St George!

One of the most striking examples which could be cited to demonstrate the manner in which the media skilfully reconstructs 'history' according to the distortions of the present would have to be BBC/Time-Life's *America: A Personal History* by Alistair Cooke, a 13-part fifty-minute series first shown on BBC television in 1974. *Halliwell's Television Guide* describes the series in the following terms:

Brilliantly-filmed historical documentaries in which the know-ledgeable and urbane Mr Cooke wanders across his adopted land and, aided by a first-class camera crew, picks up all the strands which have made up the present-day nation.[11]

In fact *America* seems to be based on the idea that the USA is a liberal-pluralist democracy and is careful to select those very historical/mythological threads which will justify and reinforce those assumptions. It is the kind of simple version of the nation's history taught to American schoolchildren. Columbus, the Pilgrim Fathers, the American Colonies, No-Taxation-Without-Representation, the War of Independence, the birth of the nation in the Civil War, the Opening of the West and the modern wars fought to make the world safe for Democracy. This is America without the extermination of the Arawak Indians by the settlers who followed Columbus, the extermination of the indigenous population of the West and the Great Land Grab, without the gangsters, the Scottsboro' Boys, Sacco and Vanzetti, serious treatment of the power politics behind the Atomic bombings, the McCarthy hearings, the whole truth about Nixon, the CIA, Jimmy Hoffa, the Vietnam War, and so on. What comes through instead is official mythology – self-help, clean living, freedom, opportunity and 'democracy' – Apple-Pie Capitalism.[12]

Such a treatment of the past, however, is not a recent development. Mark Twain called it 'the Walter Scott Disease'. Art historians term it the Gothic Revival. To some it is the Cult of the Past. Call it what you will, the revival of an interest in the sense of a past which preceded Shakespeare is an early nineteenth-century phenomenon. It is curious that the reawakening of this interest in the past should coincide with the birth of the camera. This was to lead for the first time to the attempts to present actors and actresses in roles set in the past, wearing historically accurate costume, with stage scenery and properties being likewise historically accurate and in period. In the grammar of our culture these are important elements – the lure of the past, the fascination with the possibilities offered in the future, and the painstaking novelty of historicism. Its products – the historical novel, science fiction and historical accuracy in stage production – had, and continue to have, a profound effect on cultural production.[13]

Backward-looking Middle Ages nostalgia was a marked feature of the nineteenth century. The Gothic Revival was heralded in 1818 when Parliament voted a million pounds for building new Anglican churches. Out of 214 provided under the Act, 174 were in the Gothic style. When the Houses of Parliament were to be rebuilt after the fire of 1834 the proximity of Westminster Abbey dictated a Gothic style. There was similarly a furious debate in Parliament in 1855–72 over the rebuilding of the India Office and Foreign Office.[14] The influence of John Ruskin was literally monumental in this respect.

The political manifestation of medievalist nostalgia found its expression in Disraeli's Young England movement, political arm of the cult of Sir Philip Sydney, which publicly celebrated itself in the Eglinton Tournament of 1839. Then thrived the armourers. *Ivanhoe* (1819) had started a vogue for tournaments and there were several stage versions of Scott's novel running in London in the 1820s, the most worthy at Astley's amphitheatre featuring twenty men on horseback. Librettists and composers ransacked literature for suitably chivalric and medieval subjects for operas.[15] Numerous tournament pictures and scenes from Arthurian romance were exhibited at the Royal Academy. Samuel Pratt opened his armour showrooms in Lower Grosvenor Street in April 1838. The gentry who could afford to do so built Gothic castles and filled them with suits of armour, much of it made in the Age of Steam. Edward George Bulwer-Lytton (1803–73) made Knebworth in Hertfordshire a Gothic showpiece in the mid-1840s. Charles Tennyson (1808–79) elaborated Bayons in Lincolnshire in the Gothic manner in the 1830s, after succeeding to his great-uncle's property.[16] William Russell spent an estimated £120 000 in 'restoring' Brancepeth Castle in Durham, and Charles Stanhope, the Earl of Petersham (1780–1851) totally Gothicized Elvaston Castle in Derbyshire. The return to the past seems to reach its apotheosis in the physical attempts to corporealize the past in the form of living theatre – the craze for pageants was a feature of the end of the century.

It is claimed that the pageant was invented by Louis Napoleon

Parker (1852–1944). Parker was a musician, playwright and producer, who studied at the Royal Academy and taught music at
Sherborne School, 1873–92. After deafness made him unsuitable for
music he concentrated on spectacle, mounting pageants of the past
at Sherborne, Warwick, Colchester, York, Dover and Bury St
Edmunds.[17] The craze is still with us, kept alive by the British
Pageant Society and the bizarre fad for Tolkien, in which clerks,
minor civil servants, computer programmers and other toiling
Nibelungs of advanced techno-capitalism seek spiritual recreation
in organized spurious medieval activities which include cross-
garterings, mead-swilling, heavy swordplay and other assorted
moot-hall ho-hoing.

We can yet discover a serious point in all these antics. The social
psychologist Michael Argyle argues that accent is, like clothes, part
of a person's self-presentation, and that usually as a result of
social conditioning and deliberate personal effort, regardless of
regionality and social class, we learn almost unconsciously to adopt
the accent we believe will be socially and professionally acceptable.
Under stress, people are liable to revert or regress and use an
earlier accent or dialect.[18] Thus, in a crisis, a New Yorker of Jewish
descent may shed the professional decorum and Ivy League tones
of years and revert to voice his passions in the *patois* of the Bronx.
It could be argued that the current trough of nostalgia, the fashion
for theme parks, medieval banquets, rural crafts, costume drama,
the insatiable appetite for royalty, the passion for public ceremonials
and rituals are all symptomatic of the condition of the national
psyche which is shedding layers of modernity and reverting to its
own past tones under the stress of contemporary economic,
political and social crisis. As Waldemar Januszczak writes:

> Epochs have a way of expressing themselves instinctively
> through the buildings they favour. The Middle Ages built
> cathedrals and castles. The Renaissance built universities and
> piazzas. The Baroque built churches. The nineteenth century
> built town halls and stations. We build museums.[19]

Hampton Court Medieval Banquets advertise themselves
handsomely:

> King Henry VIII returned to Hampton Court Palace to entertain
> his subjects with Medieval Banquets. At the Tiltyard Restaurant,

beside the Jousting Tower, you can enjoy Honeymead wine on arrival and be entertained by beautiful medieval folk songs played on authentic instruments by the court musicians. During the evening a five-course banquet is served with unlimited French wine and jugs of real ale throughout the banquet. Festivities including daring fire-eating and juggling displays by the court jester and continual entertainment involving your party in the acts of light merriment with the Lord Chamberlain, while buxom wenches and handsome henchmen serve you food and wine.

Beneath this splendid example of the copywriter's art lies a postulated and permanent medievalism which it is revealing to ponder. The return of Henry VIII is not located at any particular time (returning from where?) He is always coming back to Hampton Court and he is always entertaining his subjects with 'medieval banquets'.

We note in passing that other attractions include 'Strolling Minstrels, Anne Boleyn and Jane Seymour, a Dancing Bear, the Tale of the Mary Rose, the Beheading of Anne Boleyn and a Yard of Ale.' At the end of your evening you will 'Return to the Twentieth Century with Disco Dancing after the Show'.

This is diachronic tourism. The tour operators promise you a trip to the past and a safe journey home to the twentieth century and its blandishments. This seems to realize a manifest need deeply felt in modern times, to connect with the past, to trace roots backwards in time.[20] Classified advertisements in newspapers invite you to trace your ancestry. In country-town market stalls there is a flourishing trade in off-the-peg genealogies. You may mark the birthday of a relative or friend by giving them a historic newspaper which appeared the day they were born. Lack of solid evidence may often in part be compensated for if the imagination is only willing enough – witness the compelling prose from the Souvenir Programme of Walford Mill Craft Centre, published by Dorset Craft Guild. This passage of 'historical' justification comes several pages from the beginning of the booklet which has much preliminary matter to rehearse about the Mill's 'history' and its traditional crafts and workmanship:

The history of the mill at Walford is clouded in uncertainty. In David Popham's book, *The History of Wimborne*, there is a reference to 'a mille at Wimburn Town Centre end' which is believed to refer to Walford Mill, in the sixteenth century. The existing main building, however, is believed to date from 1760/1770 . . . There is, however, no evidence left in the records of any building of this period. . . .

This all seems pretty vague as far as evidence is concerned, but what is being urged is that *the mill is very old*. Even if the mill we have before us today is not the original old mill, there *was* a mill here, and if that mill had survived, then it would be a very old mill today. The programme goes on after this point to detail the existing mill's history since 1966, and to be sure there is rather more credible historical evidence available to back up the claims made for the building. Frequently we find the most fascinating juxtapositions, collisions between the past and the present, which represents a kind of creative anachronism.

Additional evidence of the craze for the past is the mania for raising the wreckage of ancient shipping. The fascination of the *Mary Rose* and of film footage of the *Lusitania* and *Titanic* cannot be disputed. But in a world where so much needs to be done immediately, the expenditure of such resources and expertise in ransacking the past seems significant. And this is precisely at the centre of much of the media industry. Although it is true to say that there has been a long history of adapting Dickens's novels for the stage, right from the late 1830s,[21] it is nevertheless the case that any truly disinterested observer of our television culture would be forced to admit we have an obsession with the past, and with resurrecting old literary texts in the form of television costume drama. The BBC's already well-established tradition of the 'classic serial' has benefited considerably from this media atavism, and in fact its spirit has generously overspilled into commercial television. Granada Television, in particular, has contributed quite outstandingly to costume drama with *Hard Times*[22] and their celebrated version of *Brideshead Revisited*.[23] Significantly the essence of Evelyn Waugh's novel was memory and the immense pull of the past on the present. Skilled media morticians earn their bread by preparing the departed for friends and relatives to enjoy one longing, lingering look. In death they are made to look fresher, cleaner, and more wholesome than they ever looked in life. In the hands of the media the past is made to lie in state.

As Mrs Thatcher first stepped over the threshold of Number 10 in 1979 she uttered the famous prayer of St Francis of Assisi (1181–

1226). The prayer is in fact bogus. As the Rt Revd Dr J.R.H. Moorman, former Bishop of Ripon, wrote to explain to readers of *The Church Times* in 1986, it was composed in France in 1912. But as long as people believed Mrs Thatcher uttered a prayer of St Francis, what does it matter?

Notes

1. See Bernard Grebanier, *The Great Shakespearean Forgery* (1965). The young Ireland wrote an account, *Confessions of William Henry Ireland* (1805). George Chalmers published a defence of his support of Ireland's case: *An Apology for the Believers in the Shakespearean Papers* (1797). The authenticity of Ireland's forgeries was strongly contested by Joseph Ritson (1752–1803) and George Stevens (1736–1800).
2. George Brandt (ed.), *British Television Drama* (Cambridge: Cambridge University Press, 1981), p. 21. See also *Theatre Quarterly*, Vol. 2, no. 6, April–June 1972, pp. 26–38 and Vol. 2, no. 8, October–December 1972, p. 82 for production history of *Upstairs Downstairs*. Cf. Colin McArthur: 'Historical Drama' in Tony Bennett et al. (eds), *Popular Television and Film* (BFI/Open University, 1981), pp. 288 ff. and Robert Colls and Philip Dodd (eds), *Politics and Culture 1880–1920* (London: Croom Helm, 1986).
3. Cole Lesley, *The Life of Noel Coward* (Harmondsworth: Penguin, 1976), p. 158.
4. Quoted in Christopher Hill, *Reformation to Industrial Revolution* (Harmondsworth: Penguin, 1969), p. 197.
5. Godfrey Davies, *The Early Stuarts 1603–1660* (Oxford: Clarendon Press, 1985), pp. 103 ff.
6. Lord Macaulay, *The History of England from the Accession to James the Second*, Vol. 1, 1842 (London: Longman Green and Company, 1869) Ch. 1, p. 1.
7. Hill, *Reformation to Industrial Revolution*, op. cit., p. 198.
8. See Graham Holderness, 'Agincourt 1944' in Peter Humm et al. (eds), *Popular Fictions: Essays in Literature and History* (London: Methuen, 1986), pp. 173–95.
9. See Christopher Hibbert, *The Personal History of Samuel Johnson* (Harmondsworth: Penguin 1984), p. 33.
10. Comment recorded in *Tour of the Hebrides*, 18 September 1773.
11. Leslie Halliwell and Philip Purser, *Halliwell's Television Guide* (London: Granada, 1979) p. 7.
12. See Robert Giddings, 'Cooking the Books' in *New Society*, 14 June 1979, pp. 652–3.
13. See David Brown, *Walter Scott and the Historical Imagination* (London: Routledge & Kegan Paul, 1979) and Georg Lukács, *The Historical Novel*, translated by Hannah and Stanley Michael (Harmondsworth: Penguin, 1969), pp. 29–69. Mary Shelley's *Frankenstein, Or, The Modern Prometheus* (1818) was the signal for a stampede of the imagination –

Edgar Allan Poe (1809–49); Jules Verne (1828–1905) and H. G. Wells (1866–1946) were the pioneers. See Brian Aldiss, *The Billion Year Spree* (1973).

14. See Kenneth Clark, *The Gothic Revival* (1950) and R. Turner, *Nineteenth Century Architecture in Britain* (1950).

15. See Mark Girouard, *The Return of Camelot* (New Haven: Yale University Press, 1981), pp. 88–110, and cf. Benjamin Disraeli, *Endymion* (1880), Chapters 59–60.

16. Elder brother of Alfred, Lord Tennyson, educated at Trinity College, Cambridge; Vicar of Grasby. He published interesting poetry and excelled in sonnet form – *Poems by Two Brothers* (1827) (with Alfred), *Sonnets and Fugitive Pieces* (1830), *Small Tableaux* (1869). He died in 1879.

17. See Louis Napoleon Parker, *Several of My Lives* (1928). He wrote successful plays – *Rosemary* (1896); *Pomander Walk* (1910) and *Disraeli* (1911), the latter for George Arliss, who took the title role in the silent film version in 1921 and a sound version in 1929. During 1914–18 Parker devised several notable patriotic pageants in London and produced *The Pageant of Drury Lane* in 1918.

18. Michael Argyle, *Social Interaction* (London: Methuen, 1969), p. 114.

19. *Guardian*, 3 September 1986.

20. Cf. David Lowenthal, *The Past is a Foreign Country* (Cambridge: Cambridge University Press, 1985), pp. 363ff. and Robert Hewison, *The Heritage Industry* (London: Methuen, 1987), p. 15ff.

21. See F. Dubrez Fawcett, *Dickens the Dramatist* (London: W. H. Allen, 1952), pp. 44–100.

22. Scripted by Arthur Hopcraft and directed by John Irvin, first shown in Great Britain in 1977.

23. This was written for television by John Mortimer and adapted in eleven parts, first shown in Great Britain in 1981. It cost £5 000 000 and starred Jeremy Irons, Anthony Andrews and Diana Quick. It was sold to fourteen countries, including the USA, Canada, New Zealand and Australia, and earned eleven Emmy nominations in 1982.

3

The Classic Serial Tradition

As Terrance Dicks says in an interview later in this volume, the novels of Charles Dickens are the bread and butter and jam of the BBC's Classic Serials. Historically it seems as if this was all but written into the 'public service broadcasting' requirements when the Corporation was initiated, as the BBC willingly shouldered the burden of broadcasting the classics very early in its career. That such a great force for popular entertainment should take on the task of bringing Boz to such a wide public might not seem incongruous, as Dickens himself was so obviously assisted – indeed to a large extent actually shaped and conditioned – by the mass media of earlier generations.

Dickens's creativity began to mature in a society which was just absorbing the impact of modern print technology latent in the steam press at the end of the Napoleonic wars, and the emancipation by literacy of a whole new readership. Although Forster's Education Act was not passed until the year Dickens died, the Sunday School movement and various religious and philanthropic organizations had already laid the foundation of modern mass literacy.[1] In 1836, the year of *Pickwick Papers*, a correspondent wrote in the *New Sporting Magazine*:

> It is the patent age of new inventions and improvements. Our outward man and our inward man, our sense, all and sundry; everything that we eat, drink, or wear, stand upon, sit upon, walk upon, or ride upon . . . all are partakers of this wondrous march. It annihilates time, confounds space, unsettles rank and distinction. . . . Once upon a time there was your scholar, your traveller, your libertine, and a just and proper distinction amongst mankind. There was no jostling over the lines of demarcation naturally . . . drawn between one class and another. But now, Lord save us! Since the establishment of the 'general-united-imperial-anti-retrogradation-reading-made-easy-society' . . . every barrier which could tend to check the progress of knowledge has been removed. . . .

Serial publication opened up a whole new range of possibilities for the small printer as well as opportunities for the well-capitalized major publisher. Eight pages could be printed in one sheet on a hand press. Even quite lengthy volumes could be printed with almost no capital. The income of one issue paid for the next. Unsold weekly parts could be stitched and sold as monthly parts. The total remainder could be bound and sold as a single volume. In effect, all pockets could be appealed to. In order to keep costs down, there was a particular interest in publishing works which carried no copyright, or works were pirated. Dickens himself, whose successful career was launched on the swelling tide of the new publishing revolution, was to become one of the most frequent victims of publishing pirates – *Pixwick Papers*, as well as *The post-Humorous Notes of the Pickwickian Club* edited by 'Bos', *The Memoirs of Nicholas Nicklebery, Dombey and Daughter* are just a few of the more amusing examples.[2]

The fiction-publishing industry took full advantage of the new technology. During the Napoleonic wars, for example, the stationers' industry had been crippled by the shortage of paper. Paper cost as much as thirty shillings a ream, plus the three-pence-a-pound tax. There was also considerable wastage (the result of imperfect sheets). But in 1801 John Gamble patented his paper-making machine. This development had been held up for a time by trade rivals but by the 1820s it had clearly begun to make its impact. When factory-made paper began to appear on the market the cost of production was cut by half. Also, the paper made by this method was of much better quality and larger in size. This made possible the rotary steam press. This was achieved by Friedrich Koenig between 1811 and 1814. William Nicholson brought about the superseding of the screw press by the cylinder press. This enabled *The Times* to print four thousand impressions on one side an hour, achieved in the production of the issue for 29 November 1814. By 1848 (the year of *Dombey and Son*) it was possible to print 18 000 impressions an hour.

Another important element was the reduction of government duty on publications. In the early nineteenth century the annual sale of newspapers in Britain was 24 000 000, with about 550 published books, in ordinary editions of approximately 1000 copies. The government had attempted to control and restrict what was published at the turn of the century. Direct bribery of journalists – an established practice since the time of Sir Robert Walpole –

was supplemented by the subsidy of newspapers and journals favourable to the establishment.[3] Direct government control of publishing was replaced by various forms of market taxation, such as Stamp Duty on each page of newsprint, advertising revenue tax and paper duty. These were imposed not so much to raise revenue as to restrict publication and circulation. Stamp Duty was originally a halfpenny, but by 1815 it had risen to four pence. After the first Parliamentary Reform Act of 1832 the tax on advertisements was reduced, finally to be abolished in 1853, followed two years later by the abolition of Stamp Duty.

The role played by the massive development of transport systems in encouraging the expansion of publishing should not be underrated. Canals, road transport and the triumph of steam meant not only that publications could be marketed in areas many miles from the source of their production but that whole new markets were created, including significantly that of the railway bookstall.[4]

The very form in which Dickens's fiction was cast was to an overwhelming extent dictated by economic and technical forces beyond the author's control. It is tempting to assume an inert relationship between Dickens and his readers. Here, on the one hand is an author of genius who wants to write fiction, and, there, on the other hand, are thousands of readers who want to read stories. Dickens supplies this demand. The relationship which the 'genius' has to negotiate with his publishers, and the means of production and distribution in shaping his fiction are too seldom examined.[5]

It is an assertion easily made and readily accepted that the very factors which resulted in so much of Dickens's fiction being serialized in the first place contributed considerably to the novels being ideal broadcasting serial material. But this needs serious qualification. The experience of reading a Dickens novel when it first came out was leisurely. *Pickwick, Oliver Twist, Nicholas Nickleby, Barnaby Rudge, Martin Chuzzlewit, Dombey and Son* – all these 'novels' came out in serial parts, several of them taking as long as eighteen months to unfold. The multiplicity of characters, the complexity of narrative, the luxuriance of incident – all the things which we tend to think typically 'Dickensian' – are in considerable part the result of the conjunction of Dickens's creative genius with socioeconomic conditions. To engage the reader's interest over such a long period a vast canvas was needed, with elaborate plotlines. Part of the result of this was that Dickens's novels, like other nineteenth-century novels, always run the risk of what E. M. Forster later called 'a certain bagginess'. Dickens generally avoids this 'bagginess', however, by the simple fact that his novels possess a coherent centre or symbolic core.

Dickens's symbolism was his response, as a creative artist, to the challenge of making a long narrative have a completeness and wholeness all its own. This accounts for the impressive and remarkable fact that although utterly and obviously all written by the same person, *Dombey*, *Copperfield* and *Bleak House* are all individually and uniquely themselves. They are quite different works. The atmosphere of each book is that of itself. This is very often the result of very carefully chosen symbolism.

But the fact is that Dickens was a writer of genius and naturally his stock-in-trade is words. This is the first, and totally unbridgeable gap we face when discussing Dickens and film, or Dickens and television. It helps us account for the fact that what we get on the screen is not Dickens. It may look like Dickens and occasionally it may sound like Dickens, but it isn't really Dickens at all.

The overwhelmingly important thing about Dickens as a novelist is not the stories he tells, but the way he tells stories. It is essentially a matter of verbal texture and point of view. These are things which are very difficult to realize on screen. It is a fact that all of Dickens's masterstrokes are achieved textually. In *Hard Times*, for example, when Bitzer arrests young Tom Gradgrind, the boy's broken father asks: 'Bitzer, have you a heart?' His former prize pupil smiles at 'the oddity of the question'. This moment of supreme irony could not be recreated in any other form. The entire effectiveness of this passage – and there are a thousand such in the novels – is entirely textual. It can only achieve what its creator imagined in the form in which he expressed what he had imagined. To deny this is to fly in the face of all the evidence. A novel by Dickens works on your imagination because of the way in which he uses words. The 'story' is only a part of his power. The real strength is in the telling.

In no novel is this more so than in *Pickwick Papers*, and this is an example well worth pondering simply because it is so frequently filmed and broadcast. In this novel the energy is expelled with unique zest and abandon in *telling the story to you*. That *Pickwick* is one of the world's comic masterpieces is beyond question. What is also beyond question is that this is so because of the way Dickens tells the story of *Pickwick Papers*. What the Pickwickians get up to is all very droll, and the dialogue is masterly, but it is in the manner and style of the narrative that the true comic spirit is to be found.

The warm generosity of Dickens's mind pours itself out in his prose with an unstinting hand. Take this account of Samuel Pickwick in his cups:

> The wine, which had exerted its somniferous influence over Mr Snodgrass and Mr Winkle, had stolen upon the senses of Mr Pickwick. That gentleman had gradually passed through all the various stages which precede the lethargy produced by dinner, and its consequences. He had undergone the ordinary transitions from the height of conviviality to the depth of misery, and from the depth of misery to the height of conviviality. Like a gas lamp in the street, with the wind in the pipe, he had exhibited for a moment an unnatural brilliancy: then sunk so low as to be scarcely discernible: after a short interval he had burst out again, to enlighten for a moment, then flickered with an uncertain, staggering sort of light, and then gone out altogether.

Now, in film or television, we can show Pickwick the worse for drink, and then have him gradually subsiding into sleep. But we cannot convey what Dickens conveys in that passage – the image of the gas light would have to go for nothing, as would the native drollery of the characters involved. Unfortunately for the filmmaker the same is true of much of Dickens's fiction.[6]

Yet the myth that it was somehow part of God's plan for the world that Dickens's novels should be suitable for film and television is almost unassailable. Kevin Brownlow writes that D. W. Griffith was called 'the Shakespeare of the screen' but goes on to argue that Griffith had much more in common with Dickens:

> The use of melodrama amid settings of complete reality, the exaggerated, yet still truthful characters, the fascination with detail, the accuracy of dress and behaviour, the sentimentality, the attitude toward religion, and the outrage over social injustice, are all points which their works have in common.[7]

Griffith did not film any of Dickens's novels, but his work – such as *Orphans of the Storm* (1922) – shows the influence of his understanding of Dickens. This construction of the 'Dickensian' has certainly affected several generations of film-makers. If we look briefly at the record, that is what we find.

Pickwick Papers was filmed several times in rather episodic silent versions. There is a rather lacklustre version with James Hayter a subdued Pickwick, Nigel Patrick a genteel Jingle, directed by Noel Langley in 1952. It came to life in the trial scene, wholly as the result of the larger-than-life performance of Donald Wolfitt as Buzfuz.

Oliver Twist, curiously, seems to have attracted little attention from the silent film-makers. In 1922 it was made with Jackie Coogan as Oliver and Lon Chaney as Fagin. Two very interesting versions contain marvellous Fagin creations – Alec Guinness in 1948 (directed by David Lean) and Ron Moody in the 1968 musical *Oliver!* (directed by Carol Reed).

Nicholas Nickleby seems hardly to have been a favourite. A one-reeler of the Dotheboys Hall sequence was made in 1903 and there was an unspirited version directed by Alberto Cavalcanti in 1947. Likewise, *Barnaby Rudge*, although filmed in 1915 starring Chrissie White, has not been filmed since.

The Old Curiosity Shop was filmed several times in the silent era. There was a sound version in 1935 with Hay Petrie, the Scottish character actor, as Quilp. In 1975 *Reader's Digest* released a musical version of this novel, directed by Michael Tuchner, entitled *Mister Quilp*. Anthony Newley was an incredible choice to play the villainous dwarf and was, on the whole, disastrous, earning from the *Illustrated London News* the description of 'a galvanized Quasimodo on a permanent high'. The film lacked a convincing Little Nell, although David Warner and Jill Bennett made a gallant effort with the roles of Sampson and Sally Brass. The exteriors (shot at Lacock, near Bath) were charming.

A Christmas Carol has attracted many film-makers. There were silent versions in 1908, 1910 and 1913, the latter with the veteran British ham Seymour Hicks as Scrooge, who also starred in a sound version in 1933. It was filmed in 1916 with Rupert Julian. Reginald Owen starred in a version in 1938 and in 1951 Brian Desmond Hurst directed Alistair Sim as Scrooge. In 1970 the Dickens centenary was blessed with the release of Leslie Bricusse's musical *Scrooge*, which had a virtuoso performance from Albert Finney as a splendidly wicked Scrooge, relishing his own wickedness, but little else. It was directed by Ronald Neame. Inexplicably it was updated from the 1840s to the 1860s and the first ghost (the child) was transmogrified into Dame Edith Evans. It was rumoured that Rex Harrison and Richard Harris were both offered the lead and declined. In the event they were proved wise.

Dombey and Son was filmed in modern dress in 1931 as *Rich Man's Folly* with George Bancroft as Mr Dombey, and directed by John Cromwell. It was not very interesting.

David Copperfield existed in several silent versions and got the full Hollywood treatment when George Cukor directed an all-star cast in 1934. Freddie Bartholomew was the young David, Roland Young was Heep, W.C. Fields played Micawber, Lionel Barrymore was Dan'l Peggotty, and Edna May Oliver created a memorable Aunt Betsy. It was written by Hugh Walpole (who also played the small role of the Vicar). By no means perfect, the film does stick in the mind, and as late as 1972 Basil Wright wrote that it was 'perhaps the finest casting of all time'. In 1969 Delbert Mann directed a film version for American television which was like a poor cake made from excellent ingredients – it has Ralph Richardson as Micawber, Michael Redgrave as Peggotty, Edith Evans as Betsy, Ron Moody as Heep and Emlyn Williams as Mr Dick.

Little Dorrit was filmed in Germany in 1933 with Anny Ondra, and remained unravished until 1987 when an impressive British film version was released. Christine Edzard's two-part version of Dickens's complex narrative is an extraordinary achievement. Even though the two parts total six hours' viewing much has been dropped from the text, including much of the melodramatic apparatus. The first part is called 'Nobody's Fault' and tells the story, through his eyes, of the return of Arthur Clennam from China after an absence of twenty years and the dreadful impact on him of the mechanisms of social injustice in modern industrial capitalized Britain, the image for which is that recurring Dickensian symbol, the prison. The second part handles much of the same material, but through Amy Dorrit's eyes. Thus a very real – indeed almost Herculean – effort has been made to deploy point of view as Dickens had used it, to present experience panoramically. Arthur's view is essentially that of the innocent returning from outside and seeing problems and villainies but not perceiving that human effects have human causes. Amy's view is sharper: a child of the prison herself, she has the prisoner's long-apprenticed wisdom and craft. The cast is, on the whole, a fine one, but somehow the very sincere endeavours to be true to the text have handicapped the movie with a stultifying *literariness* – it is

'Dickensian' rather than a Dickens film, it resembles what a Victorian film would have looked like, if the Victorians had made films. This is heavily reinforced by the music which is bang on-period – Verdi – mostly from *La Forza del Destino* which was premiered at St Petersburg in 1862. This heavy, inescapably grand operatic quality further serves to stifle the comic afflatus. It is clear that in writing this novel for the screen every effort was made to preserve the spirit of Dickens, but somehow it has evaporated in the process. The highly moral tone remains, the sense of social outrage, the dreadful tension between what things should be and what human beings have made them – but the animation, the spirit, the gushing irrepressible *life* is not there. The costumes, the make-up, the extremely high professionalism of the acting are all obviously there to be admired, but the entire performance sinks under the weight of its own good taste. The cast is the best that money could buy – Derek Jacobi (Clennam), Joan Greenwood (Mrs Clennam), Alec Guinness (William Dorrit), Cyril Cusack (Frederick Dorrit), Sarah Pickering (Amy Dorrit), Robert Morley (Lord Decimus Barnacle) and Michael Elphick (Mr Merdle). The critical response in Britain was very interesting. Film reviewers were awed by its weight and quality. Derek Malcolm in the *Guardian* welcomed the film on its release but most of his review consisted of long interview-quotations from Christine Edzard herself introduced by several laudatory paragraphs which characterized the courage, scope and enterprise of this version of a Dickens novel.[8] 'It may not be the Dickens you are used to,' he warned *Guardian*-readers gently, 'there is no sentimentality, no whimsy, no feyness and no grotesquery. This is not the Dickens we might fondly remember perhaps, from the comfortable haze of childhood. This is the real thing . . .'.[9] Philip French in the *Observer* was quite sure this was one of the best film versions of a novel that he had ever seen, 'based on the greatest novel by the man who invented the English Christmas and anticipated the language of cinema in his literary craft.'[10] The more the reviewers knew about nineteenth-century history and the novels of Dickens, the less extravagant their praise. Raphael Samuel, Tutor in History at Ruskin College, and an editor of *History Workshop Journal*, sees the film much as a product of Thatcherism. The past, he argues, can never be transcribed, it always has to be reinvented. And it is never innocently reinvented but will always bear the fingerprints and distortions of the time which reinvented it.

Raphael Samuel convincingly argues that Dickens was not a realist, in the way film-makers want him to be; his art bore only the slightest, accidental relationship to 'Victorian England'. His realism was grotesque realism, his genius caricature – and consequently this works against the efforts of film to present a 'real' world. The later 'dark novels' of Dickens were only rediscovered critically during the 1940s, at a time when 'Victorian' values were being rejected. This leads him to assert:

Christine Edzard's *Little Dorrit* might speculatively be explained by the rehabilitation of Victorian values which has been such a feature of recent years. In one aspect it reflects that urban pastoral which emerged in the 1960's as an antiphon to modernisation and slum clearance; in another the aestheticisation of dying industries. In another aspect the film reproduces the enthusiasms of conservation . . . *Little Dorrit*, though making an occasional gesture in the direction of social criticism, celebrates Victoriana. . . . In its own way it endorses 'old fashioned' family values . . . transforming a novel of alienation into a commonplace romance . . . it reflects, too, the 'heritage' industry. In the manner of a contemporary theme park, it invites us to take a Victorian Day Out . . . in which London is not a prison-house but a playground, and poverty – provided it is safely period – picturesque.

Nevertheless, this version of *Little Dorrit* will have an impact on the filming of Dickens's novels. Things will never be quite the same as before. *A Tale of Two Cities* has proved irresistible. It was filmed in 1917 with William Farnum, directed by Frank Lloyd, and again in 1926 with Martin Harvey. In 1935 Jack Conway directed a splendidly high-spirited version with Ronald Colman and a 1958 version with Dirk Bogarde was saved from oblivion by the radiance of Dorothy Tutin.

Great Expectations has always been an attractive commodity for film-makers. There was a silent version in 1917 with Jack Pickford. In 1934 Stuart Walker directed another version, with Francis L. Sullivan as Jaggers (a role he was to repeat for David Lean) and the 'classic' version was made in 1946 with John Mills, Alec Guinness and Valerie Hobson, directed by David Lean, which will be examined in detail later. A colour version was made in 1975 for US television, directed by Joseph Hardy, starring Michael York, Sarah Miles and Anthony Quayle. It was originally filmed as a musical but the version shown in the UK had the musical numbers omitted (which may have been an asset). It is not without interest. It was not heavily 'Dickensian', and Pip as a boy, interestingly enough, did have a regional accent. Joss Ackland as Joe lacked any grotesque qualities and was played as a good, simple man. The bitterness and cruel snobberies of the story were smoothed over and there was no sense of the injustice of the law or the barbarities of the class system.

Now, for an author whose work, it is so glibly asserted, was *made* for the cinema, the record is not all that impressive.[11] Apart from the recent version of *Little Dorrit*, which has a reputation still a-making, the only one of the films listed above which is universally admitted to be a great film is David Lean's *Great Expectations*. Wherever you look you will find this film acclaimed: '*Great Expectations*, as well as being pictorially superb, manages to capture the essence of the book and hold the Gothick extravagances and acute social comment in perfect balance.' That is John Russell Taylor's opinion[12] and Basil Wright was no less flattering: 'David Lean's *Great Expectations* had a quality of the highest order and, with *David Copperfield*, must be rated a secure film classic.'[13] George Perry rated it 'by far the richest evocation of a Dickensian novel of the many that have been filmed.'[14] These are very serious claims, very seriously made, and they should be very seriously considered. But to test the validity of these judgements we need first to see how Dickens's narrative works *as a novel* and then to examine the success of David Lean's work *as a film*.

Notes

1. See Louis James, *Fiction for the Working Man* (Harmondsworth: Penguin, 1974), pp. 1–4.
2. See Victor E. Neuburg, *Popular Literature* (Harmondsworth: Penguin, 1977), pp. 171–2.
3. Raymond Williams, *Communications* (Harmondsworth: Penguin, 1977), p. 15.
4. Thomas Burke, *Travel in England* (London: Batsford, 1949), pp. 115ff.
5. Edgar Johnson, *Charles Dickens – His Tragedy and Triumph* (London: Hamish Hamilton, 1952), Vol. 1, pp. 116–20.
6. For a further discussion of Dickens's textual method, see Keith Selby, *How to Study a Dickens Novel* (London: Macmillan, 1989).
7. Kevin Brownlow, *The Parade's Gone By* (London: Secker and Warburg, 1968), p. 85.

8. Derek Malcolm, 'Double Dorrit', *Guardian*, 27 November 1987, p. 22.
9. Derek Malcolm, 'The Dickens of a Dorrit', *Guardian*, 10 December 1987, p. 15.
10. Philip French, 'Let's Twist Again', *Observer*, 13 December 1987, p. 15.
11. See Michael Poole, 'Dickens and Film: A Hundred and One Uses for a Dead Author' in Robert Giddings (ed.), *The Changing World of Charles Dickens* (London: Vision Press/Barnes and Noble, 1983), pp. 148ff.
12. See Richard Roud (ed.), *Cinema – A Critical Dictionary, The Major Film Makers* (London: Hodder & Stoughton, 1980), pp. 833ff.
13. Basil Wright, *The Long View: An International History of the Cinema* (London: Paladin, 1976), p. 93.
14. George Perry, *The Great British Picture Show* (London: Granada, 1975), p. 126.

4
The Classic Novel: *Great Expectations*

The purpose of this chapter is to present an analysis of *Great Expectations* as a novel. No attempt is made to examine the novel in its broader social or historical context; instead, the concentration throughout is on the unique *linguistic* qualities of the novel.

Great Expectations belongs to the type of novel known as a *Bildungsroman*, or education novel. Broadly speaking, the education novel tells the story of the personal and moral development of its central character. By the end of the novel this central character has learnt something about the world or about himself or herself, and has become a very different person from the one we first met in the novel's opening.

In *Great Expectations* the central character is Pip, and he tells his story from the point of view of his adulthood, looking back over the events which have formed his character. All this has certain implications for the form of the novel: because Pip tells his own story directly to the reader, we have the impression of being able to see into his mind as he speaks. In addition, this use of first-person narration has the effect of creating a strongly realistic impression of the fictional world; but it also has other effects too, and we will see some of these later. For the moment, however, it will be useful merely to outline the novel's plot, for it is in considering the basic pattern of the plot that we should be able to identify the novel's major thematic concerns.

Great Expectations tells the story of Philip Pirrip, known as 'Pip', an orphan brought up by his bad-tempered sister and her warm-hearted husband, Joe Gargery, the village blacksmith.

As a child, Pip is confronted by an escaped convict on the marshes, and the convict – Abel Magwitch – forces Pip to bring him food and a file. Magwitch is recaptured, however, after a struggle with another escaped convict, Compeyson, and both are returned to their prison-ship. Some time later Pip is sent for by Miss Havisham, who, having been jilted on her wedding-day many

54

years previously, has lived cut off from society in her home, Satis
House, ever since. Miss Havisham has an adopted daughter, the
beautiful Estella, whom she has brought up as a cold, heartless
child to wreak her revenge on men. Pip falls in love with Estella,
but she immediately rebuffs him and as a result he begins to
despise his lowly origins. When Pip is fourteen, Miss Havisham
pays for him to be apprenticed to Joe Gargery, the village blacksmith, and his visits to Satis House and to Estella come to an end.

Four years into his apprenticeship Pip receives a visit from an
Old Bailey lawyer, Jaggers, whom he had met at Satis House some
years previously. Jaggers has been sent to tell him that he has
ready money to make Pip a gentleman, and expectations of great
wealth for him. The money comes from an unknown benefactor,
and the only condition attached to it is that Pip must never
attempt to discover the identity of this unknown benefactor. Pip
immediately assumes his benefactor to be Miss Havisham, and
assumes also that she is preparing him to be a gentleman so that
he may in time marry Estella. He goes to London to learn to be a
gentleman. There he becomes friends with Herbert Pocket, a
nephew of Miss Havisham's, whom he had previously met at Satis
House.

In London, Pip becomes proud and snobbish and neglects his
old friends, but particularly the loving blacksmith, Joe Gargery.
He gradually gets himself further and further into debt, and is
continually snubbed by Estella, who is now living in London. It is
at this point that Pip's real benefactor is revealed. This turns out
to be Abel Magwitch, the convict he helped on the marshes when
he was a child, and who has in the meantime made a fortune as a
transported convict in Australia. Pip at first rejects the lowly
Magwitch, and is ashamed that the source of his present wealth
comes from a criminal. Pip learns that Estella has married the
boorish Bentley Drummle, and this throws him further into the
depths of depression.

Magwitch is finally recaptured, when he is betrayed by his old
enemy Compeyson, and is sentenced to death. But he dies before
he can be executed. Pip is left penniless, although he has discovered
that Magwitch is Estella's father, that her real mother is Jaggers's
housekeeper, and that Compeyson is the lover who jilted Miss
Havisham on her wedding day. After a long illness in which he is
nursed patiently by Joe, who also pays off his debts, Pip sees the
idle foolishness of his previous way of life and returns to his home

village, intent on asking Biddy, a childhood friend, to marry him.

But on his return to the blacksmith's home he discovers Biddy and Joe on their wedding-day, and determines to put his own life in order by going to work as a clerk for the company in which Herbert is now a partner. Eleven years later he visits the ruins of Satis House (Miss Havisham is now dead) where he meets Estella. Mistreated by Drummle, Estella is now a widow and a reformed, affectionate woman. Their hands clasp, with the promise of love, happiness and marriage in the inevitable future.

A useful way to start making sense of a novel is to look for some type of pattern in the plot. This pattern can take many forms, but a good rule of thumb is to look for a situation, or a particular type of character, or a particular relationship between characters being repeated several times. This applies even where, as here, we have a fairly long and intricate plot. This in itself, however, can tell us a great deal about the novel.

One of the reasons why the plot is so complicated is that it is being reported by the first-person narrator, Pip, and Pip – unlike an omniscient narrator – cannot know everything about all the characters and all their relationships. The result of this is that things are gradually discovered, both by the reader and by Pip. What gradually comes out in Pip's story is that many of the characters are either unwittingly related to each other (such as Magwitch being Estella's father), or that they want to keep their relationships secret. When Pip is in London, for example, posing as a gentleman, he wants to keep his relationship with Joe Gargery a secret from his new friends, the Finches of the Grove. Similarly, Herbert Pocket has to keep his relationship with Clara a secret because he knows his snobbish mother will not approve of her. What we now need to consider is how all these secret relationships illustrate something about the conflict or tension at the centre of the novel.

We can begin by thinking about the concept of a relationship between people. Normally, this has to do with family ties, or sexual and emotional ties between people. One of its characteristics is that it has to do with feelings, with love for another person. Why then, should so many of the relationships in *Great Expectations* have to be kept a secret? The simple answer is: money.

Think, for example, of the various secret benefactors in the novel. Pip believes that Miss Havisham is his secret benefactor, when in fact it is Magwitch – but Pip can ask no questions, since it must be kept a secret. Later, Pip arranges, with Miss Havisham as a secret benefactor, to establish Herbert in business – but the whole thing must be kept a secret. One of the reasons for wanting to be a benefactor is presumably a desire to help somebody by giving them money. But in all the cases in the novel – with the notable exception of Joe, who pays off Pip's debts – to give financial help to somebody means hiding who you are, and hiding your relationship to that person. In other words, the thing which intervenes between characters in most of the relationships in the novel is money. Money actually obscures the expression of love, and this is a major theme in the novel. What is particularly interesting, however, is that all the characters have the *need* for love and for a relationship with another person, but this is consistently obscured by financial considerations.

In such a situation characters become utilities: Estella is handed over to Miss Havisham by Jaggers to save her mother from the gallows; Pip is bought off by Miss Havisham when she has finished toying with his emotions, and made Joe's apprentice; even Miss Havisham's original jilting by Compeyson was done for money. Looked at in this way, the whole novel can be seen to stem from a basic conflict between love and money, and it is this conflict which occupies Pip in his narrative. When he goes to London he leaves Joe's natural love and simplicity of spirit behind him. But in London, and although he has ready money in his pocket, his snobbishness forces him to keep his relationship with Joe a secret; he is snubbed by Estella, disdained by the Finches, and ultimately without love because he is emotionally alone. What this suggests is that all people, no matter what material wealth they possess, need the love and friendship of other people, but that money can make that love and friendship impossible to have.

If we accept, then, that what I have outlined above represents the central conflict in the novel, it will now be useful to look in some detail at various scenes from the novel to see how these tensions and themes are realized linguistically.

Consider, for example, the opening of the novel, in which Pip is first introduced:

My father's family name being Pirrip, and my Christian name Philip, my infant tongue could make of both names nothing longer or more explicit than Pip. So, I called myself Pip, and came to be called Pip.

> I give Pirrip as my father's family name, on the authority of his tombstone and my sister – Mrs Joe Gargery, who married the blacksmith. As I never saw my father or my mother, and never saw any likeness of either of them (for their days were long before the days of photographs), my fancies regarding what they were like, were unreasonably derived from their tombstones.

> (*Great Expectations*, Penguin, 1976, p. 35)

What we can notice about this passage is how its linguistic details illustrate the more general tension in the novel as a whole. The passage itself is straightforward enough: it introduces the novel's central character, Pip. But if you think about the way in which it does that, you will immediately notice that there is a tension of some kind between Pip the child and the family of which he should be a part. That is, this child can report who he is only on the basis of fragmentary evidence gleaned from inanimate or distant sources: 'I give Pirrip as my father's family name, on the authority of his tombstone'. He has no father to tell him anything, no mother, not even an image of them '(for their days were long before the days of photographs)'. Even his one surviving relative – his sister – is in a sense no relative to him at all, since even she does not share his name: 'and my sister – Mrs Joe Gargery'. If we now extend the idea that here we have a child curiously isolated from the family of which he should be a part, we should begin to see how the passage focuses on the novel's central themes.

For example, not only is this child wholly alone in the world, but he literally does not know who he is. Since he has no family he has relation to anything at all. Consequently, he is forced into the situation of having to provide himself with a name: 'I called myself Pip, and came to be called Pip.' A child's name is normally provided by the parents, and that assumes a child's relationship with the past and a personal, family history to support it. But Pip has no past, and hence no relationship to anything. Consequently, not only does he possess nothing (and much of *Great Expectations* is about the desire to possess), but he also has no status in the world, because he is wholly alienated from it. He has no place anywhere, and is nobody. We could safely project from this that much of the novel will have to do with Pip trying to become somebody, trying to discover who he is. The only way in which he can do this, as the above passage suggests, is by building relationships with other people, since he has none to start with. The effect of the passage as a whole, then, is that it impresses very forcefully on our minds a sense of Pip's isolation in the world, and the need for him to build relationships with other people in order to discover who he is. The novel details his successes and failures in this quest to discover a person in himself and a position in the world. This involves Pip in attempting to build relationships with other characters in the novel.

The only loving relationship in which we see Pip in the early part of the novel is with Joe Gargery, his sister's husband. Any passage in which he and Pip appear together will tell us a lot about the closeness of their simple relationship, but it may be more productive to look at Pip and Joe together being confronted by another character who is not a part of their relationship. The extract I have chosen describes Joe and Pip at Satis House, where they have been summoned by Miss Havisham who plans to pay for Pip to be apprenticed to Joe:

'Have you brought his indentures with you?' asked Miss Havisham.

'Well, Pip, you know', replied Joe, as if that were a little unreasonable, 'you yourself see me put 'em in my 'at, and therefore you know as they are here.' With which he took them out, and gave them, not to Miss Havisham, but to me. I am afraid I was ashamed of the dear good fellow – I *know* I was ashamed of him – when I saw that Estella stood at the back of Miss Havisham's chair, and that her eyes laughed mischievously. I took the indentures out of his hand and gave them to Miss Havisham.

'You expected,' said Miss Havisham, as she looked them over, 'no premium with the boy?'

'Joe!' I remonstrated; for he made no reply at all. 'Why don't you answer—?'

'Pip,' returned Joe, cutting me short as if he were hurt, 'which I meantersay that were not a question requiring a answer betwixt yourself and me, and which you know the answer to be full well No. You know it to be No, Pip, and wherefore should I say it?'

Miss Havisham glanced at him as if she understood what he really was, better than I had thought possible, seeing what he was there; and took up a little bag from the table beside her.

'Pip has earned a premium here,' she said, 'and here it is.

There are five-and-twenty guineas in this bag. Give it to your
master, Pip.' (p. 129)

The first thing we notice about this passage is its linguistic oddity.
What we can notice particularly is that in the above passage, Joe
uses language in a way which is clearly deviant. This awakens us
as readers to the fact that Joe is in some way outside ordered and
conventional society. His view of the world, as the above passage
demonstrates, is one based upon a simple love for his fellow men,
and this is brought out in the way he speaks a language other than
that used by the inhabitants of the world of money. Consequently,
we can note that in this passage, and in the novel as a whole,
there is a tension between the world of love (represented by Joe),
and the world of money (represented by Miss Havisham and
Estella). Between these two we find Pip, who is in some way
related to both. And this directs our attention to a more specific
tension: Pip's relation to Joe, on the one hand, and his relation to
Miss Havisham and Estella on the other.

. To pull these ideas together, then, we can say that the tension
in this passage is in the relationship between the various characters
and Pip, the subject of the transaction. That it is a transaction is
well worth keeping in mind, for it is this which provides the focus
of the tensions within the passage. These tensions all bear down
upon Pip, whom each character regards differently: to Joe, the
relationship is simple – he loves Pip dearly; to Miss Havisham, Pip
is a utility who has 'earned a premium', and now she has finished
with him she is selling him off to another master – 'Give it to your
master, Pip', she says, meaning Joe; and to Estella, Pip is an object
of disdain, the 'common labouring boy' (p. 89) she treated 'as
insolently as if [Pip] were a dog in disgrace' (p. 92), and whom
she now regards from behind Miss Havisham's chair. Having
identified this general tension between the characters in the passage
as a whole, we can now look at the details of the passage and
consider how these reinforce this tension.

To take Joe's relationship with Pip first. The most striking thing
about Joe's response to the situation is that he replies not to Miss
Havisham, but to Pip. This in itself is immediately amusing, and
there are all sorts of ways in which we can account for it
naturalistically. There is every reason to assume that this simple
village blacksmith is understandably in awe of this strange woman
in her strange house. But, as always, and although we can account

for the situation naturalistically, Joe's response also fits in with the thematic tensions of the passage and of the novel as a whole. When Miss Havisham confirms with Joe that he expected 'no premium for the boy', Joe fails to answer. The reason for this is plain: he doesn't answer because he has no answer. As he tells Pip, it 'were not a question requiring an answer betwixt yourself and me'. Joe is unnerved and affronted not only by Miss Havisham's strange appearance, but also by what he sees as her strange desire to turn his relationship with Pip into a commercial one. In refusing to talk directly to Miss Havisham, he is refusing also to turn his love for Pip into a commercial transaction.

Miss Havisham and Estella, on the other hand, share in their view of Pip only as an object – a point reinforced by the fact that they both see him, quite literally, from the same position: 'Estella stood at the back of Miss Havisham's chair'. Their relationship to Pip and Joe, signalled by the physical distance between them, is the relationship of master to servant; Miss Havisham, for example, is insistent that – as she says a little later – 'Gargery is your [Pip's] new master now' (p. 130), implying, therefore, that she was his master previously. Just as Joe cannot conceive of a relationship based upon economic principles, so Miss Havisham and Estella are unable to conceive of a relationship based upon love. This conflict has massive implications for Pip's relationship with Joe, and marks a turning-point in his career.

This can be seen most obviously in the way Pip describes Joe. Previously, he has told us that his love for Joe was a simple matter of equality: 'I had always treated Joe as a larger species of child, and as no more than my equal' (p. 40). However, now that he is the subject of a commercial transaction, and confronted by the world of money represented by Miss Havisham, Pip's simple love for Joe is replaced by shame: 'I am afraid to say I was ashamed of the dear good fellow – I *know* I was ashamed of him'. But not only is Pip ashamed of Joe, he suddenly enters into a new relationship with him, the relationship of master and servant. On the one hand, Joe, as Miss Havisham insists, is Pip's new 'master'; but on the other, and as Pip now sees Joe, he is a socially inept fool, and somebody to be ashamed of in front of Miss Havisham and Estella. This tension between Pip and Joe on the one hand, Estella and Miss Havisham on the other, underpins the more general tension in the novel as a whole between the world of love and the world of money, for it is the pernicious effect of money upon people and relationships which destroys the simple love Pip had previously held for Joe.

When Miss Havisham makes Pip Joe's apprentice, she is effectively paying him off for his services to her. But Pip, because of a series of coincidences regarding Jaggers, has a secret belief that she will one day make it possible for him to become a gentleman and marry Estella. That she has no such intention only serves to reinforce the revenge that she is exacting upon Pip through Estella. But the effect of Estella upon Pip, and the effect of his delusions about Miss Havisham's intentions, makes him increasingly dissatisfied with his life at the forge, and with his lowly station as a blacksmith's apprentice. In the fourth year of this apprenticeship, Mr Jaggers arrives from London, bringing news of Pip's great expectations:

'My name,' he said, 'is Jaggers, and I am a lawyer in London. I am pretty well known. I have unusual business to transact with you, and I commence by explaining that it is not of my originating. If my advice had been asked, I should not have been here. It was not asked, and you see me here. What I have to do as the confidential agent of another, I do. No less, no more.'

Finding that he could not see us very well from where he sat, he got up, and threw one leg over the back of a chair and leaned upon it; thus having one foot on the seat of the chair, and one foot on the ground.

'Now Joseph Gargery, I am the bearer of an offer to relieve you of this young fellow your apprentice. You would not object to cancel his indentures, at his request and for his good? You would want nothing for so doing?'

'Lord forbid that I should want anything for not standing in Pip's way,' said Joe, staring.

'Lord forbidding is pious, but not to the purpose,' returned Mr Jaggers. 'The question is, Would you want anything? Do you want anything?'

'The answer is,' returned Joe sternly, 'No.'

I thought Mr Jaggers glanced at Joe, as if he considered him a fool for his disinterestedness. But I was too much bewildered between breathless curiosity and surprise, to be sure of it.

'Very well,' said Mr Jaggers. 'Recollect the admission you have made, and don't try to go from it presently.'

'Who's a-going to try?' retorted Joe. (p. 164)

The basic tension we can see in this passage is a simple one: love on the one side, money on the other. Certainly it is easy to detect in Joe's manner his adherence to his feelings for Pip, and in Jaggers's manner his adherence to the facts of the case; Joe is adamant that he will not stand in Pip's way, and refuses to accept any money for releasing him from his apprenticeship ('The answer is,' returned Joe sternly, 'No.'); Jaggers is equally adamant that he is merely carrying out the actions of another ('What I have to do as the confidential agent of another, I do. No less, no more.'). What is interesting is not so much the simple honesty with which Joe responds to the suggestion that Pip be made the subject of a commercial transaction, but rather the simple honesty with which Jaggers carries out his business. Between the two it is possible to notice a subtle piece of information being conveyed by the text about Pip himself.

But to take Joe first. The situation in which Joe finds himself would seem to be identical to that in which he found himself with Miss Havisham in the previous passage: he is being made a financial offer regarding Pip. But Joe is altogether more confident in this passage. He answers Jaggers directly, 'sternly', and not *through* Pip, as he does in the previous passage with Miss Havisham. Jaggers, on the other side, is equally straightforward: 'I have unusual business to transact with you, and I commence by explaining that it is not of my originating. If my advice had been asked, I should not have been here.' Jaggers is merely carrying out the orders of another and nothing more.

Now what we have here is an interesting situation involving two apparently diametrically opposed characters, one devoted to the world of feelings and love, the other devoted to the world of facts and evidence. What the passage does, however, is to illustrate that these two characters are in a way very similar. They are clearly devoted to two opposed systems, but they serve those systems honestly. Of course, Jaggers has always received something of a bad press from critics, but the evidence of the text demonstrates that he is a wholly trustworthy person, reliable and efficient, and devoted to carrying out his clients' needs. He may not like the system in which he works – a point reinforced by the way in which he is constantly washing his hands with strong-smelling soap, as if to wash himself clean of the corrupt world with which he deals – but his work in it is carried out with scrupulous attention and devoted honesty.

What this seems to suggest is that the two characters of Joe and Jaggers share in a fundamental honesty. The systems in which they work are different, but there is a natural sympathy between them – a point emphasized by Jaggers standing with one foot on the floor, and one foot on the chair, as if to suggest this link between the two characters. And indeed, if we think about the two characters as two sides of the same coin we can begin to see some interesting parallels between them. Before the novel opens, both men have come across a woman with a child, and both respond according to their view of the world: Joe married Mrs Joe to provide love for her and the child, Pip; Jaggers had the child Estella adopted, to save her mother from the gallows. Although they both respond differently, they both respond in the best way that their view of the world allows. In a sense, Joe and Jaggers function as unchanging symbols of the two worlds of love and money, and this explains why it is that they seem never to age, while Pip most clearly does. In London, this division between love and money is apparently reconciled in the character of Wemmick who, strangely balanced between Little Britain and Newgate, leads two quite separate lives. But this is a balance of opposites that Pip never achieves, simply because he does not understand the integrity of both Joe, and Jaggers, to the systems they represent.

This idea – that Pip fails to understand the integrity of each character – is given to us in a subtle form in the above passage. Watching the exchange between Joe and Jaggers, Pip is unsure how to interpret what he sees: 'I thought Mr Jaggers glanced at Joe, as if he considered him a fool for his disinterestedness. But I was too much bewildered between breathless curiosity and surprise, to be sure of it.' The reason he is uncertain is because he does not understand the nature of these two men; he fails to understand the simple love of which Joe is the epitome, and he fails to understand Jaggers's integrity to the world of facts and money. Consequently, when he does go to London, he falls between the two worlds of Joe and Jaggers and quickly becomes a worthless snob. He cuts himself off from Joe and the love he can offer, but, unlike Jaggers, he fails to understand the consequences of being a part of the world of money: isolation from others, loneliness and lovelessness.

In comparison to the sort of honesty and integrity that I have suggested we can see in Jaggers, Miss Havisham's manipulation of Estella's character is clearly destructive. The following scene occurs at Satis House, where Pip has been asked to accompany Estella.

> We were seated by the fire, as just now described, and Miss Havisham still had Estella's arm drawn through her own, and still clutched Estella's hand in hers, when Estella gradually began to detach herself. She had shown a proud impatience more than once before, and had rather endured that fierce affection than accepted or returned it.
>
> 'What!' said Miss Havisham, flashing her eyes upon her, 'are you tired of me?'
>
> 'Only a little tired of myself,' replied Estella, disengaging her arm, and moving to the great chimney-piece, where she stood looking down at the fire.
>
> 'Speak the truth, you ingrate!' cried Miss Havisham, passionately striking her stick upon the floor; 'you are tired of me.'
>
> Estella looked at her with perfect composure, and again looked down at the fire. Her graceful figure and her beautiful face expressed a self-possessed indifference to the wild heat of the other, that was almost cruel.
>
> 'You stock and stone!' exclaimed Miss Havisham. 'You cold, cold heart!'
>
> 'What?' said Estella, preserving her attitude of indifference as she leaned against the great chimney-piece and only moving her eyes; 'do you reproach me for being cold? You?'
>
> 'Are you not?' was the fierce retort.
>
> 'You should know,' said Estella. 'I am what you have made me. Take all the praise, take all the blame; take all the success, take all the failure; in short, take me.' (pp. 321–2)

We have already noted how tightly-structured the text is in providing linguistic details which function both naturalistically and symbolically. The above passage needs to be considered very carefully to get at the way in which Dickens creates the linguistic reality of the scene. Certainly, the tension in the passage is obvious enough, and has to do with the conflict between the burning passion of Miss Havisham, and the cold indifference of Estella. This is presented in such a way as to reverse the natural order of things: Estella, young, beautiful and attractive, attributes which we normally associate with the passion of youth, is standing near the fire, and yet presents nothing but a cold, uncaring and unloving character; Miss Havisham, old and wizened like a witch, is paradoxically burning with passion. We can identify this conflict in the language used to describe the two women. Estella is 'proud', she 'endures' Miss Havisham's affection, she possesses 'perfect composure', but also a 'self-possessed indifference' which is 'almost cruel', she leans impassive against the chimney-piece 'only moving her eyes'. Miss Havisham, on the other hand, craves Estella's contact with a 'fierce affection', her eyes 'flash', she 'passionately' strikes her stick upon the floor. The contradiction is that Estella cannot feel the passion which is destroying Miss Havisham, because Miss Havisham has destroyed it in her. What we therefore see is a reversal of the natural order which draws attention to the destructive way in which Miss Havisham has manipulated Estella's character.

The whole point of the passage is to demonstrate to the reader the extent of the destruction of any normal capacity for love in Estella by Miss Havisham; but the irony of the passage is that Miss Havisham needs the very love she has destroyed. It is Miss Havisham who 'clutched Estella's hand in hers', a hopelessly passionate grasp from which Estella 'gradually began to detach herself'. All Estella can do is what her name suggests – reflect, like the cold star from which her name is derived, a beauty devoid of any natural warmth of its own.

What happens here to Miss Havisham is what happens to Pip in the novel as a whole, and as we noted in the previous analysis; Miss Havisham, like Pip, confuses wealth and love. She has given Estella everything that money can give: clothes, jewels, the ability to break men's hearts – but she has given her all this within the cold, isolated and distorting world of Satis House, cut off from the light of day and from the warmth and love that should characterize humanity. In creating Estella, Miss Havisham has created a cold automaton, incapable either of receiving or giving love. The irony is that she has destroyed the very love she most craves. This is the point which is made in Estella's final speech: 'Take all the praise, take all the blame; take all the success, take all the failure; in short, take me.' But the full implication of this speech does not come out easily. It will be worthwhile to consider this speech very carefully and to analyse precisely how it achieves its effect, because it makes use of several devices which tell us something about the unique quality of Dickens's literary style in *Great Expectations*.

First, it is important to notice the use of punctuation, and how this speech achieves its effect almost poetically. The device of repeating phrases, as this speech does, is known technically as anaphoric repetition, and its effect is to foreground or draw attention to a specific point. It works by deleting part of the grammatical order of the sentence, in this case the subject 'you'. If we insert this deleted 'you, then the meaning of the speech begins to come clear: '[you] Take all the praise, [you] take all the blame; [you] take all the success, [you] take all the failure; in short, [you] take me'. What this implies is a logical pattern of argument, indicated by the repetition of phrases and the caesural effect of the semi-colon. To make real sense of the speech, therefore, we need to insert the markers of logical argument: '[if you] Take all the praise, [then you must also] take all the blame; [if you] take all the success, [then you must also] take all the failure; in short, [you must] take me [as you have made me].' This, then, is the full meaning of the speech. Miss Havisham has made Estella by destroying the child's capacity to love, and it is therefore unreasonable for Miss Havisham to complain if Estella cannot love her. And yet, it is this very desire for love which Miss Havisham most craves, and has been unable to destroy in herself. Much later in the novel, Miss Havisham will spontaneously combust; the 'wild heat' of her own passion will ultimately destroy her, because she has turned her own capacity to love into mere passion, and, more specifically, into hate. What Dickens seems to be suggesting is that while the capacity to love is a redeeming characteristic of humanity, that same passion, when used as a threat or bargaining tool to manipulate another person, is ultimately destructive both of the person who is manipulated, and of the person who does the manipulating. Miss Havisham's spite turns love into hatred, and the natural order is destroyed.

One of the things that we can see already is that the novel explores the many facets of the relationships that exist between people. It does this by setting love in conflict with money, and demonstrates the pernicious effect of money upon people and upon their ability to care for another person. What makes the novel particularly interesting, however, is that in exploring the nature of love between people it is able to explore some of the darker areas of the human mind, simply because love itself operates irrationally. For example, there is a great deal in Miss Havisham with which we can sympathize because we know the sadness of her past. But it is in her response to the past that we lose sympathy with her.

In a sense, she attempts to rationalize a situation which is really beyond rationalization. Consequently, she chooses to use love – in her case thwarted love – as a lever upon other people, and to use love in this way is ultimately destructive.

What is worth remembering is that much the same is going to be true even of minor characters in the novel, such as Orlick and Mrs Joe. Mrs Joe is forever reminding Pip how fortunate he is to have been brought up 'by hand', and how many sacrifices she has made on his behalf, reinforcing these sacrifices with the necessary application of 'Tickler', a wax-ended piece of cane. This conflict between love being freely given and love being bought or forced out by threats sums up much of what the novel is about: characters are alone in the world and need the love and affection of others, but this must be freely given, not bought by money, nor forced out by threats. Those who cannot give love freely (like Mrs Joe and Miss Havisham) expect to force it out of others with threats. What all this is based upon is love by reward, love with a price-tag on it. It works through the operation of guilt, and Pip senses this guilt keenly: 'the pledge I was under to commit a larceny on those sheltering premises, rose before me in the avenging coals'. (p. 41) Mrs Joe's method is emotional blackmail plain and simple, and, just as distorted passion eventually destroys Miss Havisham, so Mrs Joe is eventually killed by the same distorted passion. It is this which, much later, Orlick, 'shaking his head and hugging himself' (p. 435), tells us drove him to attempt to kill both Mrs Joe and Pip: 'You [Pip] was favoured, and he [Orlick] was bullied and beat.' (p. 437) Even the lowly Orlick craves love, and, in being deprived of it, that absence of love turns into violence and hatred.

What I have tried to do so far is merely to sort out the details of what is a fairly complicated novel. This has meant looking at particular extracts which tell us something about certain characters and themes in *Great Expectations*. But what I want to look at now is *how* the novel presents its story.

For example, if you think about the type of story Pip seems to be telling, it would seem to be a classic Victorian love-story: poor boy meets and falls in love with a rich girl, and, after various trials and tribulations, a will is discovered (this is the secret benefactor in *Great Expectations*), which makes the poor boy able to marry the rich girl. That this is the type of story Pip wants to tell underlines the extent of his own delusions about himself, Miss Havisham and Estella: if Miss Havisham had planned on Pip marrying Estella she would hardly have apprenticed him as a blacksmith in the first place; Estella is unable to love him or anybody; and it is only *after* the loss of his expectations that he and Estella are united. Finally, the idea of a love-story, which brings into harmony two characters who are otherwise separated by money, class and background, is indicative of Pip's desire to find some kind of order in the confusion of life. In his desire to find some kind of order in life Pip readily acquiesces in the manipulation of his own life by Miss Havisham, whom he believes is his secret benefactress.

As we have seen, this manipulation of character is a central theme in *Great Expectations*, springing from the desire to love in a world in which love is constantly frustrated by the power of money. Pip, for example, never intimates that he wants to be morally or spiritually any better than he already is. All he needs – or so he believes – is for Miss Havisham to make him wealthy and therefore a gentleman. That done, he will be a fit object for Estella's love.

But a moral and spiritual change does occur in Pip. What is ironic is that this change occurs not because of his love for Estella, but because of his developing love for Magwitch. Furthermore, Pip's life is manipulated by two people who are curiously related to each other: Miss Havisham and Magwitch.

Miss Havisham and Magwitch never meet, and there is no suggestion that either even knows of the other's existence, but they both manipulate Pip's life in some way. That there is this relationship between them is made plain in the structure of the novel as a whole: they share in their mutual enemy, Compeyson, who betrays them both for money; and Miss Havisham is the adoptive mother of Magwitch's daughter, Estella, which provides a further link between the two characters. Given these structural parallels, it is important to examine how the novel presents their shared relationship with Pip.

In both cases, the manipulation of Pip's life is done through money. Magwitch wants to make, by virtue of the money he has amassed in Australia, a 'brought-up London gentleman' (p. 339); Miss Havisham wants to make, by virtue of her money and the jewels she hangs on Estella, a lady to break the hearts of men. That is, money creates a system in which people will buy their possession of another person's life, in recompense for the love they cannot have, because the result of not having love is isolation. Miss Havisham, jilted on her wedding-day for money, has lived cut off from the light of day ever since; Magwitch, deserted and branded by society as 'a terrible hardened one' (p. 361), betrayed by Compeyson for money, has likewise lived cut off from society in prisons and finally Australia. But Magwitch cannot resist the temptation to return to England, even at the risk of his own life, to gloat over the gentleman he has 'made', just as Miss Havisham cannot resist the temptation to gloat over Estella's effect on Pip. Both characters have been denied love, and both attempt to exact revenge because of it. Their attempt to experience vicariously through Estella and Pip the lives they should have had is initially just an act of revenge. They can now do, through the characters whose lives they manipulate, what society has done to them. What Dickens seems to be suggesting is that this desire for revenge is not only destructive of the internal, spiritual nature of the individual, but that it is a desire generated by society itself.

It is important to remember that this desire for revenge is actually generated by society, the world of money, because in the case of both Miss Havisham and Magwitch, love overcomes it. Miss Havisham's last words to Pip are indicative of her recognition of what she has done to him to satisfy her desire for revenge, but also of his compassion for her: 'Take the pencil and write under my name, 'I forgive her' (p. 415). Magwitch dies similarly contrite, his revenge swallowed up by Pip's developing love for him. In a sense, both characters have to die to achieve forgiveness for what they have done not to society as a whole, but to the emotions of other individuals. Furthermore, this manipulation of Pip's life by Magwitch and Miss Havisham is thematically and structurally at one with the novel as a whole; love, as it is seen through the characters of Magwitch and Miss Havisham and their relationships with Pip, is ultimately destructive, although both characters do experience a deathbed conversion. Set against this, we find the love-story of Pip and Estella, which should demonstrate the positive side of love, acting as a touchstone against which the thwarted passion of Miss Havisham and Magwitch can be tested. This is how Pip describes his love for Estella:

> The unqualified truth is, that when I loved Estella with the love of a man, I loved her simply because I found her irresistible. Once for all; I knew to my sorrow, often and often, if not always, that I loved her against reason, against promise, against peace, against hope, against happiness, against all discouragement that could be. (pp. 253–4).

Truly it was impossible to dissociate her presence from all those wretched hankerings after money and gentility that had disturbed my boyhood – from all those ill-regulated aspirations that had first made me ashamed of home and Joe – from all those visions that had raised her face in the glowing fire, struck it out of the iron on the anvil, extracted it from the darkness of night to look in at the wooden window of the forge and flit away. In a word, it was impossible for me to separate her, in the past or in the present, from the innermost life of my life. (p. 257)

It is the complete and utter abandonment of Pip to Estella which makes such an effect in these passages. Estella has become a part of Pip's very soul, a part of his 'innermost life', from which he can never escape. Pip can find no rational side to his love for her; he loves her simply because she is 'irresistible' to him; he loves her 'against reason, against promise, against peace, against hope, against happiness, against all discouragement that could be.' This is a deep spiritual confusion and abandonment, in which Pip gives himself over to uncontrollable passion. As if to stress the extent to which Pip is subject to Estella's phantom-like nature, she is described in terms of a 'vision', which materializes in the 'glowing fire', lurks in 'the darkness of the night', and 'flits away' from the forge window. This is love of a type which is wholly destructive. It is love of a type that should be feared, born, as Pip says, out of his 'wretched hankerings after money and gentility', and this is indicative of the conflict between the individual and society at large. The personal turmoil Pip finds in his love for Estella, motivated by his desire for 'money and gentility', serves to mirror the conflicts in the individual's relationship to the outside world. So even in the love-story of Pip and Estella, which reads on the surface much like any other Victorian love-story, we find deep spiritual and emotional turmoil, which reflects the untidiness and turmoil of society at large.

This turmoil in Pip's character and in his relationship to the outside world is given focus toward the end of the novel when, having recovered from a long illness, through which he was nursed by the loving Joe, Pip determines to put his life in order by returning to the forge and asking Biddy to marry him. There is clearly a high degree of snobbery in Pip, even at this late stage of the novel, in his willingness to give himself up to Biddy, who is

so far beneath him socially. But the irony is that Pip arrives at the
forge only to discover that Biddy has married Joe. This marriage
between Biddy and Joe is the final nail in the coffin of Pip's
expectations: he is denied the cosy domesticity of love represented
by Biddy, and he is denied the wildly passionate love which he
craves with Estella. So Pip's confusion is finally increased by his
snobbish decision to give himself to Biddy, since events again
conspire against him. This reinforces the idea that neither the
emotions, nor the world at large is a tidy collection of events
arranged to make sense; they are instead random, complicated and
unfathomable.

This sense of instability is reinforced by Dickens's choice of a first-
person narrator. First-person narrators are notoriously unstable
narrators, simply because the reader is never quite sure of the
truthfulness of their report. Many first-person narrators, for
example, tell lies about themselves and the situations they report,
in order to disturb the reader's cosy relationship with the story.
But Dickens chooses not to use his narrator in this way. Instead,
he has Pip relate his story in an historic perspective, looking back
over the events of his life, quite aware of his own failings at certain
points in the story, and willing to point these out to the reader. It
is quite true that Pip does deceive himself in the process of coming
into his expectations. But it is equally true that he makes no attempt
to deceive the reader, and that consequently, looking back over
his life, he is aware of his own self-deception: 'All other swindlers
upon earth are nothing to the self-swindlers, and with such
pretences did I cheat myself' (p. 247).

To use a first-person narrator in this way tells us a great deal
both about the novel, and about Dickens's motivation in writing
the story. First, when Dickens could so easily add to the general
confusion of the emotional and physical world he describes, he
uses his narrator instead as a touchstone of stability: what Pip has
experienced may have confused him emotionally, but he relates
that in a meaningful and ordered way. Secondly, this increases
our sense that we are being told a story, simply because we know
that life generally refuses to arrange itself in the coherent patterns
that we find in a novel. And this in turn reinforces our awareness
that the emotions and the world at large, when unfiltered by
the storyteller's art, are random and largely resistant to our
comprehension.

Having said that, the ending of the novel itself appears to deny the untidiness of the emotional world which Dickens has previously been describing. The novel ends by uniting Pip and Estella in the ruins of Satis House, with the implicit promise of marriage and happiness in the future. As you may know, Dickens originally planned to have Pip and Estella meet and part, presumably forever, but another nineteenth-century novelist, Bulwer Lytton, persuaded Dickens to change the ending to the one we now have.

It would be possible to construct some fairly persuasive arguments about which is the more satisfying of the two endings. In the original ending, for example, Pip is the confirmed loser, Biddy having married the blacksmith he would have been; in the second ending, an ideal order is created, and Pip is given another chance for happiness. I don't intend to become involved in the argument about which is the better ending of the two, but we can see how the whole question of how to end a novel like *Great Expectations* can arise in the first place, and this can tell us a great deal about the nature of the novel and novel-writing. In a sense, the story has to be resolved at the end of such a novel as *Great Expectations* because although part of the novelist's job is to make us aware of the disorder and muddle of life, another aspect of the novelist's job is to create order, to arrange life into a coherent and meaningful story. Indeed, the idea that a novel tells a story in the first place suggests that it is possible to arrange the complexities, the randomness and the muddle of life into coherence. But when Dickens came to the end of the novel and had to decide what was going to happen to Pip and Estella he was faced with trying to reconcile not just the ambiguities and complexities of Pip's story, but also the ambiguities and complexities of society at large, of which Pip's story is a reflection.

Wherever we look in the novel, we can find this same pattern in which the personal conflicts in the individual's life are a reflection of the conflicts to be found in society at large. After Magwitch has been betrayed by Compeyson and recaptured, he is brought before the judge to be sentenced along with thirty-one other prisoners:

The sun was striking in at the great windows of the court, through the glittering drops of rain upon the glass, and it made a broad shaft of light between the two and thirty and the Judge, linking both together, and perhaps reminding some among the audience, how both were passing on, with absolute equality, to the greater Judgement that knoweth all things and cannot err.

Rising for a moment, a distinct speck of face in this way of light, the prisoner said, 'My Lord, I have received my sentence of Death from the Almighty, but I bow to yours,' and sat down again. There was some hushing, and the Judge went on with what he had to say to the rest. Then, they were all formally doomed, and some of them were supported out, and some of them sauntered out with a haggard look of bravery, and a few nodded to the gallery and two or three shook hands, and others went out chewing the fragments of herb they had taken from the sweet herbs lying about. He went last of all, because of having to be helped from his chair and to go very slowly; and he held my hand while all the others were removed, and while the audience got up (putting their dresses right, as they might at church or elsewhere) and pointed down at this criminal or that, and most of all at him and me. (pp. 467–8)

The first thing we notice about this passage is what a marvellous piece of writing it is, and how it is really quite unnerving, verging, as it does, almost on the comic. And yet, tied in with this unnerving, almost comic aspect of the writing, the passage also further develops the novel's broader thematic concerns. We notice, for example, the high degree of sympathy between Pip and Magwitch. When Magwitch had first arrived at Pip's lodgings, Pip told us that 'the repugnance with which I shrank from him, could not have been exceeded if he had been some terrible beast' (p. 337), but here, Pip holds Magwitch's hand and helps him from his chair. We know what has happened to Pip by this point in the story: 'my repugnance to him had all melted away . . . I only saw a man who had meant to be my benefactor . . . I only saw in him a much better man than I had been to Joe' (pp. 456–7). Pip has realized, through his developing love for Magwitch, that his pretensions to social rank, made on the basis of Magwitch's money, served only to isolate him even further by making him unable to love. Now that his repugnance for Magwitch has 'melted away' he can see the superficiality of the social world, and yet its dreadful power to control lives.

This is the conflict at the centre of the above passage. On the one hand, society is a superficial façade; on the other, it has the power to control lives utterly, even to end them. The whole proceedings are imbued with a sense of theatricality, of spectacle and social ritual; the criminals stand before the spectators in the 'gallery', playing out their pathetic roles to the end: 'they were all formally doomed, and some of them were supported out, and some of them sauntered out with a haggard look of bravery, and a few nodded to the gallery, and two or three shook hands . . .'. Meanwhile, the 'audience' responds with a show of social ritual, 'putting their dresses right, as they might at church or elsewhere'.

The effect gained by this technique is extremely unnerving, since the whole show is almost funny in the pathetically grand gestures the criminals attempt to present to the world. And yet the scene it describes is one in which more than thirty people are being condemned to death – which is manifestly not funny. The passage achieves this unnerving effect by describing the scene in a way which seems wholly inappropriate to what is actually happening. The criminals are all 'formerly doomed' by the Judge; some of the criminals 'sauntered out', while others 'nodded to the gallery'. By describing the scene in the way he does, Dickens is able to take a sideways look at it, to see it for what it is. And it is this which gives us the sense of the ridiculous nature of such proceedings. Dickens refuses to accept the validity of conventions which most of us usually accept without question, and he does this by describing the situation in a quite literal way. It is ridiculous that these thirty people can be sentenced to death by some old Judge sniffing at a nosegay. But that is exactly what happens. By describing the scene in the irreverently literal way that he does, Dickens is able to draw attention to the façade out of which society constructs its rules and accounts for its behaviour. But by keeping his distance from it, and by describing it in the way he does, Dickens is refusing to cooperate in the idea that the law-court is anything other than an elaborate and nonsensical charade.

This is reinforced by the way in which the criminals are described in the most anonymous terms: even Magwitch, whom we have by now come to know very well, is described merely as 'a distinct speck of face in this way of light'. This sense of anonymity, not only of Magwitch, but also of the other thirty or so prisoners, reinforces the idea that these characters are merely acting out roles in an uncaring society, and this increases our strong sense of indignation at the treatment of these 'formally doomed' and helpless characters. What increases the effect of the passage still further, however, is that it unnerves us by showing just what a charade the whole show really is. And this is really very similar to how we are made to feel about Pip's abandonment to his love for

Estella. This charade of justice is a system out of control, a system over which the individual has no control whatsoever, just as Pip has no control over his deep need to love Estella 'once for all'. Both Pip's abandonment in his love for Estella, and the disruptive, unnerving way in which Dickens reports the court scene, are indicative of the confusions, ambiguities and contradictions in society itself.

What I now want finally to consider is how Dickens puts together this deep sense of uncontrolled confusion in the individual and society. The first thing to remember is that *Great Expectations* is an enormously humorous novel. Pip, in the process of stealing food for Magwitch, slips a piece of bread and butter into his trousers. The adult Pip recalls:

> Conscience is a dreadful thing when it accuses man or boy; but when, in the case of a boy, that secret burden cooperates with another secret burden down the leg of his trousers, it is (as I can testify) a great punishment. (p. 44)

The detached way in which this is reported by the adult Pip allows the reader to savour the gradual unrolling of the description, the drawing together of the psychological burden of conscience with the very real burden of a piece of bread and butter down the trouser-leg. In a similar way, Pip recalls the medicinal application of Tar-water which his sister forced him to take: 'At the best of times, so much of this elixir was administered to me as a choice restorative, that I was conscious of going about, smelling like a new fence' (p. 44). Again, the detached, reporting tone of the piece creates much of the humour, and this is added to by the drawing together of two otherwise unconnected ideas. The Tar-water is described ironically as an 'elixir' and a 'choice restorative', and this pulls together the boy, Pip, on the one hand, and the idea of a newly-creosoted fence on the other. Later, Joe is described as looking 'like a scarecrow in good circumstances' (p. 54); for his Christmas lunch, Pip is regaled with 'those obscure corners of pork of which the pig, when living, had had the least reason to be vain' (p. 56); the sergeant searching for Magwitch, having partaken of the rum offered by Pumblechook, parts from him as from a comrade, although Pip doubts 'if he were quite as fully sensible of that gentleman's merits under arid conditions, as when something moist was going' (p. 64); Joe, recalling the death of his parents,

1–3. An excerpt from *Vanity Fair*, Chapter 6, followed by an excerpt from the BBC TV script by Alexander Baron (1988), will give some idea of the adapter's role in transferring the novelist's imagining into moving pictures.

The next day, however, as the two young ladies sate on the sofa, pretending to work, or to write letters, or to read novels, Sambo came into the room with his usual engaging grin, with a packet under his arm, and a note on a tray. " Note from Mr. Jos, Miss," says Sambo.

How Amelia trembled as she opened it !
So it ran—

" DEAR AMELIA,—I send you the 'Orphan of the Forest.' I was too ill to come yesterday. I leave town to-day for Cheltenham. Pray excuse me, if you can, to the amiable Miss Sharp, for my conduct at Vauxhall, and entreat her to pardon and forget every word I may have uttered when excited by that fatal supper. As soon as I have recovered, for my health is very much shaken, I shall go to Scotland for some months, and am

" Truly yours,
" JOS. SEDLEY."

It was the death-warrant. All was over. Amelia did not dare to look at Rebecca's pale face and burning eyes, but she dropt the letter into her friend's lap ; and got up, and went up stairs to her room, and cried her little heart out.

Blenkinsop, the housekeeper, there sought her presently with consolation, on whose shoulder Amelia wept confidentially, and relieved herself a good deal. " Don't take on, Miss. I didn't like to tell you. But none of us in the house have liked her except at fust. I sor her with my own eyes reading your Ma's letters. Pinner says she's always about your trinket-box and drawers, and everybody's drawers, and she's sure she's put your white ribbing into her box."

" I gave it her, I gave it her," Amelia said.

But this did not alter Mrs. Blenkinsop's opinion of Miss Sharp. " I don't trust them governesses, Pinner," she remarked to the maid. " They give themselves the hairs and hupstarts of ladies, and their wages is no better than you nor me."

It now became clear to every soul in the house, except poor Amelia, that Rebecca should take her departure, and high and low (always with the one exception) agreed that that event should take place as speedily as possible. Our good child ransacked all her drawers, cupboards, reticules, and gimcrack boxes—passed in review all her gowns, fichus, tags, bobbins, laces, silk stockings, and fallals—selecting this thing and that and the other, to make a little heap for Rebecca. And going to her Papa, that generous British merchant, who had promised to give her as many guineas as she was years old —she begged the old gentleman to give the money to dear Rebecca, who must want it, while she lacked for nothing.

She even made George Osborne contribute, and nothing loth (for he was as free-handed a young fellow as any in the army), he went to Bond Street, and bought the best hat and spenser that money could buy.

" That's George's present to you, Rebecca, dear," said Amelia, quite proud of the bandbox conveying these gifts.* " What a taste he has ! There's nobody like him."

" Nobody," Rebecca answered. " How thankful I am to him ! " She was thinking in her heart, " It was George Osborne who prevented my marriage."—And she loved George Osborne accordingly.

She made her preparations for departure with great equanimity ; and accepted all the kind little Amelia's presents, after just the proper

* It was the author's intention, faithful to history, to depict all the characters of this tale in their proper costumes, as they wore them at the

degree of hesitation and reluctance. She vowed eternal gratitude to Mrs. Sedley, of course ; but did not intrude herself upon that good lady too much, who was embarrassed, and evidently wishing to avoid her. She kissed Mr. Sedley's hand, when he presented her with the purse ; and asked permission to consider him for the future as her kind, kind friend and protector. Her behaviour was so affecting that he was going to write her a cheque for twenty pounds more ; but he restrained his feelings : the carriage was in waiting to take him to dinner, so he tripped away with a " God bless you, my dear, always come here when you come to town, you know.—Drive to the Mansion House, James."

Finally came the parting with Miss Amelia, over which picture I intend to throw a veil. But after a scene in which one person was in earnest and the other a perfect performer—after the tenderest caresses, the most pathetic tears, the smelling-bottle, and some of the very best feelings of the heart, had been called into requisition—Rebecca and Amelia parted, the former vowing to love her friend for ever and ever and ever.

----

commencement of the century. But when I remember the appearance of people in those days, and that an officer and lady were actually habited like this—

I have not the heart to disfigure my heroes and heroines by costumes so hideous ; and have, on the contrary, engaged a model of rank dressed according to the present fashion.

2.21. INT. SEDLEYS' DRAWING ROOM.

                    DAY (5) OCT. 1813
                    (AMELIA PICKS OUT
                    NOTES ON THE
                    PIANO.

                    REBECCA KNITS
                    MECHANICALLY.

                    THE SLOW, NOT
                    VERY MELODIOUS
                    PICKING AT NOTES
                    IS A STRAIN.

                    SAM COMES IN)

SAM: Miss Amelia ...

                    (SHE JUMPS UP,
                    RADIANT.

                    HE COMES IN.

                    HE HAS A PARCEL
                    UNDER HIS ARM AND
                    A NOTE ON A TRAY)

This came for you, Miss.

                    (SHE FLIES TO HIM,
                    TAKES THE NOTE.

                    HE PUTS THE PARCEL
                    ON A TABLE IN
                    FRONT OF HER.

                    HE GOES, GRINNING)

AMELIA: (DISMAY) It's from Jos!

                    (FLVERISHLY OPENS
                    IT. READS. SILENCE.

                    BECKY WATCHES.

                    AMELIA IS STRICKEN.
                    SHE DARES NOT LOOK
                    AT BECKY'S "PALE
                    FACE AND BURNING
                    EYES". SHE COMES,
                    HEAD LOWERED, TO
                    DROP THE LETTER
                    INTO BECKY'S LAP.

                    TEARS ARE BRIMMING.
                    THEN SHE BURSTS OUT
                    CRYING AND FLEES THE
                    ROOM.

                    BECKY DOES NOT TOUCH
                    THE LETTER UNTIL THE
                    DOOR HAS CLOSED.

                    SHE TAKES IT UP AND
                    READS:-)

JOS: (V.O.) 'Dear Amelia, I send
you The Orphan of the Forest. I
am too ill to visit you. I leave
town today for Cheltenham. Pray
excuse me, if you can, to the
amiable Miss Sharp for my conduct
at Vauxhall, and entreat her to
pardon and forget every word I may
have uttered when excited by that
fatal supper. As soon as I have
recovered, for my health is very
much shaken, I shall go to Scotland
for some months, and am, Truly yours,
Jos. Sedley.'

                    (BECKY PUTS THE
                    LETTER INTO A
                    POCKET AFTER
                    CAREFULLY FOLDING
                    IT.

                    SHE TAKES UP THE
                    PURSE AND BEGINS
                    TO KNIT, MECHANICALLY.

                    HER EXPRESSION IS SET.
                    SHE IS THINKING,
                    THINKING)

2.22. EXT. SEDLEY'S HOUSE.

                    DAY (6) OCT. 1813
                    (THE FAMILY'S
                    SMALL CARRIAGE
                    WAITS, WITH
                    JOHN, A GROOM
                    ON THE BOX.

                    SAM COMES OUT,
                    WITH BECKY'S
                    LITTLE TRUNK,
                    BUT ALSO WITH
                    ANOTHER CHEST,
                    AND VARIOUS
                    BAND BOXES.

                    HE STOWS THESE
                    IN THE CARRIAGE,
                    AND GETS OUT)

SAM: There's a sight more here than
she came with, John.

JOHN: Ay, trust her.

4—5. An extract from the television script for *Vanity Fair*, dramatized by Alexander Baron
for BBC TV in 1988. Reproduced by permission of the author.

2.23. INT. SEDLEY'S HALL.

        DAY (6) OCT. 1813

    (AT THE BACK,
    UNDER THE
    STAIRS, TWO
    FOOTMEN AND
    A MAID STAND
    TALKING.

    SAM COMES IN
    ON HIS WAY BACK
    UPSTAIRS)

SAM: It's no use hanging about. You
won't get no little gifts from her.

    (HE FLIES UP
    THE STAIRS)

2.24. INT. AMELIA'S BEDROOM.

        DAY (6) OCT. 1813
    (SHE IS TURNING
    OVER ITEMS IN
    AN OPEN DRAWER.

    SAM COMES IN.

    AMELIA HAS
    OBVIOUSLY BEEN
    CRYING. SHE
    POINTS TO A
    HATBOX AND A
    LONG BOX ON
    THE BED, BOTH
    GAILY WRAPPED
    WITH DECORATIVE
    TICKETS ON THEM)

AMELIA: Take those downstairs, will
you?

    (SAM GOES AND
    GLIMPSES THE
    TICKETS)

SAM· With Miss Sharp's things in the
carriage, miss?

AMELIA: No, in the drawing-room. Put
them out of the way somewhere.

SAM: Very well, miss.

    (HE IS LOOKING
    AT HER. HE
    TAKES THE BOXES
    AND MOVES TO
    THE DOOR. HE
    HESITATES)

AMELIA: What is it, Sam?

SAM: Nothing miss ... You look so
sad, miss.

AMELIA: My friend is going away.

SAM: Yes, miss.

    (HE TURNS TO
    DOOR, THEN)

Miss, I wish you would not grieve. Not
for ... well, not for Miss Sharp.

AMELIA: What do you mean?

SAM: Well, miss, don't take on now,
but ... well, here goes and be blowed.
None of us in the house have liked
Miss Sharp ...

AMELIA: Sam!

SAM: We did at first. But I saw her
with my own eyes go into your Ma's
room, and when I looked, she was
reading your Ma's letters.

AMELIA: Sam, how dare you?

SAM: Out it comes if I lose my
place, Miss Amelia. Pinner says she's
always about your things and everybody's
things and she's put your white ribbon
into her box.

AMELIA: I gave it to her. I gave
it to her.

SAM: Very well, miss.

AMELIA: I did! Go about your work
at once or I'll ... I'll ...

SAM: Yes, miss.

    (HE GOES)

AMELIA: Oh! Poor Rebecca! Poor
Rebecca!

    (RUMMAGES FIERCELY
    IN THE DRAWER
    TILL SHE COMES
    UP WITH A SMART
    LITTLE RETICULE
    WHICH SHE RAISES
    UP)

Ah, yes!

6–7. Diachronic tourism – invitations to visit the past.

8–11. A happy hunting ground for film and TV designers has always been *London* by Blanchard Jerrold, and brilliantly illustrated by Gustave Doré (1870). These engravings are strong influences on films of Dickens novels by David Lean, Carol Reed and their imitators.

8. St Paul's from Brewery Bridge. (K. Garratt)

9. Ludgate Hill. (The Mansell Collection)

10. Dudley Street, Seven Dials. (The Mansell Collection)

11. London Bridge. (The Mansell Collection)

12. Costume design for Jos Sedley — 'Indian Party' — for BBC TV, 1988. Reproduced by permission of the Costume Designer for the series, Joyce Hawkins.

Rebecca Saire as Amelia.
"Vanity Fair"
BBC 1987.

Dress in lavender silk poult.
Trim of striped grey/lavender.
and velvet ribbon.
Turban of matching fabric.
Made at Cosprops.

13. Costume design for Amelia Sedley for BBC TV, 1988. Reproduced by permission of Joyce Hawkins, series Costume Designer.

14—18. Thackeray illustrated several of this own novels, including *Vanity Fair*. The following are from his illustrations to the first edition of *Vanity Fair* (1848).

14a. George and Amelia.

14b. Sir Pitt Crawley and Becky Sharp.

15a. Rawdon and Becky Sharp.

15b. Jos Sedley.

16a. Lord Steyne.

16b. Amelia Sedley.

17a. Dobbin and Jos.

17b. Dobbin and Amelia.

18a. Rawdon and Becky.

18b. Becky and Jos Sedley.

19. Miriam Hopkins in *Becky Sharp* (Pioneer/RKO, 1935), the first feature-length film in three-colour Technicolor. 'I can't help remembering how bright and new were all the dresses in *Becky Sharp*. Can Technicolor reproduce with the necessary accuracy the suit that has been worn too long, the oily hat?' Grahame Green, *Spectator*, 19 July 1935.

20. Promotional display for Pan Classics paperback edition of *Vanity Fair*, published to coincide with transmission of the television series.

rubs 'first one of his eyes, and then the other, in a most uncongenial and uncomfortable manner, with the round knob on the top of the poker' (p. 77).

This ability to surprise the reader by drawing together two things in an unexpected way underpins Dickens's ability to see the funny side of things not usually regarded as funny. Pip speaks, for example, of Mr Wopsle's great-aunt as having 'conquered a confirmed habit of living into which she had fallen' (p. 150), meaning, of course, that she had died – which is not particularly humorous in itself.

Much of Dickens's technique, then, centres on this ability to see things from a shifted perspective, but a perspective which we can immediately recognize as being true, or with which we can immediately sympathize. When Pip steals out of his home to take food to Magwitch, he tells us: 'The mist was heavier yet when I got out on the marshes, so that instead of my running at everything, everything seemed to run at me' (p. 48). The truth of that observation is immediately obvious to anyone who has run through mist, but it is Dickens who points it out to us, allowing us, as it were, to rediscover what we may already know, to see things anew. The lens through which Dickens filters this renewed perception is a comic one. But the comic, simply because it does force us to see things for what they really are, is not merely humorous. The comic perspective, as Dickens uses it, allows us to see behind the façade of the social world, forces us to recognize the craziness of society, the irrational impulses which motivate human beings, and consequently presents what is potentially a highly disruptive view of the world.

Think, for example, of Wemmick, who with his house cut off from the outside world by a moat and drawbridge, his cosy domestic love with Miss Skiffens, his caring love for his aged parent, seems to represent the ultimate in order, in security, and in the tidiness of emotions. But Wemmick achieves this only by physically cutting himself off from the rest of humanity. Even within the cosy domesticity of Wemmick's life with Miss Skiffens and the Aged Parent there are shadows lurking, a sense that order and emotional tidiness is achieved at too great a cost. Similarly, in *Great Expectations* as a whole, the individual is confronted by emotions, like Pip's love for Estella, which he cannot control; or confronted with a system, like the sham of the court which sentences Magwitch, too massive and irrational to be controlled.

At the centre of *Great Expectations* is, then, a comic and disruptive view of the world which recognizes the proximity of comedy to human tragedy, and recognizes, too, the proximity of the emotional life of the individual to the influences of the outside world. By presenting Pip's love for Estella as being ultimately uncontrollable, and by paralleling that with a comic, sideways glance at the systems and structures within which society organizes itself, and within which the individual attempts to organize his response to the world, Dickens presents us with a novel which is both comic and highly disruptive. Consequently, *Great Expectations* is able to hint, even within the comedy, at the darker, and largely irrational impulses that motivate human beings.

This exploration of the nature of relationships between individuals, and of the individual's responses to the world, is at the centre of *Great Expectations*. And it is this which allows Dickens to present not only a fairly scathing indictment of the surface of social existence, but to probe the darker, irrational and internal workings of the human mind. The novel achieves this through the close linguistic texture of its world, which is both naturalistic and highly symbolic. More than anything else, however, the world of *Great Expectations* is linguistic; it is a world made of words, gaining its effects through the multifarious levels upon which language is capable of working. It may be difficult to imagine how a visual representation will be capable of yielding up so many meanings simultaneously.

5

The Screening of *Great Expectations*

As we have seen already, *Great Expectations* is an extremely complex novel. What we will now consider are the various problems this complexity is likely to present to the film-maker in a dramatization. At the outset, we can summarize these problems as revolving around three areas: theme, structure and language.

The major thematic interest in *Great Expectations* is discovered in the conflict between the world of money and the world of love. Indeed, much of the novel's inherent patterning revolves around this conflict. But this conflict is in many ways an abstract one, and is obviously problematic to the film-maker. This will have even further repercussions, however, for it is through this basic conflict between money and love that we follow Pip in his attempt to discover a position for himself in the world. Consequently, much of the novel's interest for the reader is internal: Pip's consciousness, his sense of guilt and unworthiness, Miss Havisham's distorted passion, Magwitch's desire for love in the world, even Orlick's tormented psyche – these are fundamental to our experience of reading the novel. In exploring these dark and irrational areas of the human mind Dickens has the internal patterns of language at his disposal, the ability to trace out the inner developments of thought and emotion. This is central to the novel as a linguistic structure, but how will it find a place in the film-maker's realization of the novel?

This exploration of the inner workings of the human mind is assisted in the novel by the structure of the novel itself. In the novel, first-person narration serves, amongst other things, to impress more immediately upon the reader a sense of the reality of the fictional world. But in a film, attempts at first-person narration come over all too often as clumsy, ostentatiously and even pretentiously artistic. The tradition in film-making is instead an implied third-person narrative, deeply subsumed by the unobtrusive use of technology – through editing, music, camera-angles and the like – and it is likely that this first-person narration is the most fundamental aspect of the novel's structure which will need changing in moving from novel to film. But much of the novel's subtlety is achieved precisely through the use of first-person narration. If we recall those moments – such as Pip's return to his village – when he is supercilious with Biddy, baited by Trabb's boy, fêted by Pumblechook and the rest, we recall that much of the humour of those moments arises from Pip not appearing to recognize, even in retrospect, just how ridiculous he seems to the reader. That is, humour arises ironically, and depends for its effect upon the reader interpreting the text, situation and character, and perceiving the various levels upon which the text operates. In the novel, the text is open for the reader to interpret and to discover meaning within it. But in a film, that act of interpretation has to some extent already been decided upon; that is, in the film, meaning has to some extent already been discovered.

This element of discovery is in fact central to the nature of first-person narration, anyway. One of the things about first-person narration in the novel generally is that it is always potentially unstable, since as readers we are never really sure of the reliability of the narrator, nor of the status of his fiction. In *Great Expectations*, this is particularly important since it allows for information to be gradually *discovered* both by Pip and by the reader. In the film, there may be a tendency for this element of discovery to be reduced merely to naturalistic detective work. In the novel, however, this element of discovery is not merely of the whodunnit variety but functions instead thematically to illustrate something about Pip and his position in the world: that things are not always as they seem, and in order for Pip to understand himself he needs also to discover who he is in the context of the world he inhabits.

There are more practical problems also. Pip is alone in the world, an orphan, and this is reinforced by the fact that he speaks directly to us. In a sense, Pip's major relationship is with the reader, rather than with another character. On a surface level, the *picture* of Pip is of an orphan, alone in the world. But in the novel there is much more to it than that: Pip is much more than merely an orphan, as we saw in our analysis of the opening to the novel. Dickens can often be accused, although perhaps not so readily in *Great Expectations*, of gross sentimentality. But a straight *representation* of the orphan Pip, without regard for the more complex psychological and social themes this suggests, runs the risk of sentimentality of the worst kind.

This possible stereotyping effect applies to the other characters also. Take Jaggers, for example. As we saw, there is nothing in the text to suggest that Jaggers is anything other than honest and discreet in dealing with his clients. But his involvement with the underworld marks him out immediately as a stereotype. An interesting point here is that Jaggers is never described in any detail in the text. All we really know about him in physical terms is that he is continually washing his hands with strong-smelling soap and that his boots creak. But in a film, which has to *represent* the character, Jaggers runs the risk of being reduced to a moustachio-twirling con-man with a bit-part in an advertisement for Cherry Blossom or Lifebuoy toilet soap. But what makes Jaggers so interesting is in part the fact that in the novel he is *not* described. Dickens – throughout his fiction – is obsessed with dress and appearance, and this is clearly indicative of the novel's thematic concern with the show and affection of society at large. In such a situation, *not* describing a character is significant, in the context of the novel as a whole. But in the pictorially-naturalistic medium of the film, if we are to see a character, then that character must by necessity be described. But to describe, to visualize the character, destroys the very subtlety with which the novel creates this particular character in the first place.

Similarly, Joe, Jaggers, even Miss Havisham, appear never to age. They seem instead to function as agents, representatives, even, of states of mind, and it is Pip's relationship to these agents which most fascinates the reader in his or her contact with the novel. But Pip most certainly does age; his growing older is what the novel is about. In the novel, it is quite acceptable for these characters never to appear to age. Indeed, this effect functions as a part of the overall purpose of the novel. But in a film, twenty years is expected to pass with the same results of twenty years passing in life. Yet if it does, in this particular novel, we again lose something of the novel's overall design and thematic content.

This problem of the naturalistic rendering of character and situation is probably the central problem in any attempt to maintain the novel's original structural subtlety. The novel, for example, makes it quite plain that Miss Havisham, sitting by the 'cold, grey ashes', spontaneously combusts. Dickens, as we know, was obsessed with the phenomenon of spontaneous combustion, and made use of it elsewhere in his fiction, most notably in *Bleak House*.

In *Great Expectations*, Miss Havisham spontaneously combusts for a purpose, destroyed by the fire and heat of her own distorted passions. But the phenomenon of spontaneous combustion does not reside easily with naturalism. Consequently, it is difficult to imagine how the scene can be presented and still maintain its symbolic significance and integrity to the artistic structure of the novel as a whole.

This problem finds a focus in the novel's use of *language* to create its unique view of the world. Many serious-minded critics have complained that the joke-a-line quality of *Great Expectations* is tediously annoying, and that this detracts from the novel's inherent purpose. As much as anything, this tells us a great deal about the nature of British literary criticism, which always finds it difficult to know how to respond to a text which expresses its seriousness through playfulness. But the point is that, as we saw in the previous chapter, *Great Expectations* is an enormously humorous novel. Yet there is little visual slapstick in the novel; instead humour arises from Dickens's irony and sheer joy of language. More bluntly, its humorous quality is achieved precisely because it is a linguistic and not a visual creation.

Yet despite such obvious problems the novel presents to film and television, it is a curious fact that it has always had a very powerful attraction to adapters for stage and screen. Over a hundred versions are listed in H.P. Bolton's *Dickens Dramatized* (1987),[1] and David Lean's version (1946) always receives the accolade not only as the best version of this particular novel, but as being universally recognized as the best film version of a Dickens novel ever – though this assertion may be seriously qualified as the merits of Christine Edzard's version of *Little Dorrit* become recognized.

The opinion that Dickens's novels made good movies has, for the most part, always gone unchallenged. Indeed there has always been a strong suggestion that they were somehow 'made' for film. David Paroissien, for example, seems to believe that the sheer number of film versions of the novels should inevitably lead us to this conclusion.[2] But the fact that most of the novels have been filmed, several of them many times, does not so much prove something about the nature of Dickens's fiction, as the insatiable appetite of a huge public entertainment industry for stories. Mrs Leavis was of the opinion that it was Dickens's surefire mixture of comedy and sentimentality which made him suitable stuff for mass indiscriminating audiences such as filled cinemas worldwide.[3] But we need to look closer than that at the matter, and when we do, what we find is not so much the fact that the art of Dickens and the cinema have so much in common, but that in basic method and effect they are astonishingly different.

It is always claimed that D.W. Griffith's invention of the basic techniques of editing film, so that a narrative sequence may well contain a variety of shots – long shot, medium shot, close-up, various angles and reverses – was carried over from Dickens's narrative prose. Griffith's biographer, Robert M. Henderson, recorded that when Griffith first worked in the movie industry each scene was filmed from the point of view of the audience watching a stage performance, and the camera was in a fixed position, with the actors making their entrances from left to right. Griffith's revolution consisted of realizing that the nature and duration of a shot should be dictated by the dramatic essence of what was to be conveyed, not on some conception of the duration of natural action.[4] Griffith himself was given to claiming direct line of descent from Charles Dickens as a storyteller, as one who continued Boz's tradition in terms of moving film.[5] Sergei Eisenstein was similarly given to stressing his rightful place in this Great Dickensian Tradition, claiming to find in the texture of the novels what he called 'film implications' and the literary equivalence of close-up, dissolve and parallel editing to which he gave the collective term 'montage'.[6]

To take as our evidence a fine example of the art of the cinema, David Lean's version of *Great Expectations*, we should learn much of what film can do. We will need to approach it not so much to evaluate it as the film-of-the-book but as a film in its own right. It may be readily granted that David Lean's *Great Expectations* is the best film of a Dickens novel made until the appearance of *Little Dorrit* and it may be granted that it is a great film in its own right independent of its origins – but we need to examine closely the claim that this film realizes the intentions of Dickens's novel of the same name. It is when this fundamental question is examined that the real and essential differences between novel and film become apparent.

If we look at the way Dickens opens the story the first thing we notice is the first person narrative. We have the story of a boy's journey through life told by the boy-now-grown-up. There is a tension between what the man/narrator is as he tells us his story, and what he was when a child. Not only is there a difference of time (the opening is long in the past) but of social class, as the man-when-young was a member of the rural working class, whereas the narrator is clearly middle-class. The sense of time-present/time-past is non-existent. The class difference, which could have been stressed in accent, and is indeed central to Pip's humiliation at the hands of Estella, has gone altogether. Young Pip, in Lean's version of the novel, and when we first meet him in the churchyard, speaks in the smooth tones of a preparatory schoolboy. One of the leading themes of the story, Pip's search for his identity, his place in the world, goes for nothing. Dickens, it is worth noting, does not play the opening scene for melodrama. But in the film this sequence (rightly commended as a brilliant piece of editing) is pure melodrama. The text is very subtle. No efforts are spared to present the facts of Pip's situation. He is orphaned and he is in a graveyard paying his respects to his deceased family. It is essential these facts are strongly implicit in the text, as Magwitch, the convict, is in effect to be a father to him. It is important, given this implied relationship, that Pip should not be terrified of him. Indeed in the novel it is quite clear he is not as he conducts a very sensible conversation with the convict and agrees to help him. But the film plays the gloom, murkiness and terrors for all they are worth. There is a similar false emphasis in the trip back to the marshes with the stolen food and drink. In the novel the early morning fog and mists do strange, grotesque and almost comical things to Pip's perceptions. In the film, again, we have a heavy and terrifying atmosphere rather than the grotesque atmosphere suggested by the novel.

A fundamentally serious shift of emphasis is the result of the loss of first-person narrative. The entire point of the novel is the fact that the entire action – past and present – is seen through Pip's eyes. This gives us two very important qualities which contribute to the impact of the novel on the reader's imagination – everything is distorted because it is seen as Pip sees it (all the confusions of motive and identity are the result of these failures to see things as they are); and in telling his own story from his point of view Pip unconsciously reveals many things about himself which the reader recognizes but of which Pip himself is probably quite unaware. The cutting-edge of these ironies is entirely lost in David Lean's *Great Expectations*.

Although, compared with other novels of Dickens, *Great Expecta-*

tions is not disproportionately long, in making a film version, much had to be cut. The nature of some of these cuts represents very serious loss. Orlick clearly represents Pip's alter ego. He is the dark, evil side of Pip's soul. He can say and do things which Pip himself cannot. Consequently the murder of Mrs Joe by Orlick is a vital part of the novel. Likewise, Orlick wanted Biddy, just as Pip had done. All this is made quite clear in the scene where Orlick captures Pip with the intention of killing him. When he has Pip helpless before him, Orlick accuses him of giving Old Orlick a bad name to Biddy and of coming betwixt him and a young woman he liked. The attack on Pip's sister, Orlick says, was Pip's doing:

> 'I tell you it was your doing – I tell you it was done through you. . . . I give it her! I left her for dead . . . But it warn't Old Orlick as did it; it was you. . . . Now you pays for it. You done it; now you pays for it.' (p. 437)

Thus the evil, criminal dimension of Pip's character has been entirely removed.

Of course, British cinemagoers in the late forties might have found it hard to credit that John Mills, who plays the adult Pip, could have this Mr Hyde aspect to his character, having relished his virtues and heroism in such an assortment of stiff-upperlip roles as were found for him in such films as *In Which We Serve*, *We Dive at Dawn*, *This Happy Breed*, *Waterloo Road* and *The Way to the Stars*. But the loss of the dark dimension is serious. John Mills's portrayal of a working-class character who 'makes it' into the genteel classes is not at all convincing.

Similarly serious is the loss or trimming down of other characters perceived by the film-maker as 'minor' but nevertheless having a considerable quality to contribute to the total impact of the novel. Mr Wopsle does feature in the film but is given very minor status. This is a shame as he has his part to play in the general scheme of things. One of the leading themes of the novel is the destructive nature of the class system (which destroys Pip). This stands in the way of Wopsle's entering the ranks of the clergy, should the church 'be thrown open' – which, of course, it never was. It is true that the idea of entry to the ministry by means of a talent contest is droll, nevertheless a serious point is made about the class system in nineteenth-century England: if you were not sensible enough to get yourself born into the well-to-do public school/Oxbridge

classes, then the professions were closed to you. Dickens's deep
and (for most of his life, secret) awareness of his own origins made
him acutely conscious of this hard fact of life, and its searing
awareness is at the root of some of his most strikingly effective
writing. It is this which informs his brilliant creation of Pip's
psychology. Pip is rendered 'a gentleman' by the realization of his
expectations, but he is a gentleman in externals only – he can talk
like a gentleman, use his knife and fork like a gentleman, dance
like a gentleman – but deep down in himself he knows he is still
the village lad brought up at the forge. This is why he loathes the
idea of a visit from Joe so much, not only because it will embarrass
him in front of his smart London friends, but because it will remind
him of what he really is, beneath his acquired accent and silk
dressing-gown.

The reduction in the significance of Uncle Pumblechook is
another loss which affects our apprehension of the novel's intentions. He has a symbolic role to play which reinforces the major
themes of the novel: that the important things in life cannot be
bought and sold. In Lean's film version this vital theme is muffled,
and when at that terrible moment when we learn – as Pip learns –
that after all that he has done, and after all that he has done to
Joe – that it was Joe who came to London and paid his debts and
nursed him back to health like a sick child – and our eyes are not
filled with anguished tears and our throats are not choked with
emotion we cannot hide, then the dynamite of great literature has
been turned into a damp squib.

Another serious blemish in the film version of *Great Expectations*
which is curious when we consider the visual nature of the
medium, is the loss of its symbolism. The result is to make the
film curiously prosaic. Stellar imagery is a leading feature of the
symbolic structure of the novel. Pip looks up at the stars and
considers 'how awful it would be for a man to turn his face up to
them as he froze to death, and see no help or pity in all the
glittering multitude'. The stars here represent some form of
indifference, beautiful objects which shed a lustre but no warmth.
The sense of glittering coldness is perfectly conveyed symbolically
in the novel, but wholly absent in the film. As is so often the case
with Dickens the contrasting positive standards are important. The
cold indifference of Estella and the atmosphere of Satis House with
all its sunlight shut out is contrasted with the warmth and humanity
of Joe Gargery and the forge, hearth and home. Yet this goes for

nothing in David Lean's film. In fact, and although Bernard Miles makes a very interesting creation out of Joe Gargery, quite convincing in many respects, this important symbolic dimension is not realized at all.

Similarly significant is the consistent animal imagery which we find in the novel, yet which is so noticeably absent in the film. Pip is constantly referred to in animal terms by his sister and the dreadful gang who are present at the Christmas dinner. Mrs Joe calls him a monkey, and he is frequently referred to as a porker and a squeaker. This animal imagery thematicaly connects Magwitch and Pip and draws attention to the manner in which children and deviants are treated in modern society – as cruelly as we treat animals. This is noticeably absent in David Lean's film.

The impact of the novel in its movie version is further reduced by the weak manner in which several important characters are presented and their relationship with each other is hardly established or explored. The crucial personality of Biddy is played as a minor character, and the relationships between her and Joe and Biddy and Pip are only lightly sketched in. This is a serious flaw and compels one to conclude that it shows little understanding either of this novel or of Dickens. Most of the irony of Pip's deciding to go back to the marshes after his illness and marry Biddy goes for nothing in David Lean's film, and indicates a basic failure to recognize a vital pattern of relationships: Pip is sexually deeply attracted to Estella who, in her perfections, is cold and doll-like, yet Pip offers to marry the sensible and sisterly Biddy. This vital theme is entirely absent in the 1946 film.

What would a cinemagoer make of Lean's *Great Expectations* who came to it with no previous knowledge of the novel on which it was based, and consumed it just as any other film? The story line would seem straightforward, and there are some extremely impressive elements in the film – notably the first sequence with the convict in the graveyard, the scenes at Miss Havisham's house, the scene at night when the convict turns up at Pip's London apartment and the breathtaking staging of the accident with the paddle-steamer in which the evil convict is killed and Magwitch is fatally injured.

And there are also several outstanding acting performances. Alec Guinness and Martita Hunt repeated their brilliant stage impersonations as Herbert Pocket and Miss Havisham,[7] Bernard Miles was a moving and convincing Joe, Freda Jackson did wonders with what was left of the role of Mrs Joe and Francis L. Sullivan was a dominating Jaggers. The great moments in the movie, such as the fight between Herbert and Pip when they first meet at Satis House, the unexpected appearance of Magwitch in the churchyard and the paddle-steamer accident are scarcely Dickensian but are of the kind which romantic cinema of the late 1940s could be expected to handle well. In sum, the film bears about the same relation to the novel as Lamb's retelling of *King Lear* does to Shakespeare's tragedy.

But there are two major flaws which are fundamental to the whole product. The first is that David Lean and his fellow-authors (Ronald Neame and Anthony Havelock-Allan) do not seem to understand how a Dickens novel actually works, as their catastrophic omissions, excisions and false emphases demonstrate. The second is a matter of style. Dickens is neither a naturalistic nor a realistic writer and his art obviously works against the grain of the predominantly realistic/romantic style which dominated cinema art in America and Western Europe in the 1940s. To this must be added the fact that there is a very strong strain of the English-genteel in David Lean. He served a long apprenticeship in film before becoming a director – clapperboy, newsreel editor, feature editor and ultimately as co-director of *In Which We Serve* (1942). He went on to direct three other films written by Coward – *This Happy Breed* (1944), *Blithe Spirit* (1945) and *Brief Encounter* (1945). The influence of Coward is strongly marked in *Great Expectations* and needless to say, is wholly inappropriate.

John Mills might almost be described as a member of the Lean/Coward repertory company, to which he was ideally suited with his musical comedy background. Lean's *Great Expectations* is perceived through the distortions of a tremendous and stultifying gentility, which successfully masks Dickens's motivation and intentions. Dickens's novel is essentially concerned with the destruction of personality by the mechanisms of the English class system. David Lean's Pip is a nice little chap from the start. Even in the graveyard he addresses Magwitch in the tones of preparatory schoolboy. Estella and Miss Havisham might be shocked at his calling Knaves 'Jacks' but they could hardly fault his accent. Lean simply couldn't bring himself to do it properly. It wasn't in him. What impresses viewers as 'Dickensian' accuracy is really a prissy and fussy romantic historicism which is irrelevant to Dickens's intentions.

Such British costume dramas of the 1940s permanently conditioned the stylistic surface quality of the vast majority of British
attempts to film classical novels, and played a significant part in
laying the foundations for an unfortunate influence in recreating
Dickens for the screen, which almost merits the term 'Dickensian
cinematography'. Equally serious is the total failure of nerve which
grips film-makers when they undertake a Dickens novel, in not
using film to tell us what Dickens wanted to tell us, but using film
to market something which is perceived as 'Dickensian'. David
Lean's *Great Expectations* is a perfect example of the genre in this
respect. Lean could have mustered the courage to say what Dickens
wanted to say, but his courage failed him. Dickens, as we know,
did not originally intend this novel to have a happy ending.

This superb but remorseless conclusion would have rounded off
the novel harmoniously. But the novelist's friend, the successful
writer and public figure Edward Bulwer Lytton, persuaded Dickens
to change this ending, no doubt arguing that his readers would
expect a happy ending, and Dickens eventually changed it to the
one we are now familiar with in the ruined garden at Satis House:

> I took her hand in mine, and we went out of the ruined place;
> and, as the morning mists had risen long ago when I first left
> the forge, so, the evening mists were rising now, and in all the
> broad expanse of tranquil light they showed to me, I saw no
> shadow of another parting from her.

In making his film version of this novel in the late forties David
Lean might have considered putting Dickens's intentions into
effect, but he did not. In fact, the whole thrust of British film-
making at the time was against it. The very genre would resist it.
As André Bazin wrote in 'In Defence of Mixed Cinema' as a
result of the voracious appetite of the movie industry for literary
adaptations, the masterpieces of world literature were cut down
like so many redwood trees to be fed through the mass-production
sawmills of the film industry – Victor Hugo, Shakespeare, Dickens,
Austen, Brontë. They all come out looking very much like one
another: 'worse, they looked like every other film of the period.
Classic cinema . . . has an official look which depersonalizes every
film and treats every subject alike.'[8]

This is a very serious effect the movie industry has had on the
production of Dickens's novels – that they all come out very much

the same. There is a terrible sameness about all the Dickens films (with the exception of the recent *Dorrit*) which flies in the face of all the evidence. Anybody who knows anything about Dickens will know that although all the novels are unmistakably the creation of the same extraordinary imagination, each individual novel is nevertheless uniquely itself.

Yet the sausage-factory style survives from one generation to another. The BBC began very early in its career to broadcast radio versions of classic novels and dramas as part of its responsibility to educate and inform (as well as to entertain). Some of these productions were outstanding. Particularly memorable was the version of *Great Expectations* by Mabel Constanduros and Howard Agg, which starred Cyril Cusack as Pip and Laidman Browne as Joe, transmitted in Autumn 1948. With this and other radio serials a very important tradition was gradually established and the British broadcast classic serial genre was constructed, a model which survived and indeed thrived in the age of television. The mainstay of the classic serial division was Dickens, but there were regular forays into Trollope, George Eliot, the Brontës, Jane Austen and Thomas Hardy. The classic serial was a Sunday treat, usually scheduled for tea-time or early evening, and was broadcast to run from the Autumn to Christmas time. Outstanding among the early British television examples were *Oliver Twist* (1962); a fine version of *Great Expectations* written by Hugh Leonard and broadcast in 1967 which used the original, 'unhappy' ending; *Dombey and Son* (1969), which used the music of Sibelius and had a fine Mr Dombey in the person of John Carson; *The Old Curiosity Shop* (1978) had everything except a passable Little Nell, but the 1980 version of *A Tale of Two Cities* brilliantly realized itself with a small budget and economy-sized French Revolution to win an Emmy. Outside the BBC's 'classic serial' slot some interesting things had begun to happen. In 1977 Granada Television made an outstanding version of *Hard Times*, starring Patrick Allen as Gradgrind and Timothy West a superlative Bounderby. The exterior locations and artwork were extremely impressive and it clearly broke new ground in style and tone. It was adapted for television by Arthur Hopcraft, and the BBC bought in Hopcraft to write their evening serial version of *Bleak House* in 1984 which had many good things but rendered Dickens's masterly exposition almost incomprehensible.

Meanwhile BBC Radio broadcast three brilliant serial versions of *Pickwick*, *Bleak House* and *Little Dorrit* which were all written by

Betty Davis and produced by Janet Morgan. A feature of the productions, particularly useful in the case of *Bleak House*, was the retention of much of the narrative voice, which added tremendously to the descriptive colour of the productions and deployed the important feature of point of view.

The main problem seems to be that adaptation has not yet been granted much status – even when achieved by writers of note and distinction (Dennis Potter adapted *The Mayor of Casterbridge* and John Mortimer adapted *Brideshead Revisited*). The unquestioned assumption is that adapting a novel or a play for film, radio or television is an act of secondary creation. Its practitioners are not given the status of writers, so much as that of media journeymen. This is demonstrably unreasonable. Even Shakespeare created dramas by adapting source material for the stage written by other people.

Film, radio and television are media with their own languages – languages no less worthy of respect than the printed text. But it is in the nature of the production and consumption of 'high culture' in our society that there is an inbuilt snobbery about print. Bernard Levin recently wrote of an author in a review: 'his technique of undercutting . . . has a cinematic gloss but also a cinematic superficiality'.

Such cultural snobbery has always demonstrated itself by its allegiance to the immediately preceding mode of production. This is an essential part of the grammar of our culture. It is the argument between fashion and anti-fashion that we see in clothes. Uniforms, formal clothes, the costume of royalty, the law, church and state are all frozen, all from the past, which represents all that is permanent, immutable and unchanging. The fashionable and the trendy are here today and gone tomorrow. And the classics, of course, are relics from previous modes of production.

The ability to adapt to change, it will be remembered, was one of the qualities which Charles Darwin believed enabled life to survive. But we still resist new forms. Very recent cultural history will show how this cultural grammar actually works. Hollywood musicals of the 1930s and 1940s were originally regarded as shallow, ephemeral entertainment. The next stage was the development of a camp interest in the genre. And now the 'best' of them are regarded as 'classics' worthy of being shown on BBC-2, the channel of Jane Austen.

And the classic serial is a particularly interesting case. As a media construction it clearly stems from the intention to educate and inform as well as entertain. Consequently it has taken on a high sense of duty, an obsession with period 'accuracy', high production values and a devout respect for the text. This is a relatively recent phenomenon, and a product of the age of the mass media, of the mass-production of works of art. Shakespeare is our best witness. Ever since his death in 1616 his plays have been adapted to the changing modes of theatrical production. The first full text of *King Lear* was not produced until William Charles Macready put it on stage in 1838. But as we have seen, historical accuracy only dates from the nineteenth century. This respect for the text and the manner in which the media recycle the classics are very much matters of cultural convention. The conventions themselves are in considerable part formed by market considerations. Even Shakespeare had to eat. Just as Dickens himself was required to write long narratives for serial publication which would have a fairly popular appeal so as to attract good advertizing revenue, so the television companies who make classic serials today have to bear in mind the pressures to satisfy overseas markets.

It is worth bearing in mind the kind of money we are talking about. In 1983 British television and filmed earned a surplus of £101 000 000 from overseas sales. This is the highest figure ever recorded. The Department of Trade and Industry reported that sales rose by £23 000 000 to that peak and that sales are now running at ten times the level of the 1970s. Economic considerations will always have to be taken into account when the British make classic serials. Quaint Dickensianism and prissy Austen-Bronterie is good for trade. James Andrew Hall, who adapted several Dickens novels for British television, wrote:

> It would . . . be helpful to an adapter to be blessed with a sense of humility . . . The danger of an adapter being overawed by his subject matter is the same as that of a surgeon operating on a member of his own family: he may shrink from applying the knife deep enough.[9]

He has a point, though the real dangers may lie elsewhere. It should be possible to recreate our classics for the new media, instead merely of preserving something of their essence in the aspic of media footage.

Notes

1. H.P. Bolton, *Dickens Dramatized* (London: Mansell Publications, 1987) pp. 416–29.
2. David Paroissien, 'Dickens and the Cinema' in Robert Partlow (ed.), *Dickens Studies Annual*, Volume 7 (Carbondale: Southern Illinois University Press, 1978), pp. 69ff.
3. Q. D. Leavis, *Fiction and the Reading Public* (London: Chatto and Windus, 1965), p. 156.
4. Robert M. Henderson, *D. W. Griffith – His Life and Work* (New York: Oxford University Press, 1972), p. 39.
5. See A. B. Walkley, 'Switching Off – Mr Griffith and Dickens, A Strange Literary Analogy' in *The Times*, 26 April 1922, p. 12.
6. C. W. Ceram, *Archaeology of the Cinema* (New York: Harcourt Brace and World, New York, n.d.), p. 120; Keith Reader, *Cinema – A History* (London: Hodder and Stoughton, 1979), pp. 18ff.; Gerald Mast and Marshall Cohen, *Film Theory and Criticism* (New York: Oxford University Press, 1979), pp. 394–405 and Ralph Stephenson and J. R. Debrix, *The Cinema as Art* (Harmondsworth: Penguin 1965), pp. 189ff.
7. The adaptation by Alec Guinness performed in the Rudolph Steiner Hall, London, in December 1939 was produced by George Devine and starred Marius Goring as Pip. The same adaptation was successfully staged at the Liverpool Playhouse directed by John Moody, 1943–4, and a further production toured England in 1946. It was staged again at the Bristol Old Vic in 1957.
8. J. Dudley Andrew, *The Major Film Theories* (New York: Oxford University Press, 1976), p. 175.
9. James Andrew Hall, 'In Other Words' in *Communication and Media*, Volume 1, no. 1, October 1984, p. 17.

6

Case Study: The Dramatization of *Vanity Fair*

What follows in the remainder of this book is a case study of one particular dramatization: the BBC TV Classic Serial presentation of Thackeray's *Vanity Fair*, broadcast in the Autumn of 1987. The aim of this chapter is to examine the practice of adaptation through an analysis of some of the problems confronting the production team. Consequently, we rely heavily in this chapter and the next on interview material from members of the production team. Chapter 8 examines promotion, audience response, marketing, and critical reviews of the programme.

The edited interviews which follow were all conducted by Chris Wensley, during Autumn 1987 and Spring 1988, and include a wide-ranging analysis of the work of the scriptwriter, producer, directors, script editor, production associate, production manager, designer, costume designer, two of the major actors, and with representatives from BBC Enterprises and Pan Books. The topics discussed in this chapter focus on *Vanity Fair* as a novel, and seek to explore the relationship between the producer, directors, designers, composer and actors to the novel and to the dramatized script.

Before we turn to the interviews, however, it will be useful to summarize some of the problems likely to be encountered in dramatizing *Vanity Fair* for the screen. One of the initial problems is, of course, the length of the novel itself: there are well over six hundred pages of prose, with many characters and incidents, as well as large sections of authorial comment and description. The 1987 BBC Classic Serial opted for an eight-hour serial version, approaching the length of time it might take a reader of the text. When one considers the length of a cinema film version – not more than two-and-a-half hours, normally – then the problem of what to omit which confronted the various adapters for the cinema screen can be realized.

More fundamental, however, is the problem of tone. Thackeray's novel is a comedy of manners; the object of his satire is not the various characters with all their variations of goodness and wickedness, but rather the social system which has produced them. They live in a society in which money, status, and greed are the dominant characteristics: Thackeray's criticism of Becky and George Osborne must be seen in the context of the social pressures surrounding them.

For example, George recognizes this when he describes to Amelia a rival to whom his sisters have shown much affection:

> 'I wish they would have loved me', said Emmy wistfully. 'They were always very cold to me.'
>
> 'My dear child, they would have loved you if you had had two hundred thousands pounds,' George replied. 'That is the way in which they have been brought up. Ours is a ready-money society. We live among bankers and City big-wigs . . . and every man, as he talks to you, is jingling his guineas in his pocket.' (p. 203)

And in a direct address to the reader, Thackeray adds later:

> For I defy any member of the British public to say that the notion of wealth has not something awful and pleasing to him; and you, if you are told that the man next to you at dinner has got half a million, not to look at him with a certain interest. (p. 205)

It is, therefore, essential for a faithful screen dramatization to try to show not individual struggle, vice, or achievement, but to demonstrate that social pressures are the dominant shaping influence. To complicate the task further, Thackeray manages to present many situations from a variety of points of view; there are variations upon a theme, repetitions of events, and retelling of incidents from different perspectives to demonstrate the inescapable relationship between the characters and their desire for wealth and social position. When this is realized, then Thackeray's subtle control of our responses to Becky can better be understood: the moral perspective in which she is presented manipulates our sympathy for her predicament, our admiration for her drive and nimble wits, and our repugnance at her selfishness, always in the context of the moral contrast with Dobbin. The danger, therefore, for a faithful dramatizer is the risk that this subtlety of treatment becomes merely a humorous character study of a spirited but heartless individual, Becky.

As can be seen from the interviews which follow, those involved with the BBC TV dramatization of *Vanity Fair* saw their role as an attempt to represent closely and faithfully Thackeray's novel on to the screen. Such a faithful adaptation will try to reproduce as much as possible the detail and spirit of the original prose. Certain passages in the novel inevitably raise particular problems. For example, Amelia's character is developed by Thackeray in passages such as this:

> It was arranged that Amelia was to spend the morning with the ladies of Park Lane, where all were very kind to her. Rebecca patronized her with calm superiority: she was so much the cleverer of the two, and her friend so gentle and unassuming, that she always yielded when anybody chose to command, and so took Rebecca's orders with perfect meekness and good humour. Miss Crawley's graciousness was also remarkable. She continued her raptures about little Amelia, talked about her before her face as if she were a doll, or a servant, or a picture, and admired her with the most benevolent wonder possible. I admire that admiration which the genteel world sometimes extends to the commonalty. There is no more agreeable object in life than to see Mayfair folks condescending. Miss Crawley's prodigious benevolence rather fatigued poor little Amelia, and I am not sure that of the three ladies in Park Lane she did not find honest Miss Briggs the most agreeable. She sympathized with Briggs as with all neglected or gentle people: she wasn't what you call a woman of spirit. (p. 140)

The problem here is the irony, the conciseness and the precision of the prose: 'was so much the cleverer,' 'always yielding', 'continued her raptures' and 'sympathised . . . as with all neglected or gentle people'. What is being narrated here is not an event, a specific moment in time but rather a continuing state, a situation or a relationship which has developed during several previous meetings: the past, the present and probably the future are all conveyed by the simple use of an adverb such as 'always', or the verb 'continued'. To convey this subtlety without the clumsy clichés of fades, flashbacks and dissolves will be a major problem for a screen dramatization.

The text contains frequent examples of intervention by Thackeray, when in a direct address to the reader he points up moral dilemmas or philosophical issues. For example, within a few paragraphs of one another, the following examples occur:

> We are Turks with the affections of our women; and have made them subscribe to our doctrine too. We let their bodies go abroad liberally enough, with smiles and ringlets and pink bonnets to disguise them instead of veils and yakmaks. But their souls must be seen by only one man, and they obey not unwillingly, and consent to remain at home as our slaves – ministering to us and doing drudgery for us. (p. 175)

> When one man has been under very remarkable obligations to another, with whom he subsequently quarrels, a common sense of decency, as it were, makes of the former a much severer enemy than a mere stranger would be. To account for your own hardheartedness and ingratitude in such a case, you are bound to prove the other party's crime. It is not that you are selfish, brutal, and angry at the failure of a speculation – no, no – it is that your partner has led you into it by the basest treachery and with the most sinister motives. From a mere sense of consistency, a persecutor is bound to show that the fallen man is a villain – otherwise he, the persecutor, is a wretch himself. (p. 175)

Such comments are clearly a major part of the experience of the text for a reader. They are not in some way inferior to the plot and the characterization, odd snippets of philosophical rambling which can be excised with no loss; rather, they point up the meaning, generalizing the application of the events, and contributing fully to the construction of meaning.

Thackeray recognizes one of the privileges of the novelist over other storytellers, his ability to achieve an internal psychological realism by taking the reader within the mind and thoughts of the characters, not being restricted as is the dramatist for stage or screen to revealing thought through action or dialogue:

> And now she was left alone to think over the sudden and wonderful events of the day, and of what had been and what

might have been. What think you were the private feelings of
Miss, no (begging her pardon) of Mrs Rebecca? If, a few pages
back, the present writer claimed the privilege of peeping into
Miss Amelia Sedley's bedroom, and understanding with the
omniscience of the novelist all the gentle pains and passions
which were tossing upon that innocent pillow, why should he
not declare himself to be Rebecca's confidante too, master of her
secrets, and seal-keeper of that young woman's conscience?

Well, then, in the first place, Rebecca gave way to some very
sincere and touching regrets that a piece of marvellous good
fortune should have been so near her, and she actually obliged
to decline it. (pp. 152–3)

This raises, as has already been discussed, one of the major
problems for the dramatist. Does he abide by the realistic convention and attempt to show by the actor's expression the thoughts
in her mind? Does she rather artificially write her thoughts in a
diary or letter? Or in his search for a psychological realism does
he make use of voice-over or soliloquy? As Becky rehearses the
problems in her own mind, the extent of the problem for the
dramatist is revealed. How can all this information be conveyed?
But equally how can it be omitted?

In the first place, she was married; – that was a great fact. Sir
Pitt knew it. She was not so much surprised into the avowal, as
induced to make it by sudden calculation. It must have come
some day: and why not now as at a later period? He who would
have married her himself must at least be silent with regard to
her marriage. – How Miss Crawley would bear the news – was
the great question. Misgivings Rebecca had; but she remembered
all Miss Crawley had said; the old lady's avowed contempt
for birth; her daring liberal opinions; her general romantic
propensities; her almost doting attachment to her nephew, and
her repeatedly expressed fondness for Rebecca herself. She is so
fond of him, Rebecca thought, that she will forgive him anything:
she is so used to me that I don't think she could be comfortable
without me: when the eclaircissement comes there will be a
scene, and hysterics, and a great quarrel, and then a great
reconciliation. At all events . . . the die was thrown, and now
or tomorrow the issue must be the same. And so . . . the young
person debated in her mind as to the best means of conveying

it to her; and whether she should face the storm that must come, or fly and avoid it until its first fury was blown over. (p. 154)

One of the problems often quoted with regard to prose description is the inevitable consecutiveness of the list of items. A film can reveal all the details concurrently, closer to our experience of reality when the eyes reveal the whole scene at once, and then often randomly fix upon details. By contrast, a prose description can seem systematic, and laboured. However, consider the following description of Jos Sedley at Amelia's wedding:

Jos Sedley was splendid. He was fatter than ever. His shirt-collars were higher; his face was redder; his shirt-frill flaunted gorgeously out of his variegated waistcoat. Varnished boots were not invented as yet; but the Hessians on his beautiful legs shone so, that they must have been the identical pair in which the gentleman in the old picture used to shave himself, and on his light green coat there bloomed a fine wedding favour, like a great white-spreading magnolia. (p. 216)

The cumulative effect of the list presented is an essential part of its meaning. Thackeray is not presenting merely a vulgar, over-dressed figure, but by isolating details for our attention, and linking them with previous items, both describes the outer appearance, and also mocks the character of Jos: his shirt frill is 'flaunted gorgeously', and had varnished boots been invented, we can be sure Jos would have owned a pair! His wedding button-hole is no mere flower, but blooms 'like a great white-spreading magnolia'. As he has become fatter and more pompous, so his vanity has grown like the spreading magnolia tree in the image. A costume designer can hint at the above, but will inevitably lose the precision of the verbal construction.

There is a sense, also, in *Vanity Fair* in which Thackeray, presenting lists of things, is making an attempt to understand the world by its details, and by the relationships between those details. The world may be too enormously complex and baffling for us really to understand in any other way. But it may be, Thackeray seems to be suggesting, that when enough of these apparently isolated details are described, and their relations discovered, the truth behind each will be liberated – a truth which will be both particular and universal.

Issues of tone, style, and mood present themselves to any group undertaking the transfer of a novel to the screen, but the detailed problems discussed above are particular concerns if the aim is to reproduce the novel as faithfully as possible, and with the minimum of alteration. Such is the aim of the BBC TV Classic Serial dramatizations.

The BBC has a long tradition of dramatizing classic novels for its Sunday afternoon teatime serial slot, as we have seen already. Paul Kerr has commented: 'The BBC's conception of literary classics does not differ remarkably from Leavis's *The Great Tradition*, or the Penguin Imprints, Penguin Classics, and Penguin English Library.'[1]

The BBC's first TV Classic Serial was a six-part version of Anthony Trollope's *The Warden* in 1951; when BBC-2 opened in 1964, it transmitted a classic serial *Madame Bovary* in its first weeks, and also in 1967, the first TV Classic Serial in colour, *Vanity Fair*. Clearly the most successful classic serial was *The Forsyte Saga* which attracted an average weekly audience of fifteen-and-a-half million viewers, and, it has been calculated, has been shown in 45 countries worldwide, with an estimated audience of 160 million viewers. Mike Poole has described the phenomenon as: 'cultured soap operas, an episode by episode unfolding of a reassuring pattern of identification and resolution which hooks mass audiences while respectfully paying its dues to literature.'[2] Or, as Hanif Kureishi writes: 'It's as if the real passion of the writers . . . gets lost in the peripherals which are to do with the look of the thing, and with the kind of softening out and flattening out that you get . . . it's as if the stories are pulled out, whereas the ideas are left behind.'[3]

Gardner and Wyver see the Classic Serial as:

The production of a mythologised British 'history' and 'tradition' . . . in strictly domestic economic terms, [they] are expensive but become 'a good investment' when guaranteed foreign sales are involved. The marketing of British culture as a televisual commodity has become almost a corollary of the British tourist industry, and fulfils a similar role in international terms.'[4]

It should be noted that there are two BBC TV Classic Serial styles: the relatively lavish BBC-2 production, designed for mid-to-late evening transmission, with a relatively sophisticated adult audience in mind; and the BBC-1 production, usually made with a smaller budget, and designed for transmission at Sunday teatime, and generally watched by family audiences.

The rest of this chapter, consisting of interviews and analysis, takes as a case study the BBC-1 Classic Serial dramatization of *Vanity Fair* of which Episode 1 was transmitted at 5.50 p.m. on Sunday, 6 September 1987, with subsequent episodes each Sunday until 20 December. This was in fact the third time that *Vanity Fair* had been dramatized as a BBC TV Classic Serial. This was, however, the most lavish production attempted, making use of 37 locations, 44 sets, 200 wigs, 2200 costumes, 80 carriages, 1023 extras, 250 horses, 32 goats, 18 dogs, 35 geese and several dead horses.

Chris Wensley interviewed key members of the production team[5] and discussed with them the style of the BBC-1 Classic Serial which almost always is naturalistic, historically accurate, and very faithful to the plot of the novel. We started with the question of the relationship between the literary text, in this case *Vanity Fair*, and the actual business of making a television serial drama. He began his interviews with Terrance Dicks, the producer of the BBC-1 Classic Serial.

CW: Do you have any feelings about Jonathan Miller's argument, put forward in his book *Subsequent Performances*, that film and television dramatizations somehow have a deleterious effect on the original literary texts on which they're based?
TD: I actually had that argument with Jonathan Miller at the Edinburgh Festival. He argues that the dramatization of a novel inevitably damages the original, that future readers are corrupted and previous readers are disappointed. I think it's nonsense, basically. As I said he gave this idea in a speech at the Edinburgh Festival where I was also appearing on another panel and I was in the audience and leapt up and said, 'I am the producer of the BBC-1 Classic Serial and you have been trying to put me out of business for the last hour!' – which got a nice laugh. What I said was that I thought that we had three classes of viewers. People who knew and loved the book and therefore would have a very firm idea in their minds and could then compare our version. People who had not read the book but would see it on television and would then be led to go to the book and read it: obviously it's not for nothing the publishers do tie-in editions. There is always a huge upsurge in libraries when anything appears on television, a lot of people

go to the book, so we gain readers. The third lot are people who have not read the book and who never will read the book and they get something of the book from the television version – they get all they will ever have. I think it's insulting the intelligence of the viewer to say that; it's also insulting the writer. The impact of Thackeray or Dickens is so strong I don't think its actually possible for this process to take place to a damaging extent. Obviously if you have seen Simon Callow's Micawber and then you read *David Copperfield* there will be overtones of Simon Callow in your head but I think you will very soon be swamped by the genuine Dickensian Micawber. It is certainly true, there is a saying that the best books make the worst television and alternatively a bad book can make very good television. If we do something like *Beau Geste* we are actually giving everything that is in the book and more, so that there is not a question of ruining *Beau Geste* for everybody which is actually a pretty terrible book, it's just that it has got this sort of mythic status. The other side of it is that if you do something as good as Dickens, say, I am always aware that one is only able to put a certain amount of what's in the book on the screen. The book is always infinitely better; they would all do much better to stay home and read the book. So the greater the genius the less you can put on the screen. I still believe it's worth doing for the reasons I've said.

We then turned to Alexander Baron, the adapter of *Vanity Fair*, to discover how he felt about his relationship to the novel.

CW: Do you feel it necessary to do some research on the author before you begin, on his life and other works?
AB: Because my background is writing novels I usually bring to it some knowledge of the writer. I would sometimes need to do some reading beforehand and sometimes this is of practical use. I remember when Julian Mitchell once did a dramatization of a Jane Austen novel, he said 'What do you do when you've got to make up dialogue?' because it's up to us to make up Thackeray, to make up Jane Austen and he found that he was able to go to Jane Austen's letters and take suitable passages so that he felt that he was doing plastic surgery on Jane Austen rather than impudently putting in bits of pastiche. I find it useful, also from this practical

point of view, to be able to fall back on what I know about Thackeray. My own technique for supplying conversation is to go to other parts of the book we're not using. Sometimes the narrative or to his commentary, of which there is a great deal, and to use that for conversation between characters.

CW: Was it your intention to try to reproduce Thackeray's tone, the grotesque, the satiric and so on, and is it possible even to translate those elements into the naturalistic medium of television?

AB: The problem of reproducing the tone, of fidelity in general, confronts you every time you dramatize a novel. After all, you've got to start off with respect and determination not to do the dirty on a writer whom you admire. But in fact the first decision that had to be taken with *Vanity Fair* was that really Thackeray is addressing the reader all the time and talking about life and then he illustrates it with scenes, and there is no way that you can carry that over into the television version. . . . It's awfully difficult to honour the novel fully. One can't, and the last line of defence would be not to violate the spirit of it. There is a kind of problem of conscience involved in dramatizing books that you like if you profess to be serious. We think about this and talk about this all the time.

CW: Can you tell me a bit more about how you try to get Thackeray's point of view across in the dramatization? In the novel it's very clear because he keeps stopping the reader and saying, 'This is what I think about it and what you ought to think.' How do you manage to get that into the script?

AB: Well, it was awkward. I'll say a number of fragmentary things. First of all I wanted, and we proposed until quite late in the day, to keep the fundamental of the framework thing, of the showman opening his box of puppets and putting it away at the end and we found that wasn't possible, or we just didn't want to do it. It was a question of, I don't know, pace and finding the most apt beginning, the most apt ending. At the end it would have been tedious after the particular ending that we, again, contrived. It was the last of several versions. It would have been intolerable to have tried to have had any kind of ending commentary or narration and the most one could do was to simply say, 'Well, we've got this from the book and somehow what we write has got to be impregnated with it.' In a minor way what helps is that there are certain scenes which were invented or certain interpolations into scenes which are passages of his commentary at certain points of the book which one has been able to put into the mouths of characters. But that's really quite a lame answer, because this is a fundamental way with this particular book in which one can't undertake to render the whole book on television. Lots and lots has to go. I mean, the book is the book and there is no substitute for it, but the viewer who has read the book has to judge to what extent he feels Thackeray in what he has seen.

CW: Were there any major differences between the script as you perceived it when you were writing and as it was eventually realized on the screen?

AB: No and yes. No – because I'm very fortunate to be with Terrance and in that routine. We always seem to be so much of one mind from the beginning that the scripts that I give in are not very different when they are handed over to the directors and they work strictly to them. But, so much is added in production that I enjoyed the episodes enormously when I saw them, and I really felt almost in the same position as my family because I was so pleased with what the directors had done, what most of the cast were doing and so on. Very often things are being brought out that I hadn't been subtle enough to do and yet they had seen them and brought them out in the performance. But no. I have never found that they had departed from the script.

CW: Did you feel that there were some places where television was actually able to cast light on parts of the novel that perhaps the reader of the prose narrative wouldn't have been able to appreciate? In other words that the television version added something to the novel?

AB: Well, I doubt that. I doubt that that could happen. If it's a realization of the book that you have in mind you can only lose by conveying it to any screen, cinema or television, and I don't even think you can claim that making things visible helps. No, I don't think it does add to the book.

CW: Jonathan Miller has argued that any dramatization of a novel inevitably damages the original and his argument is that future readers will be corrupted, previous readers will be disappointed and a lot of people will regard reading novels and watching television as somehow interchangeable. Are you conscious of these issues as you work on the dramatization?

AB: I am indeed, and that is, I think, the problem of conscience. I can't say that we lose sleep over it but there is a kind of niggle there all the time. Something one talks about in the pub but I can never solve. I don't know that it does disappoint previous readers. It may conflict with what a lot of individuals have got previously from the novel or with people who have been taught the novel or are teaching the novel, but most people seem to be delighted with the dramatization, and they never notice the differences. Where you have had to interpolate a scene or so on, they take it all as Thackeray or all as Dickens. I think Miller does overlook the fact that the two entities can exist side by side without one being a violation of the other. I think it can become so if you have a vulgarized thing. But you see, whoever is reading a book, I would like them to read it with there being an interchange involved. That is to say that the reader's thoughts and the writer's words have some kind of discourse going on between them. Perhaps a critical discourse, and I think even the ordinary reader if he comes freshly to the book is capable of this. I suspect that if you have previously seen it on the screen, that becomes the version in your mind and you may then read the book without interjecting thoughts of your own. So if corruption is not too strong a word to apply to that, I think that does happen.

We then turned to Diarmuid Lawrence, one of the two directors of *Vanity Fair*, who explained how he prepared himself for such a task.

DL: I had never done an adaptation of a classic before and the first thing was to reach for the book and to read it and read it and read it. I can't conceive of it not being enormously important. But . . . in terms of his [Thackeray's] shadow – because that sounds intimidatory – no, I wasn't aware of his shadow. I was aware of his support in a way. I never felt that intimidating in that sense and this might be rather worrying because it might be that I have underestimated the problems or the pain it might cause to his friends and admirers, and that is whether we are going to address ourselves to 100 pedants up and down the country who want every jot and tittle untouched and who will be genuinely alarmed at almost anything that departs from their expectations. All the people who broadly admire the work, remember the work and are affectionate towards it – certainly in the feedback we have had, a lot of people who are affectionate to it have been very affectionate about the series, despite the fact that, clearly, it is going to be a different event. It comes into such a broad country in that sense and unless you are doing *Nicholas Nickleby* or doing this kind of adaptation that stretches over 8 hours or you are doing *Little Dorrit* [Christine Edzard, 1987] in the way that it has been done recently on film, you can't hope to encompass all the book. So certainly in feature films I am aware that I will be wary of going to see something that I have formed a strong affection for as a book, because I know that disappointment is going to come and sometimes I will be wary of listening to a recording or going to a concert of something that I have become very fond of because the pacing and everything will be different and I will resist it at first. Then after a while I will actually start playing two things for those very differences, and it was very interesting that comments constantly came up from the feedback we got and the letters we got. For instance people had said, which I think is very informative about this whole argument, a lot of people said that Eve Matheson's face wasn't what they expected. But they then immediately said what a good idea it was. Now that seems to me that if one is stepping past 100 people who will not be moved, into the vast mass, for people within the first episode to say, 'This wasn't what I expected because I expected to follow the Thackerayan thing of a sharp face for Becky, and here was this lady with a broad face and open eyes and what have you' – and then to actually fall for that as being an embodiment, an embodiment, not the embodiment, not a definitive version but an embodiment of Becky, shows that people can be moved from their base very quickly. There is a tendency for the argument to become slightly precious – about not wanting to upset people. I cannot begin to go the route of this idea of permanent damage to the novel which I think tends towards intellectual pretension and prissiness.

What has happened on this, we got audiences between a disappointing 3 point something million and a very agreeable 6.8 or whatever it was. I was very chastened the other day because I went to the Mermaid Theatre and was reading the programme notes and discovered that since its opening, up to the point of its renovation, it had had 3 million customers. You are talking about our lowest figures being everybody who had been to see anything at The Mermaid in all those years. It kind of puts those figures into perspective. But of those people, although you can't, obviously, come up with mathematical absolutes, certain things are reasonable to assume. One is that of, say, the 6 million, or take an average of four-and-a-half million, that the vast majority of those will never have read the book, probably will never read the book again. Some of them may as a result decide they will read the book, and not read it; and some as a result will decide to read the book and go ahead and read it. If we are talking about those people who have come to the adaptation knowing and loving the novel, and were upset by it, we seem to have proved or indicated that there is a large number who will be perfectly able to take the adaptation for what it is. . . . In terms of people who may be damaged for approach to the novel, (a) would they have gone to the novel anyhow? There may be a very small number there who, some might argue, would have gone to the novel unsullied by TV at some point in the future and now they will never be able to approach it in a neutral fashion. That may be probably true, but I'm not sure they are that sullied. I'm not sure that you can't remove one picture from your mind and paint in another, especially as going in that direction is always an enrichment. If you then go there, because you can't get the mental images of one person out of your mind, clearly the opposite track that we have had from the letters is that people have been able to remove one image from their mind, go along with another, find that agreeable and possibly end up with both. I'm not sure people can be trapped like that. The idea that to protect a minority that might possibly go to the novel later on outweighs moving a lot of people to either having some knowledge of the book via us, even if they never want to pick it up, or intend to pick it up and never get round to it. Or the other, which is more likely, that there will be some considerable number, maybe, probably young people, who will be moved to pick up the book, do pick up the book who would never have picked it up before. None of these things can you prove, but they seem to me to far outweigh this rather delicate point that you have somehow permanently damaged the novel.

CW: From what you say you are obviously quite conscious of the novel all the time. You see yourself as representing it in visual terms?

DL: Absolutely yes. I think there is unquestionably a duty to the novel. It's often interpreted by people who write you the most critical letters as a pedantry, and I don't think there is a pedantry because an adaptation is, by essence, different. It is not the novel. But it must be true to the novel and true to the flavours and the feelings of the novel so that you would hope that if Thackeray could come and look at it he would say, 'Well, it's not what I wrote, but it's got an awful lot of what I wrote.'

The other director on *Vanity Fair* was Michael Morris, who explained his relationship to the novel and how he prepared himself for the production.

MM: I had never read any Thackeray before I did this and when I was told I was doing it, I thought, 'Oh that will be nice, I can get into an author I don't know at all.' I got hold of the book as soon as I heard I was doing it and started to read it and I thought 'Oh God!', because the first 100 pages of that book are a heavy slog, they really are. But once I had got past page 100 I got really wound up in the story and it was smashing. Then having got through it, one goes through it again just to fix everything in your mind as to where the thoughts and ideas of what Thackeray was trying to do go. Then I think it is quite important to leave the book alone.

Alexander Baron delivered the 16 scripts, but with the best will in the world in 8 hours of television he cannot put those 800 pages all there. So you've got to find a way – we are not doing *Vanity Fair*, we are doing an adaptation of *Vanity Fair*. I think that has to always be borne in mind by the people that make the television programmes of it. You are doing the script, not the book. Alex has his own ideas and there will be ways he just wants to move things slightly and emphases he wants to give to different parts because of the dramatic construction of what he's written. He stuck very rigidly to what Thackeray wrote, he is a brilliant adapter and the scripts were of such a high standard there was no problem anyway. I think had he not been so good, then maybe we might have referred to the book a bit more. . . . But it was never a case of going back and saying, 'Why can't we do this bit which isn't in?' One has to appreciate that you can't do it all, and in fact some of the stuff that we did actually do, we weren't able to get to the screen anyway, because some of the scripts were just slightly too long.

CW: Were you conscious of the shadow of Thackeray when you were directing, and the reactions of his admirers and readers, people noticing little differences in the text that you had changed or omitted?

MM: One was aware of Thackeray, yes, but as I've said, because Alex's adaptation was so true to it, we didn't have to worry whether we were getting it right or wrong. It was right on the line – at least we thought so. It was a very loyal adaptation.

It would be possible in a television version of *Vanity Fair* for Thackeray's hand to weigh quite heavily on the nature of design, as he illustrated his novel himself. Chris Wensley discussed the influence of the book on television designers. He began by talking to Gavin Davies.

GD: I think you have to work primarily from the script, because that is actually what you are doing. You can't work to two masters. You have to be careful not to imagine doing the book when you are actually doing the adaptation. It's quite a common problem that a slight characterization or a situation may have changed. If you adhere to the book you could find yourself falling foul of the adaptation and that is actually what we were doing. What I tend to do is to read the novel. I actually outlined some descriptive passages, but that was more to give me the general feel of the period and the time, and Thackeray's attitudes. From there on in it was very much script-based. The script tells you the actual practical things that have to be resolved.

CW: You obviously have to provide far more detail than Thackeray, because he only draws attention to the key details. Was that a problem, having to fill in so much of the background?

GD: No – because it is a creative process. You can't slavishly work from his total reference. In the end it's an individual act on my behalf to create these interiors and rooms and a lot of it comes from your own research and your own feelings about it. It is not a direct illustration of anything either described or seen. It is something new and has to be something that has got its own integrity all the way through.

The costume designer, Joyce Hawkins, also commented on

Thackeray's influence in the look of the television version of *Vanity Fair*.

CW: Do you work mainly from the script provided by the writer, or do you go back to Thackeray's own descriptions?
JH: Thackeray. Which is something different from what I noted in the *Radio Times* about another production, but yes, I do. I think it's important because I think your intelligent viewer will have read the book, perhaps, and if a description is in the book the viewer would expect to see that.
CW: Was the fact that some of Thackeray's illustrations were wrong a problem? Did you use his illustrations?
JH: No, I didn't use his illustrations, because they were wrong. His illustrations were of the time he wrote the book whereas his descriptions really were better, they were much more like they should have been.
CW: So in your research you would go back to an 1815 infantryman and see exactly what he looked like in contemporary drawings?
JH: Yes. It was a special regiment, you see. Thackeray says, I think, the 115th Foot, doesn't he, which is ridiculous, so we made it the 110th because I think there are 109 or something like that, so we made it just one different.
CW: Did you get any letters about detail?
JH: The only thing which rather upset me was the fact that somebody wrote in and said that the cartouche was on the wrong shoulder on Rawdon and I checked and, yes, the viewer was right. It was on the shoulder it would have been on for an infantryman, and a cavalryman would have had it on the other shoulder.
CW: Your order of priorities then is historical accuracy first, then Thackeray's descriptions and finally the script?
JH: Yes, well the script should be from the book, shouldn't it?
CW: Were there times when you found that there was any sort of dilemma between what Alexander had described and what Thackeray had described?
JH: I don't think I ever actually put them close together to see. What I did when I read the book was to mark all the references to costume or to character. Then I compiled what I called my Bible and I put the name of the character, and eventually filled in the name of the artist who was going to play the part, and wrote the description in underneath, I always do that. Then when you have

got your artist at a costume-fitting you can say, 'Thackeray says' –
and read it out to them and you've got something to pin on to.

CW: Do you try at all to reflect the nineteenth-century view that
costume is symbolic of character?

JH: To a certain extent, yes, because your first impression is from
the costume. It's the first judgement you make of anybody so to a
certain extent, yes. We tried that with Becky. What I said to the
director was, 'How I see this first scene, I want all the girls like
little butterflies and I want Becky as a little plain brown moth.'
That's what we did and I think that worked. I was quite pleased.
The girls would have been all in white so we gave them all
differently lightly-coloured sashes and they fluttered about while
she sat there and I thought that worked. Then gradually we made
her more and more come out, and Diarmuid [director] wanted her
to look at her most surprising, the first time we really see that she
is developing – because the book says that she only had two
dresses – so she only had the little brown striped one and one
white muslin dress. Then in the text Amelia gives her a dress
which she subsequently wore, so she then had three dresses. So
when she went to Queen's Crawley, the first day, she goes down
and meets the mother of the children. She was wearing Amelia's
dress which we have seen Amelia wear before. I don't think that
viewers would know, but I knew.

CW: Were there other characters where the costume was telling
us something important about the character?

JH: There wasn't so much character development with Jos. I loved
doing him as a dandy and his over-the-top style of dressing and
then gradually, I think, at the end he was totally broken down
and depressed. We took off his padding then so that he lost weight.
I loved doing the pretence of his uniform. He invented a uniform –
he says in the book it's his own version. So they made one for us
at the costumiers and I didn't like it when it arrived, I thought it
was horrid. So we refaced all the front part with a piece of original
paisley of the period which had a border. So it was scarlet with a
paisley edge, we remade it so that it was much more fun.

Amelia was originally all pink and white, the pampered darling,
then when she goes downmarket and gets depressed we actually
had her in an original frock. Miss Schwarz had an original dress
as well, the bright yellow dress was real dress of the period in that
colour. It says in the book yellow and turquoise so we spent a lot
of time on that because it was absolutely yellow and we kept

looking at it saying we've got to put something with this. We kept looking at it over a period of weeks but not quite knowing how to do it then suddenly at the last minute we did it with that yellow and turquoise hat. Amelia, Rebecca Saire, got a sort of hang-up about 'I'm not really a milksop. I'm not a soppy sort of person. I've really got strength of character. Could I have bright colours for the later part?', and I said 'Well, you can't actually have bright colour because that's not what's right.' There was something that worried me a bit because mourning was something that went on for two years and because of the span of time and because of the little boy we had to squash it in. I knew that viewers might mind that we hadn't moved on in time enough for her to give that Indian party because she would still have been in mourning, so she is in mauve, which is half mourning. They shouldn't have had the beach scenes either, because people didn't have beach holidays until the railways came along. They wouldn't have had that picnic on the beach and that worried me, designing clothes for a 'wrong' scene!

What is already beginning to develop in the interviews, as you will have noticed, is that the primary relationship of the directors and producer to the novel is via the script they received from the writer. The designer and costume designer, on the other hand, take their cue directly from the novel, with a proportionately lesser relationship to the dramatized script. This is clearly because part of their function in the production is the visual creation of reality, while the directors and producer are possibly more concerned with the visual recreation of reality; that is, filming the historical verisimilitude provided by designer and costume designer. One of the people who might liaise between these two areas of historical reality and the style in which that historical reality is recreated is the composer, who provides much of the non-visual atmosphere of the production. Composer Nigel Hess explained to Chris Wensley how music could be used to reinforce mood, character and situation and help bring out what he believed was explicit or implicit in Thackeray's novel.

NH: I don't think people realize how important music is in manipulating what they think about a scene. In *Vanity Fair* with the character of Becky Sharp I had the power in the music to make her a lot more evil if I had wanted to and I discussed with the directors as to how sinister I should make the character of Becky Sharp and we decided not to go overboard on that. But musically I could have made you think she was an out-and-out villain, depending on what kind of music you put underneath her, but I tried to keep it ambiguous, and obviously that applies to every character, going all the way through. For Amelia I tended to use a sweet solo violin every time we saw her. She was the goody-goody and so sweet and innocent. Whereas for Becky I tended to use a clarinet or a bass clarinet, slightly more snarling, a bit more uncomfortable. I always like to try and get different sounds for different characters as I go through, so that Rawdon is French horn; not one person in 10 000 would notice that on the screen but that's not the point, the point is it gives me a through-line to a character and how the music is going to help that character.

CW: Did you find that it was useful to get to know the novel quite well before you did the music, or did you work almost exclusively from the script?

NH: I worked almost exclusively from the script. I would sometimes go to the novel to see what Thackeray said about a certain musical point and he was nearly always wrong. For instance he has them waltzing at the Duchess of Richmond's ball; well, they wouldn't have waltzed. It was only just coming in on the Continent at that time and it would have been a terribly risqué thing but, because at the time he was writing people were waltzing like things possessed, he decided that they would dance a waltz. It was difficult deciding how much to go with him! As it happened, in the TV version they did dance a waltz but it was a bit touch-and-go as to whether they actually would or not. But no. I worked from the script, because inevitably so much of the book is missed out in the script and it was no good wading through pages and pages of the book when it wasn't going to be included. I had read the novel earlier on but after that I just put it to one side.

At the centre of this whole question of the relationship between the historical reality being recreated and the tone or style in which that is recreated are, of course, Becky and Dobbin, who are both the subject and the creators of their own historical recreation. Eve Matheson, who played Becky Sharp, and Simon Dormandy, who played Dobbin, had much to say about the relationship they saw between the literary text and a modern television production. Chris Wensley began by asking Eve Matheson whether she was influenced by Thackeray's portrayal of Becky.

EM: I was enormously influenced and it got in the way sometimes, but I couldn't do without it. I actually didn't think I had the right to disregard it or disobey it because it is a very famous novel and she is a very famous character. I don't think I've got the right to change it in any way to impose anything on it.

CW: Were there places in the script where you felt that something important from the novel had been omitted?

EM: Occasionally, and I said so and occasionally it was taken up and sometimes it wasn't.

CW: Can you remember any examples?

EM: There was a point when Becky is in Brussels and there is the contretemps between Becky and Lady B and that had been diminished rather, sadly out of necessity as always. There was a point in the book where Becky sits on the windowsill of her hotel bedroom and yells out of the window at Lady B this beautiful, disguised insult. She has no shame at all; she doesn't care who hears and she says exactly what she likes. In fact it's not disguised at all, it's quite blatant and I laughed outright when I read it and I was mortified when I didn't see that in the script; and I said 'Oh please' and it was put back in, but that sort of thing can be very intrusive because the script is worked out very carefully by the people who are writing and producing it and they have been looking at it for a great deal longer than you. Of course you have ideas and fortunately the things that I suggested were listened to and a lot of things were explained to me: why something hadn't been included or why such a thing was this way round and you either take it on board and appreciate it and say yes I understand, fair enough, or you try to insist on its importance; I found the production team were really good about this.

CW: Did your understanding of Becky change during rehearsals and recording or did you have a clear understanding of the character at the beginning?

EM: Well, obviously, as you go on you understand more and more, and there were some things that I got wrong but what I found was that I really did love her as a sort of person you hate to love, you can't help to like everything and I found I was very defensive of her. She came in for a lot of flak from other people all around who in joking would say she's abominable, what a bitch! And what I wanted was for the audience not to think that, for the audience to feel what I was feeling, that they hated loving her and they hated her for making them love her. There were two occasions when I was reading the book before we had started rehearsing when I thought she was awful and really had gone too far, and those were when she tries to steal George from under Amelia's nose and when she hits her child, particularly the latter. But then I thought with George, what a frightful thing to do, but when it came to it in the production my understanding of Becky's appreciation of George and Amelia was such that I realized Becky would have thought if you can't look after yourselves then it's your loss, and I can therefore I will, and to hell with it and have a damn' good time doing it and I loved that attitude of hers. It's dreadful but she feels that she is dealing with fools, with George who's such a pompous young twit and Amelia is such a silly piece of nonsense that it's all their own fault, and she thinks if you feel something, stand up and say it and fight for yourself – and they can't do it, for whatever reason, so she thinks she should get on with it. I know that I can be over-reverent towards the original text but in this case the brief for the series was a dramatization of the novel as faithfully as possible. If somebody said, let's take *Vanity Fair* and set it in the twentieth century, I'd say fine, but you are not doing the original novel: you would be taking a storyline and you would have to change the people and the settings to fit. You would lose something central: the social delineations of gender which is what she's fighting against throughout.

Simon Dormandy played opposite Eve Matheson as Dobbin. In the novel, Thackeray presents Dobbin as an extremely clownish but he comes over as much more purposeful in the television production. This, clearly, might tell us a great deal about the actor's sense of his relationship to the character he plays, and implicitly, therefore, to the novel itself. Chris Wensley followed up these ideas with Simon Dormandy.

CW: Do you feel that your portrayal of Dobbin on screen differs in any significant way from Thackeray's portrayal of Dobbin in the novel?

SD: It does, yes. I do think the clownishness is definitely part of Thackeray's point of view. The directors and the writer, before I even got to the casting stage, had decided to play that down and it really went altogether. One was just aware of him being shy and I think the danger was he might have come over a bit stuffy as a result of not being funny. I think that stripping away the sentimentality is a big plus for me. There is a lot about Thackeray's novel that I can't stand. I think it's a brilliant novel but I think there is the essential story, which I think is superb, but then there is a great deal of comment piled on top of it and surrounding it, some of which is brilliant and some of which is actually destructive of the actual work that he has created. It is a very complex piece of work and I think stripping away some of those layers actually benefits it in a way.

CW: But you always went back to the novel before preparing a scene?

SD: Yes, I did.

CW: And you obviously feel it's important to try to be as faithful as possible to Thackeray.

SD: Yes. As faithful as possible within the constraints that you've got. In the end you've got to say, 'Well, I'm making a television serial, I'm not reliving the novel. I'm making an entertainment from scratch but the novel is the source of it. The novel is where all your riches come from.'

CW: What do you feel about the argument that the dramatization of the novel inevitably damages the original?

SD: You might just as well say that about critics' work. You could say that criticism inevitably damages a novel because if you read the criticism before you read the novel then that's going to affect the novel. What are we supposed to do, shut up about novels? It's rubbish, absolute rubbish.

CW: So what's the justification of taking a novel and dramatizing it?

SD: To make it more available to people. There are tremendous riches in Thackeray's novel and I think that dramatically the nineteenth century is only just being reassessed but certainly the great dramatic writers of the nineteenth century wrote novels and so, until Ibsen comes along, we don't have the great moral and political dramas for the stage. They all happen in the novels, and so if we want to examine that part of our history and if we want to benefit from that wealth of writing then we have to plunder the novels.

CW: There is some strength in each side though, isn't there? Television can add things to the prose narrative?

SD: I don't know that television can add that much subtlety actually, although it can obviously give you the close-up on reactions. I remember there was one particular scene when Becky was introduced to Jos Sedley right at the beginning and there is a description in the book of her raising her eyes right to Heaven and then right down again and Eve Matheson actually did that eye-motion, although it wasn't in the script at all, because she was aware of what she was thinking. So she would hope to be able to reveal that on her face, and if you are in close-up on television that does show a lot, but it can't show quite the wit of it.

However the debate rages over the desirability or otherwise of dramatizing classic novels for film and television, the fact remains that it seems to be good for the book trade. Chris Wensley concluded his interviews with a discussion with Joanna Webb of Pan Books, who published the paperback edition of *Vanity Fair*.

CW: How did your tie-in publication of *Vanity Fair* originate?

JW: Of course *Vanity Fair* was out of copyright, and we had a Pan Classics available with a tired-looking cover on it, published several years ago. So when we heard of the BBC project, we were invited to bid by the BBC. The system is that all relevant publishers are invited to submit secret sealed bids to the BBC. We decided we wanted the rights because Pan Classics was something we wanted to develop, and we were keen to beat Penguin at their own game. We got it and we paid a lot of money for it.

CW: What exactly did you get for your money?

JW: The exclusive use of the photograph of the cast in the production on the cover and also on our point-of-sale material: we did a point-of-sale dump bin with a headboard and a poster as well. (See plate 20.)

CW: How much did you pay?

JW: Between three thousand five hundred and four thousand pounds – which for us is a lot of money, really. In fact our Managing Director at the time was very keen to go for it and so we were prepared to pay that much. Normally when we do film and TV tie-ins, very often we don't pay at all: unless it's like *Vanity Fair*, open copyright, or it's a real biggie. For example, a film of *Nostromo* is coming up, and we'd like to get that one, too. Penguin brought out a cover version of their own. That's standard practice; we would have done the same if Penguin had got it. We did pretty well with sales, and got our sales kits in the shops early.

CW: What sort of change in sales do you notice after there is a tie-in publication with a TV dramatization?

JW: Generally they go up – on the whole a lot, but it depends on the type of book, but say, fifteen to twenty thousand extra sales on average, quoting off the top of my head. With our detective-story literature, for example Inspector Morse, it's a smaller increase – I suppose because people know who did it once they've seen the programme! In those cases, we try to get the book out well before the transmission, so that people will read it first.

CW: How did you market *Vanity Fair*?

JW: We had a nice dump bin, header and posters. We sold over 200 bins, and 1000 posters.

CW: And specifically with *Vanity Fair*, what sort of sales did you achieve?

JW: Well, it was over thirty thousand. We published it in August, so we were selling it in June; subscriptions came in from the shops for publication date, with a few repeats for September, assuming the stock had sold out. So, thirty thousand was our sale during August and September.

CW: And what were you selling of the old *Vanity Fair* edition for the similar period last year?

JW: About fifty copies a month. So you can see the sort of increase we achieved! Of course, with our extra sales, you can't really tell why people buy the book. . . . Some people probably buy the book because they like the bloke on the cover, or as a souvenir, or hopefully to read it. We can't really tell either whether more copies are sold before the transmission or afterwards – since we sell it to the shops well before transmission. Anything that's on TV makes our sales shoot up. We employ a full-time film and TV officer specifically to find out exactly what is coming up, when and where, so that we can get our tie-ins ready. And there are a lot of adaptations coming up. We publish an 'advance warning' list for our sales force.

There are several things we have seen emerging from the

interviews so far. The first is the division between the past as historical artefact and the past as historical atmosphere, the difference between the creation and the recreation of the past. Next is the high degree of professionalism of all the people involved with the realization of *Vanity Fair* as television, the scope of their research and the breadth of their creative thinking and planning that goes into the production. Last of all, of course, and this is something we might particularly note from the final interview in this chapter, the media industry *is* an industry, and as such, is concerned with making money: Pan Books' sales of *Vanity Fair* increased from about fifty copies a month to about thirty thousand in two months, due almost entirely to their tie-in publication of the novel with a new cover and plenty of well-directed publicity. It is this side of the media industry to which we turn our attention in the following chapter, which is concerned very much more with the nuts and bolts of planning, creating and then broadcasting a media product.

Notes

All quotations from *Vanity Fair* are taken from the Pan Classics edition first published in 1967 by Pan Books, London.

1. Paul Kerr, 'Classic Serials: To Be Continued' in *Screen*, Vol. 23, no. 1 May/June 1982, p. 9.
2. Mike Poole, 'Englishness for Export', *Time Out*, 7 March 1980.
3. Hanif Kureishi, *The Media Show*, director Peter Orton, Channel 4 TV, May 1987.
4. Carl Gardner and John Wyver, quoted in Paul Kerr, 'Classic Serials', op. cit., p. 9.
5. It will no doubt be useful for the reader to have some information about the interviewees. The following is a brief biographical and credit list for all of the people interviewed, although some will not appear until the next chapter.

ALEXANDER BARON, a successful novelist in his own right, undertook the epic serialization of *Vanity Fair*. He has written many original television plays and has dramatized a considerable number of novels including *The Black Tulip*, *Poldark*, and *A Horseman Riding By*. Past dramatizations for BBC-1 Classic Serials are *Sense and Sensibility*, *Stalky and Co.*, *The Hound of the Baskervilles*, *Jane Eyre*, *Goodbye, Mr Chips* and *Oliver Twist*.

MICHAEL DARBON read English and Drama at University College, Bangor and then took a Post-Graduate diploma in Theatre Studies at

University College, Cardiff. His first job was as an assistant stage manager at the Belgrade Theatre in Coventry. He joined the BBC as a floor assistant in 1978. He is now a production manager with the BBC's Series and Serials Department and has worked on many projects, including *Juliet Bravo, Dr Who, Tender is the Night, The Singing Detective, Vanity Fair, Blind Justice* and *Bergerac*.

GAVIN DAVIES trained at Glasgow School of Art. He joined the BBC in 1969 and has since designed a wide variety of plays, series and light entertainment programmes. The plays he has designed include: *The Enigma, Artemis '81* and *East Lynne* and amongst his many serial credits are: *The Brothers, Poldark, The History Man, Bird of Prey, Dead Head, A Very Peculiar Practice* and a recent BBC-1 Classic *David Copperfield*.

TERRANCE DICKS worked for five years as script editor on BBC-1 Classics before becoming a producer. He had previously worked for six years as script editor on *Dr Who* before leaving the BBC to write children's books, including about sixty *Dr Who* books, *The Baker Street Irregulars*, a series of detective stories, *Star Quest*, a sci-fi trilogy and *Cry Vampire*, a series of children's horror stories. As producer on the BBC-1 Classic Serial, he has the following titles to his credit: *Oliver Twist, Alice in Wonderland, Brat Farrar, David Copperfield* and *The Diary of Anne Frank*.

SIMON DORMANDY has already played the part of Amelia's loyal admirer Dobbin in an acclaimed portrayal for the Cheek by Jowl Company. Recently he has appeared in the BBC drama serial *Boogie Outlaws* as Constable Toy. In the feature film of *Little Dorrit* he played Edmund Sparkler in scenes with Alec Guinness, Eleanor Bron and Michael Elphick. Other film credits include *Castaway* and *Whoops! Apocalypse*.

ALISON GEE started her working career in the Capital Taxes Offices of the Inland Revenue and joined the BBC as an Assistant Allocations Officer in 1978. Since then she has worked as film editing manager and production associate on several drama series and serials, including *One by One, EastEnders, Call Me Mister, Vanity Fair* and *Thin Air*. She later worked on the BBC production *Shadow of the Noose*.

PHILIPPA GILES was script editor of *The Diary of Anne Frank* before taking up the same post for *Vanity Fair*. She has worked also as an assistant producer and director on *Jackanory, Take Two* and *Johnny Briggs*.

JOYCE HAWKINS joined the BBC in 1958 as the sole member of the Costume Department in the Midland Region. She has now taken early retirement from running the Department (which now has over thirty staff members), in order to move freely into designing for theatre and film. During her years with the BBC she has worked on numerous programmes as diverse as *Newcomers, Brothers, All Creatures Great and Small, Nanny*, and many one-off plays and serials. *Vanity Fair*, for which she received a BAFTA nomination, was the last production which she designed as Senior

Costume Designer at BBC Pebble Mill. She was awarded the John Logie Baird Award in 1988 for her outstanding contribution to costume design.

NIGEL HESS works extensively as composer and conductor in television, theatre and film. In 1981 he was appointed Music Director of the Royal Shakespeare Company, and has composed scores for fifteen RSC productions, including *Much Ado About Nothing* and *Cyrano de Bergerac*, both playing in repertory on Broadway, and for which he received a New York Drama Desk Award for 'Outstanding Music'. Recent television scores include: *A Woman of Substance, Anna of the Five Towns, Father Matthew's Daughter, To Us a Child, Vidal in Venice* and *All Passion Spent*. His concert works include *The Way of Light*, recently performed in St Paul's Cathedral in the presence of Her Majesty the Queen and the Prince and Princess of Wales.

DIARMUID LAWRENCE's first production as a freelance director was *Ladies*, a BBC Play For Today which was shortly followed by *My Dear Palestrina* for BBC Playhouse which won the 1980 RTE/Jacob's Award. Since then a wide range of work includes episodes of *Grange Hill, The Practice, Juliet Bravo, By the Sword Divided* and for TVS *The Young Person's Guide To. . . .* He has just completed his first feature film, Thomas Hardy's *Our Exploits at West Poley* which was shown at last year's London Film Festival.

EVE MATHESON takes the role of Becky Sharp in *Vanity Fair*. She has worked widely in the theatre, including playing alongside Vanessa Redgrave in the recent production of *Ghosts*, and has appeared on television in *Fireworks for Elspeth, What If It's Raining* and *Jane Eyre*.

MICHAEL MORRIS began his career as an ASM, working at the Thorndyke Theatre, Leatherhead, and with the Young Vic and Volcano Productions. In 1973 he joined the BBC as AFM and production manager on a wide range of programmes. It was in 1982 that he embarked on the BBC Director's Course and his subsequent freelance credits include: *Tenko* (series III, 1984), *Juliet Bravo, Bergerac* and the series *Strike It Lucky*.

JOANNA WEBB started in publishing as a secretary in the Sales Department of Collins Publishers. She then moved to become copy-editor at Pan, then film/TV officer, and is now promotion manager with the same company.

7

Case Study: The Production of *Vanity Fair*

Our aims in this chapter are twofold: first, to identify the nature of each individual's responsibilities involved with the making of the BBC's *Vanity Fair*, and to consider how his/her work relates to that of colleagues; secondly, to examine, again through interviews with the production team, issues relating to the overall style of the production – the choice of naturalistic style, and consideration of whether a BBC 'house style' for TV classic novel serializations has developed. One of the things that particularly interested us was to try to discover whether, if there were such a thing as a BBC 'house style' for Classic Serials production, this would run the risk of subsuming the distinctive voices of individual novelists into a continuing monotone of costume dramas.

We started, however, with the question of each individual's responsibilities as a member of a production team. This is obviously an extremely important aspect in any production. Making any television programme is a highly complex operation, requiring almost military precision and planning, and a smooth meshing of the various responsibilities so that each stage of the process is achieved as required. With an eight-hour drama serial the complexity is clearly made that much greater.

MAKING THE PROGRAMME

The first interview is with Terrance Dicks who, as the producer, is very much the linchpin on whom the production itself depends. Chris Wensley asked him to outline his role and to describe his professional relationship with other colleagues in the production.

TD: The role of a producer generally is to be a kind of focal point. He is in charge of everything and has final responsibility for everything under the head of department. It's where the buck stops . . . . The first thing you do is to get the scripts in. You decide which writer you want to do it, talk to him/her and then work with your script editor to get the scripts in.

CW: How do you select the adapter? Are certain writers suited to certain novelists?

TD: It's a small field, adaptation, so in a sense that narrows the choice. Some writers have a particular gift for it and specialize in it so you would probably be thinking of a smaller field of names than you would have for anyone to do an original. In my case it was simply because I've worked with Alexander Baron before on other shows. Two things: he is very good, an extremely good adapter and, equally important in this case, where there was enormous pressure of time . . . that he is also immensely reliable. . . . He was producing about a script a fortnight for us and the scripts came in like clockwork for the whole 16 episodes.' We never had script trouble because if we had we couldn't have done the production, we really couldn't.

We found the stress Terrance Dicks put on the importance of a good script very interesting. Television programmes, and despite popular beliefs, do not write themselves. We next turned to Alexander Baron, who dramatized *Vanity Fair* for television.

CW: Can you outline briefly your role in the production, when you become involved and how your work relates to that of other colleagues?

AB: I have worked for the BBC Classic Serial for many years and when Terrance Dicks, the producer, has a project he wants me to consider, he lets me know well in advance. I read the book once generally to see if I want to do it and if I am okay to do it, then I need fairly minutely to decide broadly how I intend to do it. Then I have a meeting with Terrance and tell him what I think are the main problems and how I propose to tackle them and we generally find that we are already of the same mind but in any case we come to agreement. He decides beforehand how many episodes it is going to be and then the BBC likes to have synopses of the episodes, which I think are referred to somebody upstairs, you know what upstairs is in the BBC! I find it easier for myself to go directly to doing a scene-breakdown of each episode which, more or less, I find I am able to adhere to as a skeleton, a framework when I write the episode. Terrance finds it very useful because from it he can roughly estimate what he is going to want in the way of cast, what he is going to need in the way of sets for each episode – and, indeed, for this show, he told me he was able to work out the first budget from them. Then I write the episodes and we don't revise them until they are all in and then Terrance and the script editor meet and we work on them. The directors don't at this stage, come in, so that they are presented with not so much finished scripts, but scripts on which the producer himself can take a stand. That really is most of my part in the thing except that I always go to the first reading and we do learn quite a lot from the first reading when it's spoken by the cast; and then Terrance, the director and I meet after each first reading, whether it is an episode or a group of episodes and discuss it and we may have further changes to make. After that the director has a producer's run-through. It used to be episode by episode, but now, of course, they don't shoot the thing by episodes, they group all the scenes in, say, Sedley's drawing-room together, so when he's done a group of scenes he has a run-through for the producer, which I go to and so we work all the way through it and we come to final amendments and offcuts then. Really my part in it is then finished.

The movement we can perceive here is from writer and producer towards the director. But acting as liaison between these three is the script editor, in this case Philippa Giles, who outlines the production from start to finish.

PG: I start really at the conception. . . . As soon as the idea has been given the go-ahead by the Head of Department, it's our job, the producer and myself (with really more emphasis on me in a way), to come up with a writer. Although on this occasion, the writer had already been chosen before I got there because Alex Baron is somebody that Terrance has worked with for years, when he was script editor before me; Alex is somebody who has a reputation for doing that sort of adaptation and obviously we needed someone that we weren't taking a risk on to get 16 episodes in, which is a tremendous amount of work in the time that we had available. . . . We needed somebody who was going to come up with good first drafts that we could go straight into rehearsal scripts with. . . . Then basically, Alex goes away and writes it and I keep in touch with him. I'm mainly supportive, but also do any research he might need doing into the period or any specific aspect or some particular piece of music or something like that which might come up. I liaise with him when first drafts come through, but . . . in this case there were no big hiccups, there were only small things that needed to be discussed so he just kept going. We needed him to keep going! The next stage is when the director joins, although we actually had two directors on *Vanity Fair*, because it was so big. The director is cast by the producer and so he is the other key casting decision after the writer; and when the director joins and the script is at first draft stage, I have quite long, intensive meetings with the director over the scripts. He will have a lot of things which won't work for him which we have to make work, or sometimes just general views on the script, but often more from the slightly technical side: which Terrance and I wouldn't necessarily have foreseen. Once the director is fairly happy with the rewrites that have happened, we go to the rehearsal script. The rehearsal script then goes to the read-through with the artists, and at that stage a more accurate, timed script is made, and if we need to cut the time, we cut at that stage. That's one of the first stages. Then once it's in rehearsal I'm there to represent the writer – because the writer is not always available or may not want to be there at rehearsal, although it is his right to be there. Sometimes directors are not happy to have the writer there. All these are very individual situations which depend on personal relationships, but I tended to go to quite a lot of rehearsals and if things weren't working I'd sometimes do things myself or sometimes ring Alex up. So after rehearsal then there is the producer's run where we go through the whole thing which is going to go into the next studio: so it might be any number of scenes, because as you know we call it 'out of sequence': it could be a scene from the end and a scene from the beginning but just because they are in the same set they are recorded. . . . Then you get to the studio, and in the studio again it's my job to represent the writer though a lot of writers like to attend the studios. Alex didn't. It's a question of a fine line between being pedantic as to whether every word is correct on the script, which of course it's not, and making sure that things aren't going drastically wrong, like characters being called by the wrong names, which can very easily happen. Then also I keep a general overall view on what's happening – on location as well, where possible. Once it is being edited the director often does a rough cut which puts things together as they are going to be assembled but not cut down to time; it's still quite loose and at that stage both Terrance and I looked at the cassette and had notes to give the directors on how to get it down to time. . . . When it's edited together, you see the full version without all the sound added professionally. Before the sound is done, because that's a pretty irrevocable step, you show it to the Head of Department and he might have some views; but again in practice he doesn't have too many views after the first few episodes because he expects it to be going along the right lines by then and it's just not practical for time purposes and it would cost such a lot of money to have it re-edited. Then my specific job at the end of production was the publicity side, which is something you can make as much or as little of as you like. My job has not got a real job description; I think my job is to support the producer and to be his right-hand man whatever that involves you in. If the producer likes to look after special areas then you keep out of those areas, and they give you things which they are not so interested in.

As both Philippa Giles and Terrance Dicks have mentioned, because *Vanity Fair* was going to be such a lengthy production, it was decided to use two directors, in this case Michael Morris and Diarmuid Lawrence. We spoke first to Michael Morris.

MM: On *Vanity Fair*, I was one of two directors. They chose two because it was done over 16 episodes and logistically one director can't do that amount of work because by the time you have got to start editing the other director is in production. . . . My position is that I am employed to work with the production team in order to put the script on to the screen in visual and acting terms and then to chop it all together and make sure we've got a programme that will hit the screen in as good a way as we can at the end.
CW: Were there any particular problems involved in sharing the production between two directors?

MM: No, there weren't. We were very lucky in that both Diarmuid Lawrence, the other director, and I joined at the same time, which sounds a little luxurious in terms of money because I wasn't starting until way in, but the preparation time was useful for me anyway. But it meant in fact that we could actually cast it together. Because there are so many characters that go right the way through the whole piece we felt very strongly that what we wanted to do was get two minds on it, so that when I did take over I wasn't working with anybody I didn't think was right, so that it wasn't just one person's idea. So we were able to sit down and cast all the regular and semi-regular characters together, with Terrance as well. I mean he has final approval, and that was extremely useful and valuable. . . . The only real problem was a practical one, because when we did the exteriors on OB [Outside Broadcast] we were sharing the OB time and it meant that he was on one day and then me the next day and then him and that was not terribly satisfactory. Only because you get into a rhythm of working and we both have different styles of working. Obviously we are both different people and, although that style on the screen should look the same, our approach to it might be slightly different. When that rhythm gets disrupted, it's difficult for us, there is the frustration of not working, of knowing that we are there and not being able to do anything, and there is the frustration for the actors as well of having to deal with two different people so quickly. If we did a week each it would be easier but we were doing it piecemeal because we had to do it location by location. Otherwise we would have found that we would have spent a lot of money going to a location once, and then if Diarmuid finished all his stuff then I would have to go back to the same locations because a lot of them were common to the episode and we would be paying double the fee, basically. Plus it is a huge upheaval technically.

Diarmuid Lawrence, the other director, identified some of the problems of two directors working together similarly.

DL: There were real problems, there were potential problems and avoided problems and I think there were both real and imaginary problems. I think, Michael . . . probably had the worst part of it, simply by coming in second. Because of the nature of the production last year and because we had amongst other things a strike . . . [there was a BBC Electricians' Union strike beginning in January 1987 which affected the production] it did make what was already going to be a long time before he got his foot in the water a very long time, and this could have affected how the thing looked as a whole.

As we can see from the above interviews with the two directors, a point of major significance for them both was the question of style, of how the programme would look. The finished look of a programme is a complex issue, the achievement of both the directors and a team of designers. Gavin Davies was the designer on *Vanity Fair*, and we asked him to outline his role in the production.

GD: What I'm responsible for is the overall look in scenic terms. That means the building of sets, the search for properties, the selection of locations, the dressing locations, almost everything that happens behind the heads of the people on the screen is my major responsibility. And I am responsible firstly to the producer and more directly to the director, really fulfilling his interpretation of the text. It's not fulfilling my own, although obviously I would have views on it. But the main thing is to be aware and to fulfil the director's interpretation and make it practically possible.
CW: Are you responsible for the look of the costumes as well? Do you give the costume designer a brief?
GD: In the BBC the functions are split. But . . . in practical terms, although I wouldn't at all influence any individual costume, because normally, the set designer is involved at an earlier stage, very often the tone and the approach will have been developed with the director by the set designer and that will have an effect on the costume designer. . . . I would discuss with the costume designer in broad terms things about colour, tone and general feel – with the director as well. But from there on in I would have no direct input into the costumes just as I expect the costume director to have no direct input to the sets, but we do have an agreement and discussion all the time.

The costumes for *Vanity Fair* were designed by Joyce Hawkins, who described her involvement and responsibilities on the production.

JH: I can't actually tell you when I first talked to a director but then Gavin (designer) and Lesley, who was doing the make-up, were in communication quite a lot of the time. From my point, I worked rather more closely with Lesley than with Gavin. We would discuss whether or not somebody was going to be wearing a hat at this particular point or whether they would wear a cap and when possible I showed what it would be like. She came to one or two of the costume fittings certainly, so that we could see the sort of hair and hat that we were talking about, so that it all went together very well.

CW: Your responsibility is what – to design all the costumes that are used?

JH: Yes. Except that, because there were so many [about 3000] and I didn't think I could do the research for the uniforms as well, I had three assistants working with me on this, which is the largest number of assistants that I've ever had. So to one I gave the responsibility for researching and finding where we could get uniforms and then looking after the whole design of the uniforms and the medals and the livery, because that all came from one particular costumier, except for Jack Klaff (Rawdon) and his uniform was made by Morris Angel. Then I had one other assistant, who was responsible for all the logistics because of the enormous number of extras and who they were, and what costumes they were to have, and where we were meeting them out on location and where they were doing their fittings, etc. So she did all that coordinating and sending in the hire forms that have to be filled in for the costumiers. Then the third assistant was my loyal lieutenant by my elbow and I would send him out for fabric samples and he would come back in with them and then we would say, 'Well, how are we going to trim this?' and we worked together artistically very closely.

Joyce Hawkins has begun to draw attention to the huge logistical planning that has to be undertaken on any production. This is the major responsibility of the production manager, who on *Vanity*

Fair was Mike Darbon. He described his role as falling clearly into three categories.

MD: My role splits into three component parts:
(i)   The scheduling and day-to-day organization of the programme;
(ii) Location Manager – finding all the different locations for the production and organizing them;
(iii) Working closely with the director, as first assistant – standing beside the director at rehearsal/recording and organizing everything around the camera.

CW: What were some of the particular problems involved in organizing *Vanity Fair*?

MD: To do the production manager's job properly, you need all the scripts from the start, but in fact it never works like that. Here we had the book, of course, which was very useful for background information. From my initial contacts with the producer, script editor, the early scripts, and from consulting the book, I had some idea of the areas we would be going into. From this, I was able to produce an initial breakdown of location and set requirements, and try to block them together. This has, of course, on a long project like *Vanity Fair*, to take account of the seasons, and so we had to think when was a good time to do the OBs in terms of good weather and good light. So we started planning in October for the following year's shoot. . . .

I also worked very closely with the designer, Gavin Davies. We were shooting at Pebble Mill, and the studio there is not very large; because *Vanity Fair* was such a big project requiring very large, varied sets, we had to sit down and work out how we could organize all the set requirements. The other early decision was to schedule the order of shooting the various scenes – sets and locations – because that has to be done before you can start booking any of the major artists. . . . For a lot of the actors, because of the length of the project, it was necessary to contract them from the start until the end of the period – actors like Eve Matheson (Becky) and Jack Klaff (Rawdon). But a lot of the more senior actors in it who have character parts are not too pleased if they have something in the first studio and nothing else for a couple of months – but they are still expected to keep that period free. . . . It's my job to take into account all those elements and produce some coherent pattern. . . .

Penny Bloomfield, our location manager, had worked very hard on location-finding. Unlike, say, a Victorian programme where there are still a lot of useable locations around, especially in the London area, for *Vanity Fair* we needed pre-Georgian buildings, and finding them was not easy. We initially concentrated on cathedral closes to try to find something like the London squares described by Thackeray. We had problems with this all the way through. We liked Salisbury Cathedral Close but because of problems with a previous recording of a Hardy adaptation in that location, the Salisbury authorities were not keen. We did some sequences in Winchester, but still had a problem finding locations for the main London squares described by Thackeray. In the end we settled on Bath, substituting the Circus for the Square – but then at the last minute there was a new Police Chief Inspector appointed. He was briefed on a previous – ITV – programme recorded in Bath, which had caused problems with a false police car with sirens, etc. – and with only a couple of weeks before shooting he said, 'No, you can't do it here!' So we were left high and dry again . . . So then we tried to use Lincoln's Inn Fields – we've used it before – to replace Bath, and we hoped to set up there for the Easter period. They agreed, until they discovered what our designers had to do! Lincoln's Inn is nicely laid out, and is ideal, say, for a Sherlock Holmes, because all the street-fittings are perfect for that period. Unfortunately they are not right for Georgian London. They got very frightened when I told them we would need to take cables off walls which fed main-frame computers, lift the lampposts, etc. So there was no way they would have us!

I work very closely with the production associate. I look at the manpower, allocation of resources, what we actually need, and the production associate says how much money or how many man-hours we have available. We had a very tight and precise OB schedule, and there wasn't much scope for over-runs or pick-ups. . . . I worked on a production board which entails your putting all the details of a scene or a group of scenes on a large card. It turns out like a large graph, using a number and colours system. It's an American invention, but a lot of BBC production managers now use it. You see groups and patterns of information emerging which can then be put together into your blocks of shooting. This information is then presented as a weekly schedule. We started shooting our OB on 12 April 1987, and finished on 23 May 1987.

One complication I had was that the BBC London week starts on Saturday, whereas in Birmingham they work from a Sunday! This caused problems with my initial scheduling! You are also restricted by the engineering managers as to the number of hours you can work each week. Officially, we are allocated 50 hours of shooting in one given week with the crew; although there is a certain amount of flexibility allowed. The weekly schedules are prepared in conjunction with the location manager: I say, 'This number of days in this place, we must move on this day, etc.' The location manager is at the same time trying to set up groups of locations to limit the number of moves you make. Obviously it's better for everyone if we can be based in a central town and not have to travel far to the various locations, because each move eats into a day, and you only have a limited number of days altogether. Unfortunately, with *Vanity Fair*, it was necessary to move about quite a lot, so we had to compromise as far as possible on artistic ideals versus geographical realities. . . . Of course, we also need venues which can cope with the logistics of a large crew arriving to shoot; I mean, hotels, restaurants, etc. for all the actors, technicians and so on. And that can be a problem, finding a suitable base for the whole unit. . . . And that can change too, because OB crews must have two days off each week; film crews are much more flexible, and work all the hours God gave. Hence, the schedule has to show two clear days each week, so that the OB crew can head back to base for their break – they have a strong homing instinct – yet another complication when designing schedules. Night-shoots are another problem: you end up with complete days off in between, of course. Because of the two directors, we often had two OB camera units at work at the same time. Then, we had to 'share' the actors between the two units. One day, for instance, Eve Matheson (Becky) had a night-shoot with one unit in Winchester, a morning taxi ride across country to the other unit in Sidmouth and another shoot when she arrived. Also, one crew would have the battery camera with no playback facility and the other the scanner; and that would cause problems when deciding who needed which. You can't always tell how long a scene is to shoot; think of the problems with horses and carriages – saddling them up, turning the carriages round, etc. Or the Battle of Waterloo, one page on the script, but hours and hours of location work. We only got through our schedule because of the good will and professionalism of everyone involved.

In such an enormous logistical task, Michael Darbon worked closely with Alison Gee, the production associate on *Vanity Fair*. Chris Wensley asked her to comment on her role in the production.

AG: First of all, I am the person who should set the budget up, but in this case Dave Edwards set it up. He was originally going to be production associate on the show and he actually took the book away and worked out how much it would cost to make the show. He then went on to another show and I took the programme over, so I was given the budget and then it was a question of working with the producer and script editor and the production manager to make sure the budget was adhered to. Also I do all the scheduling, the basic scheduling of the show in terms of studios and OB; all the post-production scheduling, then day-to-day coordinating and running of the show. There were two teams and I worked with both of them, so it was a question of communicating with both of them and passing information between them and things like that.

CW: Assuming you were responsible at the beginning for the budget, you work that out from the book itself, from the novel?

AG: Dave Edwards did because that was all there was, there were no scripts. The budgeting is usually done a year before you get into production so it has to be done on the basis of something and so he did it on the basis of the book.

CW: So how would you do that if you were approaching another one, do you count the number of characters and locations?

AG: That's right, you break down the number of sets. First of all you want to know whether it's all in the UK or whether it will be abroad. Then you work out the number of sets, the number of characters, the number of extras you think, the cost of building the sets and all that sort of thing. You build up a budget of cash and then you build up a budget of the resources that will be required to make the show, and you would obviously multiply it by the number of episodes you were going to have. But it's a little bit difficult doing it from the book because you never know how exactly it's going to be adapted and I think that was probably Dave's problem. He wasn't absolutely sure how it was going to be adapted and so he just had to take a rule of thumb that only so many characters would be involved, etc.

CW: Can you briefly outline the arrangements for the casting of actors, the assembling of the production team, the choice and reservation of studios and the selection of locations?

AG: The casting is very much the director, but they would also go through the producer and sometimes Head of Department, but not in this case. I don't actually get involved in casting at all, it would be between the director and the producer, I would only get involved in terms of how much we were going to pay them and whether it was exorbitant or what. The actual production teams are allocated by our manager but with me going in and chatting about who it's going to be. . . . The choice and reservation of studios is done by Planning. When the original budget is drawn up by the associate he would work out which way he thought was the most economical and best use of resources so we would probably be told that it couldn't possibly be all film because it would be too expensive and then you would have the choice of either going studio with film inserts or studio with OB or electronic inserts. Most people these days who do studio work would prefer electronic inserts because they match better. Planning would have decided where they would like to go, and in this case it was Birmingham, so the studios were all in Birmingham; all the servicing staff came from Birmingham and had to be booked through Birmingham and the dates were given to us by Planning as to when we could do it.

CW: So you request, say 20 studio days and they allocate which days those will be?

AG: Yes. About the selection and preparation of locations. We have a locations manager these days. It used to be the production manager and the associate who did it, but nowadays the shows are getting so big and complex that we have location managers who just deal specifically with locations and on this occasion it was Penny Bloomfield, and she obviously had a list of locations to find and went off on the road to find them. She would find maybe one or two locations that she thought would do for a particular thing and then the director would go off with the designer and have a look at them. Then they would say, 'No, we don't like those,' and she would go back to the drawing-board. It's a very arduous, physical task to go rushing round the country. We were having a great deal of difficulty in finding what we and the directors wanted and we had a great deal of discussion about the fact that I felt that the more we could do in one area, the better, and I was trying to stop them going to the four points of the compass to find what they were looking for; but in the end we ended up with a little bit in Aylesbury, something in Sidmouth, we went to Winchester and then we ended up for the last three weeks of the OB in the East Anglian area. Norwich was our central base and from there we found a lot of very good locations. We went to Thetford Plain for the Battle of Waterloo and for various other locations, we were in Hayden Village – we were there for two weeks and had a wonderful time because the village was one set and the Hall, the Manor House, was another set, and round the back of the Manor House was yet another set, so we got three major locations out of one little village, which was very good.

CW: What is the major cost with a location shooting? Is it the preparation of the site or is it moving people about and getting them there?

AG: Going to large houses, historical houses, is very expensive, you are paying a thousand pounds a day these days. They are either National Trust properties or the owners are members of the Historical Houses Association and they have a scale of rates you have to pay. We went to one house and all we did was an exterior of the house and the moat that went round it and it was £750, just to shoot the exterior, which is quite expensive. But if you are going for period shows there is not a lot you can do about it, you have to pay the money. The actual OB itself is very expensive. Once you are on the road it is exceedingly difficult to control what is being spent, and catering is one of the major expenditures once you are on the road. Reinstatement can be a bit of a problem because of a lot of these places are owned by people who want everything just so. If you spoil anything they want it put right. Hayden Hall was a vast problem with reinstatement because we left a scanner on the drive and the drive had actually subsided. We didn't realize but it was weak underneath and so, of course, we had to pay for a whole new drive, and they are the sort of things that you cannot take into account until it happens. Just general wear and tear: you have got an awful lot of big heavy lorries charging about and they tend to do damage wherever you put them. You try and avoid all that, of course, by putting down special racking over large areas of lawn when you think that the lorry is going to sink in but that costs quite a lot too. You do need an awful long time to plan a show like this. I don't know whether we really had quite enough – we should have had another year. The equation is time, money and resources.

In the midst of such massive technical, economic and logistical planning, it is almost difficult to remember the artistic input being made by each member of the production team. Yet every decision made will, as the above interviews have suggested, have an important effect on the finished aesthetics of the production. This was something of which Nigel Hess, the composer for *Vanity Fair*, was particularly aware.

NH: Normally when I am involved in a television production I'm brought in at the end, after the editing is nearly finished, because you can't write the music until the picture has been finished and edited and the timing is right. But for *Vanity Fair* there was so much music in the production – characters had to play, they had to sing and they had to dance. All that had to be sorted out before any filming could be done, so I was brought into the production quite a few months before they started filming which was lovely, because I was there right from the first read-through and rehearsal. But that is unusual. That's because, as I say, the piece had so much source music in it and so much you could set about beforehand. I started out by trying to research Vauxhall Gardens, the Duchess of Richmond's Ball. I tried to research dance music from the period which was a useful exercise but in the end I wrote it all myself. It was pastiche music because then you could be guaranteed that it was the right length, that it would fit the action. So all that had to be done before filming could start. And from a technical point of view, although I had to select all the pieces for those sections, the musicians that you saw on the screen actually weren't playing because if you have the musicians playing as you are filming, making the sounds, it makes terrible editing problems. So what I had to do was to do a piano guide-track which they would then play at the time into the earpieces and they mimed. I had written out all the parts, so it had been arranged for the orchestra, but they mimed. The violins soaked their bows so that they wouldn't make any sound and they mimed to the piano track that was going on in their earpieces but actually they weren't making a noise. That, of course, is doubly complicated because the dancers can't hear any music to dance to, so the key dancers were also wearing little radio pieces so they could hear that piano guide-track. There were people offscreen clapping in time silently so that the dancers at least kept to time! Then at a later date at Lime Grove we do all the music. We then recorded the music properly. Doing it that way means that because there is no sound on the set if the director wants to edit out a problem, he doesn't have to worry about joining the music. So all that had to be done beforehand.

CW: But for the background music and the incidental music, that process takes place much later?

NH: Oh yes, after everything is finished. And that is normally the point where I would come in on a production. At that point they send me round a video cassette which has a time code on it. I tend to do my own identification of where to put the music first. Then I get together with the director and say, 'Look, this is where I think the music should go, this is where you think the music should go,' and generally we would agree but sometimes have to talk it through. Then I have a couple of weeks to record two episodes in each music session – so I would be writing two episodes at once. But that really is the final stage, the background music, that's the easy bit.

CW: You are writing with a specific number of musicians in mind. That's a restriction placed upon you by the producer?

NH: Yes, it is. They gave me a certain number of heads per session that I was allowed to use. Within those number of heads I could use any combination of musicians that I wanted, obviously, but it settled really at virtually the same combination for each session. So we had between 15 and 17 musicians.

CW: What do you feel is the role of music in films?

NH: Desperately important. . . . There is a time and place for it, of course. We made a decision fairly early on that the music was almost like another character and it was really more than the icing on the cake. It has actually a tremendous part to play: the obvious thing is showing where the drama is going but also to sometimes explain things that maybe because of time or pressures of editing or whatever may not necessarily have been clear from just the pictures. So the music is telling you how you should react and how you should feel for that particular character. I guess that applies to TV drama in general and I find that when people say to me when I have written maybe half an hour's worth of music for a TV programe, 'Well, I didn't really notice there was any music there,' now to me that's terrific, because it shows they were so involved in the drama they didn't notice the job that the music was doing. And I think that's a great compliment to the composer because it means that the music was so integrated that you are not aware of it being there, it's just another part of what you are seeing.

This final idea that the music is 'just another part of what you are seeing' usefully summarizes the whole thrust of the preceding interviews: that the final production, as an artistic whole, is the memento of a complex series of production decisions. Taking this idea further, allowed us to discuss the question of whether there is indeed such a thing as a BBC 'house style' for the Classic Serial. Certainly, it does seem to be received wisdom in the media industry that the serial version of the classics is something the BBC does singularly well and that this is the result of the long-established 'public service' tradition. Is this really the case? Is there such a thing as a BBC Classic Serial house style? Or does the production team of each individual production bring something of themselves and make each product their own? These are the questions we address in the following section.

THE QUESTION OF BBC CLASSIC SERIAL HOUSE STYLE

Chris Wensley began by talking over matters of production style with Terrance Dicks, the producer.

TD: I think there is probably a tradition but it is also affected by the character of the script editor and producer – what they see as being good television. Mine was very much a carrying-on of what I had worked out with Barry Letts, my immediate predecessor, when I was script editor, and we both saw alike on this – which was basically that you put the book on the screen as faithfully as possible. The 'as possible' has to have a certain amount of margin in because you can't literally take a book and put it on the screen. There are creative reasons and there are also practical reasons why you might have to make changes, but what I always have in mind is that the changes you make should be changes which are forced on you; they are not changes because you think you know how to do it better than Dickens and Thackeray. So basically that was always the intention: faithfully to transfer the book to the screen.

CW: What is the difference in style between the BBC-1 Classic Serial and the BBC-2?

TD: It's largely a question of money. By and large the BBC-2 serials are bigger-scale productions. There is an expression 'flagship productions' which, in other words, is something of a spectacular. They are not done on such a regular basis and they are much more of a one-off; they will, generally speaking, be a fairly big, prestigious project, like *Fortunes of War*, like *Bleak House* some years ago. They are in a sense a showpiece, whereas we are, I think, much more a part of a routine programming strand; we are one of the things the BBC does, the BBC-1 Classic Serial, but then so is *Howard's Way* and lots of other things, so we are much more down in the marketplace. I personally feel at least some obligation to go after audiences, to do something that will pull in a reasonable audience because we are going out at ten-to-six or thereabouts on a Sunday which is not an esoteric time slot! That's another factor certainly.

CW: There is no pressure to do modern novels instead?

TD: I think there is something of a feeling that perhaps we rely too much on the Victorians; it is Dickens, you see, Dickens is our bread and butter and jam and that's basically what people expect. It is nice when you can, to get away from that slightly, to do something like *The Diary of Anne Frank* which is forties, which is still period. We are doing a thriller now which is set in 1947 – which for practical intents and purposes is as much period as 1847. You've got all the same obligations.

CW: You have partly touched on this already, but why did you choose *Vanity Fair*? Did you have any doubts about the suitability of the material, and were you influenced as well by the time-gap since it was last dramatized?

TD: *Vanity Fair* was very much tied up with the spectacular, with doing something that would sustain for 16 episodes. Some Dickens would, I think, but there is a slight feeling among the public, and perhaps in the BBC, that in this slot we over-rely on Dickens. Even when I decided to do *Oliver Twist*, there was a slight feeling both in-house and in the public – not again! So I didn't particularly want to go for another Dickens, especially having just done *David Copperfield*, and the thing about *Vanity Fair* is that it is absolutely loaded with plot. A lot happens in it. Someone like Jane Austen for us is a problem because the action tends to be interior and psychological and in emotional shifts, which is wonderful in literature and, of course, will work wonderfully in a certain kind of production but, in my terms, tends to come down to people standing in beautiful locations in beautiful frocks looking soulful! And *Vanity Fair* is not like that. There is a lot going on: there is a lot of plot and counter-plot and deviousness and all sorts of things, so I liked that kind of busy, bustling element. And it's a name, one of the things that we go for over and over again is the resonance of the name, and I thought then that *Vanity Fair* was a name everybody knew – very often one of the things we say we are in the business of doing are books everybody has heard of but nobody has read – or relatively few people have read – and I think *Vanity Fair* came into that category. Again there was the hope that when people saw it, they would see that there was rather more to it. Sometimes people just remember – they saw *Oliver Twist* and they think: 'asking for more' and Fagin; they don't actually remember the book unless they happen to have read it fairly recently, and with *Vanity Fair* people think, 'Oh yes, Becky Sharp, young girl on the make', but not much more than that, really.

CW: Did you have doubts about it for the family slot?

TD: I didn't at the time; retrospectively I think perhaps I should have done. In fact there is very little in *Vanity Fair* for children; with hindsight I am inclined to think it certainly wasn't as suitable for our slot as *Oliver Twist* because the concerns are purely adult and, as I say, a lot of our audience comes from people who sit down with the kids and say, 'You ought to watch this'; hopefully, you have got something for the kids and something for the adults as well, but in fact with *Vanity Fair* young boys wouldn't watch it, I don't think; adolescent or sub-adolescent girls would – they would become interested in Becky and in the romantic side of it but basically it is much more BBC-2 sort of work than the kind of thing I normally do.

The idea that *Vanity Fair* may have been a more suitable production for BBC-2 rather than the teatime BBC-1 slot seemed a significant one. We followed this up by asking Alexander Baron, the writer, about ways in which the traditional Sunday afternoon teatime slot might have affected what he wanted to write.

CW: One thing that struck me was that Thackeray was in some ways inhibited because of Victorian morality and the things he could hint at. Were you in the same way inhibited because you were aware of the teatime audience or would you have treated it in exactly the same way if it had been a late-evening BBC-2 serial?

AB: Well, I think it's going out again as an hour show in the evening, anyway – but no. From the time I went to work for them they said, 'Don't think of this as the kiddies' show, don't think of it as the family show. Write what you think is the right dramatization of this book', and here and there in the book we did, in fact, go outside the bounds of family entertainment and made quite clear what Thackeray genteelly suggested. But there is a kind of decorum which I believe in generally. If you are going to show Becky as Steyne's mistress, I don't think anybody would be foolish enough to do a Ken Russell and show them rolling about together.

CW: Are you influenced at all by previous adaptations? Do you take the opportunity to try and look at them if you can?

AB: No. Each time, if we know that there has been something previously, we float at our first meeting but decide we ought not to.

CW: So you don't deliberately look at it and then react against it?

AB: No. There is no virtue in that, is there?

CW: In your very early thinking were you tempted to use a narrator other than just at the beginning and the end?

AB: No.

CW: Why not? Do you think that's a sort of cliché now in dramatization?

AB: I think that you can't really do that now. It's a cop-out unless you can find a creative way of doing it. The best example of that is Jack Pulman's version of *I, Claudius* where he brings Claudius in, and the action at the end of the book proceeds all the way through it. So that Claudius is not just appearing and narrating, from the very beginning he is bringing the story to its close and at the same time taking you back to the past. And that, I thought was an absolutely great way of weaving the whole thing. So I think you've got to be empirical about that, but in the case of most writers I think it's still a cop-out, that they could very often find a better way of doing it.

CW: Is it your aim to produce a good television drama script or to produce a faithful representation of the novel, or are you trying all the time to balance the two?

AB: Well, it is a question of balancing the two. What the BBC wants is a tremendous lavish sort of soap, really. That's not quite fair to them, because they still want to be the better end of television. What the producer wants is something that does some credit to its subject. People who run that spot have always been quite serious about it but, above all, they are involved in the ratings race. They are given a big budget and they have got to justify it and, above all, it's got to be good drama. All down the line, whenever we are talking about things at production run-throughs right up to the last moment, even after I've left it and Terrance and the directors are discussing it over the editing and so on, they are always having to face up to this problem. How shall we play this scene? How shall we edit this scene? We'll get a big laugh here, or we could do this and we could do that, but at some points they have to say, 'Well, we are not just doing an early nineteenth-century *Dallas*. That's wrong. That's wrong for Thackeray so we've got to stop there.' I want, in the last resort, to attract people to books or back to books, and I also feel that we've got a responsibility to Thackeray or Dickens or Charlotte Brontë or whoever it is, and that we've got to keep that in mind while we work to get this ten-million-audience drama serial.

Chris Wensley followed up the idea again with Philippa Giles, script editor.

CW: Do you think possibly it was in the wrong slot – that it was too sophisticated for the Sunday teatime audience?
PG: Yes, I do, in a way. The problem with that is that because we knew we were in that slot, we went for the less sophisticated elements of the book and so we dealt with it that way. If you are told: 'That's the project. Where do you want to put it?' That would be wonderful because you could do exactly what you wanted with that project. But when you are given the slot and then the project, then you have to make the project fit the slot and that's where you start making compromises – as soon as you know you've got to go out early evening on BBC-1.

This took us on to a more specific question about the novel in relation to the tea-time Classic Serial slot: whether it was possible to keep Thackeray's constant and often ironic commentary in a television version of *Vanity Fair*.

PG: I don't know. In a way I think I would have liked to have found a way for that to have stayed. It still actually worries me. To me that's one of the things which I feel is most wrong about our adaptation, the fact that we missed a whole level or more than that. What we have done is just a stripping out of the plot. That is very worrying, I think. The specific things that went wrong were the timings and the fact that we were so way over on each episode and that had damaged it. In that sense it was not what I visualized on the page. Seeing the edited form of programmes, it is lacerated and that's something that we hope to correct if we can actually re-edit. But that went wrong at all different stages. That went wrong in as much as early on we didn't realize how over it was, even though we did time it at run-throughs. As you can imagine, without actually shooting the shots, you might have a page of dialogue which looks, when you time it, just right, but then there are various fancy bits that are added in. Both directors went equally over, so it wasn't down to one director putting in more arty shots than the other or anything like that. . . . A lot of people who have not read it and have talked to me about it found it quite hard to follow. I think that's another problem with doing a novel, not of this size, but of this scale and scope with so many characters who don't always appear in every episode. I think doing 16 episodes is too much. I wouldn't advocate doing that again ever. It was more like a publicity exercise or an exercise in logistics rather than an exercise in doing something artistically good over 16 episodes, because you know people aren't going to be able to sit down and watch 16 episodes. You know they are going to miss episodes and that makes it very difficult to sustain. Also I think that half-hour formats for this scale of adaptation was wrong. I don't think you can reintroduce characters and develop them again in half an hour, that's expecting too much. Even with Dickens you've got a problem, but I suppose you can perhaps contain it a bit, but there are still a lot of characters. With *Jane Eyre* the half-hour thing works but, as you know, almost all other adaptations apart from us are fifty minutes at least and I think that's got to be much more sustainable.

As we have pointed out already, because of the length and

complexity of the project, it was decided to use two directors –
Diarmuid Lawrence for episodes 1–8, and Michael Morris for
episodes 9–16. When interviewing the directors, Chris Wensley
began by asking Diarmuid Lawrence if he was conscious of a BBC-
1 tradition of dramatizing classic novels.

DL: I had never seen any earlier adaptations of *Vanity Fair* at all
and I hadn't actually read the book myself. It was a gap. I knew
there had been the Susan Hampshire 20-year-old version but I
didn't want to look at it. I didn't want to look at it because I knew
that if I had I wouldn't get those images out of my mind and I
really didn't want to be wondering whether I was affected by it or
not. I thought it would be pretty swish and a pretty good job, so I
left it. There were a couple of tele-recordings of one episode that
had been transferred to video so I did order one up and I kept it
in my bag and I started looking at it during the editing when
everything was safely out of the way. I fell about laughing, I
thought it was really, really bad. It was bad in ways which were
forgivable and understandable in that it obviously was made at a
time when there was twopence-halfpenny resources. It was a
mixture of rather poor film in small quantities which came totally
unexpectedly, with dreadfully-lit studio, with street scenes which
are really awful and dreadful crowd scenes. I remember one crowd
scene, looking through an arch over the heads of a crowd, and
soldiers were going by and you saw the hats going by; with the
benefit of freeze-frame, we froze it, only to find that they were
hats on sticks! Those were forgivable problems at the time bearing
in mind the equipment. More particularly it was a really rotten
adaptation and extraordinarily badly cast. Susan Hampshire was
there being lovely, but I don't think a patch on our Becky in terms
of interest. But mainly because she was surrounded by a rotten
script and a cast who seemed, although there were some nice
actors in there, dreadfully miscast. I did not understand the casting
of it at all and I didn't understand the adaptation at all. So I
breathed a sigh of relief and fell about laughing, having been so
worried about looking at it. Because it will be another twenty years
before somebody else does another one for television, you feel
rather responsible if you are going to cover this for two decades.

Michael Morris responded by saying that he did not know there had been a film version, but he was aware of a previous BBC television version.

MM: I remember the BBC version of it, which I think was the first colour production, in fact – with Susan Hampshire. When you look down that cast list, you think 'My God, it must have been done an awful long time ago!' You would never consider these actors for the parts now at all. Diarmuid did get episode 1 of that first series out just to look at it, just out of interest. I wasn't available so I didn't watch it. I would have done, but purely out of interest, not for any comparison with what we were trying to do.

We then moved on to wider issues. In particular, to try to discover if the directors were influenced by the critical debate about dramatizing novels or whether each script was just another job – regardless of whether it was an original play or a dramatization.

CW: Critics have argued at length about the dangers of dramatizing novels. For example it has been argued that a screen dramatization damages a novel and that it can never be the same again afterwards. Are you influenced by that debate or do you see your role really as delivering a good programme from a given script?
MM: I do, really. Although one doesn't want to desecrate the original, my profession, my job and my love is making television programmes and I thought that *Vanity Fair* was a very good story to make. One didn't want to do it badly, one didn't want to spoil what was there and I don't think we did. Certainly it is there in your mind, yes, that you want to be true to what the author has written all the time. It also has a lot to do with why you make the programme: what is the point of dramatizing a thing in the first place? Some people have said that because of the slot it was in, *the* Classic Serial slot, at teatime on a Sunday, that it is a kid's programme. At one point that was true, and the thing they set out to do, I think, when the Classic Serial slot was conceived, was to get kids to watch and say 'Oh, I'd like to read that.' They never said this is the definitive interpretation of what is being done, but rather tried to foster further interest in the novel. I think that is

now slightly old hat. I think we now try, more so than we did, to say that this is not definitive, but this is one interpretation of *Vanity Fair* and whether you want to follow it up and read it afterwards is irrelevant. I think the actual story of *Vanity Fair* is certainly not a kid's story, it's far too complex in the thoughts that go on. It's not an action piece as such. It's not like *David Copperfield* or *Oliver Twist* which has got goodies and baddies who are obvious. There is so much more in the minds of the people in *Vanity Fair*. Thackeray is not Dickens, it's as simple as that; they write in totally different ways and different styles.

CW: Were there problems in relating the tone of the novel, the satiric and the grotesque elements to the naturalistic style of TV?

MM: I don't think so, I hope not. I'm not really the person to give you the answer to that, it's the viewing public that should answer that, really. We felt that we had succeeded with it. It was something that we were all, again, very conscious of, that we were into a satirical, more conscious, inward thing than is normal for that sort of programme and that is how we set about it, that was our creed as we went and I think we succeeded. Everybody was on the same wavelength about it, there were no huge, violent discussions saying you've got this totally wrong. It never happened – it can happen often, with adaptations of maybe more modern novels. But no, it wasn't a problem, given the fact that one can't develop every line all the way, and there are threads of the story that you have to let go, which you would follow up in the book and maybe tie up in a sentence; we very often just didn't have time even for that one sentence. Because, to take a sentence from the book you have to actually build a scene around it in order to flesh it out. If you can throw something in as a reference later on, then yes, you do, but then there is a danger of it standing out like a sore thumb. So, once you've got the shape you have to stick to that and just use what is in there, bearing in mind as I say all that one has gleaned from the original.

Chris Wensley raised similar issues with Diarmuid Lawrence.

CW: If there was a decision to make, between good television on the one hand and being faithful to the novel on the other hand which way would you go?

DL: Well, it puts you in a hypothetical situation that suggests that those are always mutually exclusive. I think ultimately you've got to make good television in order to follow the logic that people are going to watch it and enjoy it. I think if the route to good television was something that just totally cheapened what you were doing, then I would resist that. I'm not sure that one is always forced into a situation unless it has been very clumsily adapted, where it's an absolute one way or another. For instance, Alexander decided not to employ a voice-over. In fact the original scripts had a voice-over at the very beginning of episode 1 and the very end of episode 16 and I mooted getting rid of them, and Michael went along with it because we felt it was such a halfway house. Also I just had an abhorrence of voice-over, although it has worked very well, and I thought that if I put up the first few frames and people hear the voice-over and think, 'Oh God, here we go again,' and it seemed an enormous switch-off to a lot of people. In doing that one has lost Thackeray's capacity to whisper in the ear, because one of the most engaging things he does is to actually dialogue a scene, play the scene virtually as dramatic script from which Alexander took a lot of his dialogue, obviously. Then you come to a conclusion at the end of it and then he promptly tells us something entirely different to think about it. So he cheats all over the place wonderfully well. That capacity is lost a great deal and so with things like that one can't be faithful to the novel, but I don't think in transferring, that is a genuine loss. I think that's something that cannot be covered.

CW: Were there problems in relating the tone of the novel – the grotesque, the satiric – with the naturalistic demands of television?

DL: In that the adaptation is quite straight in a way, I think that's quite useful. The choice would have to have been taken earlier than I had come into it, in that the gun had been fired and we were off and running, to go for a much more theatrical, a much more grotesque style. What we came down to was a fairly straight adaptation but with energy and with very good character work. There are possibilities, yes, for making it more of a cartoonish sort of event, reflecting the cartoon work and the lampooning of the day. But it would have been a very different event. I think we would have had to go the whole hog and do a very, very different adaptation indeed. Given the scripts we had got, which I think are good but conventional, it wouldn't have worked to start going that route. In a way the novel is quite strange in that sense. It has areas where it goes into that and areas which are really quite straightforward and simply narrative. It's such an extraordinary masterpiece in the sense that it wanders through various things and, like many masterpieces, you get the feeling that a lot of it was experimental and therefore the style isn't consistent in the book either. I would have loved to have explored the possibilities – if we had had this a year earlier and taken a completely different approach to the scripts. But I think if we had done it half-measure, it would have fallen flat on its face. So without the voice-over technique as well, we came down to straight adaptation and making the characters credible. I'm told I coined this phrase 'heightened reality' and I got chased by it all over the place and I kept trying to remember in what context I had come out with a thing called heightened reality. I think it was because we were trying to talk to the actors about what sort of scale of performance to give this, and I always felt that these characters, however incredibly they behaved, had to be credible characters. In the context of the adaptation we were doing, they were real people and appeared to be real people, however extraordinary they became, and we hung on to that throughout and I think that was right.

Both directors admitted to feeling somewhat inhibited by the 'family audience' slot of the Classic Serial. Clearly, *Vanity Fair* deals with sexual, moral, and social issues which would allow a fairly sophisticated treatment. Chris Wensley asked the directors whether they would have done anything differently had they known initially that the programme would be given a later evening slot.

DL: I think yes. More explicit. The only bed-scene is the one between Rawdon and Becky and I think they played that beautifully. I think you would probably have them without any clothes on simply because it looks coy to have clothes on.

Michael Morris agreed:

MM: Yes, I think we probably would. I think we would have gone maybe a little more raunchy because it is all there – the things with Betsy Horrocks and Becky herself. Yes, it's there to be done and I think you've got to brave and do it if it is. There was a possibility when we started off that we were going later. We didn't really know until we were well into it that we had been lumbered with the half-hour at teatime, so we tried to push it to a certain extent, further than it had gone before in terms of the Classic Serial. But there comes a time when you've got to stop and say, 'Well we might still be going out at half-past six and there we had better temper it a little.' But yes, I think had we known we were going out a lot later – only in certain areas – one would have gone maybe a little bit further.

Turning to issues of visual style, Chris Wensley spoke to both directors about their methods. We were interested to try to discover why one had used mainly single-camera, whereas the other had preferred multi-camera. Initially this would seem to be a source of problems, with one director's work differing in style from the other. Chris Wensley spoke first to Diarmuid Lawrence.

CW: Were there long discussions about the way to treat the material – technically and aesthetically?
DL: Well, there kind of were and there kind of weren't, because, like many things, it's very difficult to say this is a case study for how any particular project gets underway, because it had its own unique birth. It had difficult birth pangs and it was nearly stillborn because there wasn't nearly enough money available from the beginning. So I'm not aware that we have ever had large intellectual conversations about style. We had a lot of conversations about how we could keep the project alive, although those things did emerge. They did emerge an awful lot later on, but I'm not sure that Michael and I ever sat down and had prolonged conversations about that. We were aware that we had some differences in approach, which I think we have to this day. Mainly in terms of technique. I think in terms of our view of the piece we were broadly similar.
CW: Is it possible to see differences in approach or technique between you and Michael?
DL: I can clearly notice them, but I think mainly in terms of style.

I was much more concerned to make it, as much as possible, a video film early on, and I had particular views of its vigour as a piece. I had an abhorrence in my head, stylistically, of going back into the very domestic, cosy stillness that's associated with most of the classics. Hence, as I was allowed to choose the title music and allowed to choose the composer, I banished floaty oboes completely so it was going to be really quite brassy and quite vulgar music and that sense of energy should run throughout. I went for a much more filmic approach and I think Michael was more concerned, purely as a technique but it nonetheless shows, that he was much more multi-camera orientated. In a way I would call it more conventional, not because he was tied by convention but I think he thought he would get better performances out of his half. The two halves of the story, which, of course, aren't halves, mine covering 18 months to two years, his covering the whole of the rest of the book, even though they do halve the novel, have very different demands. In a way he may have chosen a technique that was more appropriate to his half and I chose a technique that was more appropriate to mine. But from the outside I might not spot these things at all.

CW: What exactly do you notice as the difference – rhythm, pacing or what?

DL: We both suffered from the fact, which is a broader thing, that we felt that we were shoehorned into too small a slot and really the pacing wasn't completely in our hands because the scripts never were really 30-minute scripts. They were 40-minute scripts which we managed to shoehorn in and we are now going to be able to expand slightly when we re-edit. As a result I think he suffered more from pacing duress than I did. How much that is to do with his style – I think most of that is to do with outside things imposed, but he did have scenes, for instance, like the return to Queen's Crawley, when Freddy Jones's character is absolutely pissed out of his mind and the wee girl and the butler are all over the place, which is broad farce. I think he certainly wanted to achieve those kinds of scenes, of which he had several, as multi-camera if he possibly could because he would get a more theatrical style, rather than breaking it down to the extent that I did. He paid for that, I think, to a large extent in terms of less control over lighting and shooting – which were stylistically very important to me. The lighting guy and I had come very much to particular terms about how we were going to light it, how we were going to treat it. I think he found it much easier to work with my style than with Michael's but I can see very clear reasons why Michael wanted to do it his way, as I think he had more of that kind of material. But he then had the hectic slalom effect towards the end of those episodes where Becky goes romping round Europe and five minutes later we are in another country and another scene and it gets faster and faster and faster.

CW: Were you really completely free to choose whether to use single-camera or multi-camera?

DL: Well, no. The freedom was snatched from the circumstances. The dominant circumstances about the setting-up of this is a Catch-22, and this is a very particular BBC thing. That is that having committed to do it and having committed to do it for transmission in the Autumn, the gun having been fired and the scripts coming in, the scripts and the budget didn't come within a million miles of each other. Therefore we went into a painful process of gradual, allowed, controlled and then finally less controlled, overspend. We refused to call it an overspend, we called it an underbudget, which is precisely what it was. Now that then dictated other things. It was never written down as a single-camera video and it was certainly never written down as a single-camera studio, which is not an accepted thing as such, because of the time and expense. We had studio slots. What was given to us were the facilities that would normally have made a BBC-1 classic, and a little bit more money. Those facilities blew wide open because it was just not possible to do. Partly the electricians' strike did that, and the strike played into our hands and helped.

The complexities of the set and the complexities of what we were trying to do made it apparent, in terms of studio early on, that it would be possible and arguable (and Terrance and I have actually had this conversation since), as to whether Michael's technique, which he stuck to more rigorously in terms of studio, not OB, of multi-camera, and mine which was split down into single-camera work – as to which actually, at the end of the day took longer. I think it probably came out much of a much, because Michael would have horrendous problems to resolve because of doing it multi-camera, and mine would take longer in a planned way from the word go. I think they probably ended up broadly equal. Now when we got on to the OB, this was very complicated and always bordering on disaster, because it was six weeks in which we eventually had to schedule for both of us to be working at the same time when possible. A lot of the time, that wasn't even a starter because there simply weren't enough costume and make-up crew and there weren't enough separate characters who would be available to mount scenes. Also our OB schedule was completely constrained by the fact that we had six weeks in which to do it, plus travel. So we had to be in a certain place, say, if it was Wednesday evening and we were supposed to be doing the Duchess of Richmond's ball and then on. There was no opportunity to come back. There was in the whole six weeks, I think, an afternoon of pick-up, which was ridiculous. And we were thrown on the mercies of the weather and unbelievably we got through it. We got through it not least because of the professionalism of the crew but also because the weather was just ridiculously kind to us and we had an enormous amount of luck.

But that then dictated other things: to what degree we could go single-camera or multi-camera. Sometimes it was quicker to have two units working with single-camera, Michael working on one thing and me working on another in different places. So it was never written down that this was going to be a single-camera job. It emerged as a working practice and in many ways it emerged as the only way. And occasionally if we had a suitable scene we would cross-shoot. I came upon a technique which I used quite a bit because we didn't have much rehearsal for the studios, and I used it sometimes in the studios and even sometimes on the OB and I wouldn't vision-mix. I would actually record split feeds – we would have two cameras. I used those particularly in the studio on dinner scenes of which I seemed to have a large number. Around the table we used minimal movement so that we could get very close to the table and keep the lighting very naturalistic, for candlelit scenes. To do that and to get through it in anything like the time necessary, I would use two cameras at a time which could be paired into shots which were complementary in terms of lighting and not getting in each other's way. So I put up pairs of shots at a time and then ran those on to split-feeds to separate machines and then edited it all afterwards. So that just meant I could romp round in pairs; so if there were 16 set-ups I could get them done in eight goes rather than 16.

CW: Were you free to choose whether to use locations or studio as you wished, or were there restrictions; in other words, because the studios exist, did you have to use them for a certain number of days?

DL: Yes. That was clear from the word go. There was never the money available to do it all on location. We were very, very tight-pressed on the location shoot. It was six weeks and that was it. We came up with, I think, some ludicrous number, something like 18 or 19 versions of the schedule ultimately, to try and maximize the work. We had screwed ourselves into a corner too, financially, to try and make the bookings more attractive to the actors we wanted to get. Obviously any lady being offered Becky Sharp who is of that age is going to leap at it; some of the other ones like Freddy Jones and Sian Phillips would love to do it, but BBC money is not as good as ITV money and the bookings then sometimes spread enormously, so as an actual weekly wage it ain't so hot! Therefore we had to try and contract their periods as much as possible. So we ended up painting ourselves into a corner with both the studio and the location schedule and therefore locations (when we found them because they were suitable and would have us and have this bloody great circus!). They also had to be in a convenient part of the country to actually minimize the travel in between them and also to fit into these wretched artists' schedules. Choices of location were hard to come by because by the time you've narrowed down which you can travel to, which is suitable, and which will have you, and what is right for the day, you come out with the answer. If saying yes to that is choice, yes!

Chris Wensley raised similar issues with the other director, Michael Morris, who summarized how he felt about decisions he took about shooting, and particularly why it was he chose to use multi-camera rather than single.

MM: It's the way I prefer to work. I like to play scenes from beginning to end. I think I get better performances. The actors that I've talked to about it prefer it because it means it's slightly more stagecraft in that they do get a beginning, a middle and an end to a scene and they can see the development of emotion through it. Whereas in filmic terms, where everything is broken up so much – to sustain the thoughts and performances more times through it – I mean I'm not saying that we do it all in one, we go 9–10 takes maybe on a scene. And I do drop in the odd stuff and I say, well, I don't really want to do the whole scene again, I'll just pick that bit out of it. But at least I've got the master-shape of a scene before we ever get into that. Actors seem to prefer it and I think they benefit from it as well. One of the problems with it was that the whole thing was done out of order. Because of the size of the studio we were in in Birmingham, and the size of the sets that were required, you couldn't get them in episode by episode. You had to put the Queen's Crawley set in and do it all, episodes 1 to 9 and in fact the first scene I ever shot was the very last scene in the show. You think, well that's crazy, but one is governed by factors. The last scene in the show was actually done on location but there was only one day we could go to that location and it happened to be the last scene in the show. That's difficult for the artists as well, the first day I have ever worked with them I'm asking them to assume that everything has gone before and played the last scene. Now if you've done your homework on it and you talk about it well enough then you succeed. If you haven't, then it fails.

Clearly, the designer of the dramatization has a major responsibility for the visual style of the programme. Crucial decisions concerning such aspects as authenticity and naturalism have to be taken at an early stage. Chris Wensley's discussion with Gavin Davies, the designer, started at these basic choices.

CW: Is there a BBC TV Classic Serial house style that you felt constrained to work within and was that the reason that you abandoned a non-naturalistic approach?
GD: Yes. There is a house style but it isn't a static thing, it's a developing house style and it has changed over the years gradually to become more like film. It's more naturally lit. I think it's a heightened sort of reality, what we're aiming for isn't just sort of historical. It's not factual. We are not making a documentary programme about life in the 1820s. It is a dramatic reconstruction and by that it is culturally bound by where we are at the moment and what we expect the audience to see; the audience have an expectation of these things and we are aware of that. They expect the past to be slightly glamorized, a golden age and very appealing, and you are actually using that within the design.

CW: At what stage did you decide to use a naturalistic style; was that very early on?

GD: It was very early on and it wasn't totally my decision. That was very much the decision made by the producer and the two directors: that it should be within the bounds of the normal television naturalism and that we shouldn't try and do anything that was going to distract from the text. There is no accepted grammar, really. Television has failed to turn up an acceptable alternative grammar for drama except in a very few circumstances. You have to be careful not to allow the design to dominate the text. It's about the story and it's about people. If you go into a curious new grammar, you may alienate the audience and actually add very little; it's only worth considering if you are totally convinced that it would be an addition. Would it really enhance the final production? It could have been a way to do it but I think it would have needed much greater build-up time and analysis of really what the goals were.

CW: Do you try to appeal to the twentieth-century viewers' vision of the period or do you go for a 'complete' historical accuracy?

GD: It isn't an historical document. We are not saying this is exactly what it was like in 1820, because nobody really knows what it was like. There is lots of reference available, lots of pictures and descriptions but it is very hard to get into the minutiae of the way of life of people of that time. So that it is a creative recreation of what we imagine it to be, but bound by our own attitudes and our own way of life. If you watch a film made in 1935, you can set the Georgian period within three or four seconds of watching that film, [and] you will know exactly what period it was made in. . . . We can identify just curious little details like, say, hairstyles or the way people are talking and moving and you say, 'Oh, that's 1935.' Just as if you watch a Classic Serial made by the BBC 15 years ago, there are all sorts of technical and cultural reasons you can tell it's 15 years old. Whether we like it or not, we are bound by that. We don't purposely set out to do that, we purposely set out to try and make it as accurate as possible within the bounds of our own knowledge and within the things that are actually available to us. But there you have it, it always turns out to be a reflection.

CW: Do you think there is a danger sometimes that the historical quality of the setting causes the action to become rather cosy and sentimental and secure and that you might lose some of the harshness and hardness of the text?

GD: Yes, well, I think that the television image glamorizes anyway. Our desire to make things beautiful or pretty or satisfying as images enhances that, so you get the double-edged thing there. I think with Thackeray there are advantages, in that if you can come out of that feel and that environment and actually hit the audience with something quite hard, an audience that will have been lulled into an expectation of something cosy and warm and pleasant, only to see a totally immoral tale with these tremendously horrid characters . . . and if they are coming out of something that has the appearance of cosy naturalism, a golden age, and the romance of it all, then I think that's actually quite dramatically interesting.

CW: Looking back, what pleases you most and what don't you like about the finished programme?

GD: I never liked the short episodes and the truncation of the situations and scenes where it becomes slightly *Comic Cuts* without really letting the emotional charge follow through. Visually I felt it terribly difficult with a studio and video OB-based production to really hit the finish and polish on the visual side. There is something antipathetic about the video image to a period production. When you are trying to get the romance and the softness and that expansiveness about it – it's a huge story and we should have been very expansive – it is made smaller by the technique that we were actually using. I think given exactly the same production to be put on film with a bit more time, I think we would have had something that was visually more satisfying.

CW: Do you mean film then transmitted as television?

GD: Yes. It's almost impossible using outside video cameras to achieve perspective and distance. Video cameras especially, used for exteriors, were designed initially for football and things like that and it makes everything just a little bit too sharp, too real and all on the same plane; to get distance and mystery and perspective to the image is terribly difficult. If you are faced with a nice fine day when you are actually shooting you get everything – the background comes hard up against the foreground, there is hardly any depth in it. You can pour a colossal amount of effort into dressing a street and it vanishes before your eyes, it looks hard and it looks modern and that's the quality of the picture rather than what you have actually done in terms of design. Because film has got subtler tones, you can do a bit more manipulation. Video's getting better though, a lot better.

CW: Does the same apply to interiors and studios?
GD: Not quite, because that's under much more controlled lighting and because in the studio it is totally artificially lit, there is quite a lot you can do to soften. But when you are actually competing with God, with natural light, you don't have that degree of control of the image so quite often you can get a satisfactory mix using film exterior and video interiors in the studio where you can match the lighting quality. But there is still a problem with video exterior, I think, that it is still too hard. But that's a professional quibble. As for whether the audience really noted that, I'm not sure.

We were interested to know whether Eve Matheson, who played Becky Sharp, had been influenced by any previous interpretations of the role in film or on television, and whether this caused her to create the role in a Classic Serial convention.

EM: It's very tempting, but I had enough of an influence sitting on my shoulders with the book let alone another person's portrayal. . . . Of course, you can read it today and appreciate it today; it's a bloody good novel and it's timeless and any good piece of writing or painting or acting will last if it means something. But any intention to drag it up to date, I think it's limiting it. You must understand that it's about a very particular class at a very particular time and then you can see the similarities, but to go back to your question – no, I didn't strive for anything in particular; you do have to move in a certain way, but costumes help that and you speak in a certain way; a certain class moved in a different way from nowadays; people do behave differently and you have to find what suits what's being demanded by that character regardless of the situation. But I also didn't want it – it can be very easy sometimes from what I have seen in the past for period drama to look chocolate-box, for it to look idealistic and a little bit pretty-pretty, but that wasn't the case here. People had smelly breath and sweaty armpits – and I am all for showing everything, to show that those people lived and were real. I know they are characters in a novel and slightly larger than life sometimes, but this is where you have to leave the novel behind. You have to make those people live, otherwise they are going to seem like cardboard, one-

dimensional with no substance to them. But I certainly didn't want
to be a modern girl in period dress.

CW: If you were doing it differently, if you had known it was
going to be shown at 9 o'clock and not 5 o'clock you wouldn't
have played it any differently?

EM: I don't think so, because often there is a great deal more
power in what you don't say than in what you do say. Once again
I'm all in favour of presenting the book as it was written. Thackeray
chose not to talk about certain things – why should we open up
doors which had been deliberately left not tightly shut but with
chinks left invitingly open for you to have an idea of what was
going on on the other side, rather than give it to you on a plate? It
is much more fun if an audience is left to make up its own mind.

   When Chris Wensley spoke to Simon Dormandy, who played
Dobbin in the dramatization, the discussion concerned the naturalistic convention of most television dramatizations. In the light of
Simon Dormandy's experience of having played Dobbin in a stage
dramatization of *Vanity Fair*, we were interested to discover if he
had felt at all inhibited in his television role, which clearly lacked
the freedom and experimentation with narrative styles available to
him on stage.

SD: I wouldn't say so at all, no, I didn't find it difficult at all, not
from the period point of view. I had to make some very definite
decisions about how to play Dobbin which were related to adapting
Thackeray's style to television style. I don't think that's to do with
period, I think that's to do with the narrative style which one
might well come across today. I think I feel this more acutely than
I would if I had simply played it on screen because I did play it on
the stage as well. In our stage adaptation, there were six actors
playing all the parts in *Vanity Fair* and, interestingly, we got at
least as many, if not more, incidents into a three-hour stage
performance than we got into eight hours of television. We did
that by using a very particular style of theatre which was developed
by Shared Experience and people like that, where one frankly uses
a great deal of the narrative, of the authorial voice, so that you can
'tell' an episode and you can get right to the heart of a scene more
quickly because you don't have to use dialogue. You can say, 'So

and so came in and this is what happened and that's what happened,' and then you get to the core of the scene and you play that core of the scene. When you are working that sort of way you have, initially at least, to characterize very boldly because you are jumping in and out of character all the time. You may have seven or eight characters to play in the space of fifteen minutes and you also have to let the audience know clearly who you are at the beginning of the play. So in the first hour of this three-hour show, I would say I played Dobbin in a fairly cartoonish sort of way, playing his ungainliness as a comic quality and playing his gawkiness and shyness so he was quite adolescent in the early period. Then as the show progressed, as the characters fell away and it became concentrated on fewer and fewer people, and as the scenes got longer and richer, and as the characters got older, one was able to go fully into good, hearty, naturalistic acting. I think that that variety of style is, in a way, closer to the novel than the naturalism which is imposed by television style. But I think that this style of television does demand naturalism, whereas perhaps in a film one could depart into more daring ways and different forms of performance and more alienated – in a Brechtian sense – performance techniques; so that you saw the camera or you saw Thackeray or whatever, to get across the sense that one gets in the novel of 'I am writing the story and I could write it differently, and this is what I think about the characters, what do you think?' But in television, unless you are really going to do something quite extraordinary, which I don't think has been done, you have to concede to the naturalistic, almost soap-opera framework. When you've done that, that demands certain things from an actor and so you do have to adapt. I had to make decisions, for instance, about Dobbin's clownishness. I decided to make Dobbin less clownish, with the director's help, and with the prodding of the writing and the structure of the scenes, it was inappropriate for Dobbin to be clownish. There weren't the scenes to show it and it would have upset the balance of the relationship, because Dobbin starts the television serial in the avuncular relationship to George and it would be very hard to explain how he had this avuncular relationship if he was a clown, if one didn't see the schoolboy. So I feel that a strand of Dobbin's character doesn't appear in the television show, which is his clownishness but I think that's just as well because I think that would undermine what you can get from Dobbin in a TV serial.

SOME CONCLUDING NOTES TO THE INTERVIEWS

One of the first things we set out to demonstrate in this book is that there is a considerable body of critical literature concerned with the adaptation of prose fiction into film and television drama, and that central issues such as point of view, tense, and imagery have been analysed and discussed by a large number of critics. Many critics have attempted to categorize types of adaptation, from the faithful literal translation to the dramatization which seeks to shed important new light on its original text. There are also those who have warned of the dangers and even futility of the whole exercise. However, when one attempts to relate this body of theory to the work of practitioners, specifically the BBC TV adaptation of *Vanity Fair*, it becomes apparent that in the face of such huge logistical, economic and practical considerations, there simply is not a great deal of room for massive critical debate to take place.

There is a strong sense gained from the interviews that, with one or two exceptions, the majority of those involved in the dramatization saw themselves engaged in a continuing production-line of Classic Serials, reproducing a certain style of production already well-established. The main aim seems to have been to reproduce the events and characters of the novel as faithfully as possible in the hope that some of the audience will be encouraged to read the original text, and that the remainder will at least have a veneer of literary culture applied to them. Having said that, the intelligence and creativity that goes into any good production is also obvious. Many of the interviewees stressed how they *would* have undertaken the project had they had the time and opportunity to do so. The fact is, that as in any industry, such luxury very rarely exists. For example, there seems to have been very little opportunity for discussion among the production team about the style of the programme. It seems that naturalism just had to be accepted almost without question as the dominant mode of expression, simply because the public expect to see naturalistic representations of the classic novel. And that's what the Classic Serial slot is there to do. But this means that – as many of the production team accepted – such things as some attempt to search for visual equivalences for the style of the author, for example, surrealistic sequences, montage, multiple points of view, and the grotesque had largely to be ignored. Also, the notion that a 'faithful' dramatization reflects the mood and tone of the novel better than a dramatization which seeks fidelity through transformation seemed almost to be explicit from the start. One of the problems about such implicit assumptions is that details about a horse's harness attract more attention and discussion than a moral analysis of a competitive society. It can become a cosy world of escape from contemporary problems, and a chance to luxuriate in the glories of the English heritage, a continuous soap opera in which characters like Becky Sharp, Miss Havisham, Oliver Twist, and Jane Eyre make regular appearances over the years, with the individual style of the various authors smoothed out in the production-line process. This, of course, is no criticism of the production team involved; rather, perhaps, a criticism of the structure within which their creativity operates. We do not live in an ideal world: the practitioners of the media industry find themselves so busy with the pressing demands of producing eight hours of historical drama in three months that they are never able to reassess purpose and direction. The industrial processes of a major institution like the BBC weigh heavily upon their shoulders. To close with Joanna Webb from Pan Books, who publish *Vanity Fair*: 'There are a lot of adaptations coming up. It's big business now!'

8

The Transmission and Critical Reception of *Vanity Fair*

The major publication for the *Vanity Fair* serial was a glossy brochure issued by the BBC. Featuring photographs from the production, and details of the cast and production team, its aim was to achieve recommendations from TV reviewers that viewers should watch the series, and to stimulate preview features, articles about members of the cast and the production. The text of the brochure begins:

> This is the most ambitious production ever mounted for the BBC-1 Classic Serial slot on Sunday evenings. The sixteen half hour episodes, stretching from September to Christmas, have all the scope and visual bravura to match Thackeray's colourful novel. The passions, the betrayals, and the rivalries of this boisterous classic are played out against the glamorous backdrop of European society during the Napoleonic Wars. Location work includes such major set pieces as: Vauxhall Gardens, the Duchess of Richmond's Ball, and the Battle of Waterloo.

This brochure was supplemented by standard press-handouts listing career details of those principally involved in the production, and other publicity puffs.

However, before any of these publicity releases, even while the series was still in production, the *Star* newspaper offered its own preview, on Saturday, 21 March 1987, five months before transmission:

> The BBC is set to spend like never before – coughing up a whopping 8 million pounds for a lavish new production. The price tag of the 16-part adaptation of the classic Vanity Fair is believed to make it one of the costliest British products ever.

The magazine *Televisual* ran a two-page feature on the making of *Vanity Fair* in its June 1987 edition, under the headline 'The Making of a Cultural Dallas'. Budget is again referred to, but this time more obliquely:

> Putting an exact figure on the production is hard, considering the back-up facilities supplied by the BBC. . . . but if an independent company had made the same production, the bill would have run into millions.

In the first week of September 1987, to coincide with the transmission of the first episode, there were several features and previews in the press. The *Daily News*, for 4 September continued the fascination with budget: 'Costly Entertainment Worth Every Penny: 2 million pounds spent on Vanity Fair' while also explaining 'Why Eve loves Wicked Becky' in an interview with Eve Matheson who played Becky Sharp. The *Daily Mail* of 5 September developed instead the soap-opera potential of the story: 'At last it's Dynasty Fair. Bitchy Becky finds soap stardom. . . . 140 years on!' The article compared the characters of Becky Sharp and Amelia Sedley through interviews with the two actresses who played them; it also referred to budget: 'At a cost of 2 million pounds, the lavish production is the most expensive classic serial ever made by the BBC.'

The *Today* newspaper on 5 September headlined its preview 'Beeb Repairs to the Drawing Room', while the *Brighton Evening Argus* of 2 September ran an article which stressed both the 'modern soap opera' and the local connection – part of the location was in Brighton: 'Dynasty touch in old Brighton! A tale of sex, war, power, and glamour'.

The *Bath and West Evening Chronicle* (5 September) and the *Daily Post* (8 September) both ran the same syndicated article: 'When Becky Sharp's dance with her best friend's husband ends, the glance of longing, lingering sexual tension tingles and smoulders. It's enough to make Sunday tea time quite lively.' And: 'When Becky Sharp dances with her best friend's husband, his lingering parting look crackles with sexual longing. It's more than enough to wake you up on a sleepy Sunday tea time.' One is headlined 'A Little Bit of Sauce for your tea on Sunday' and the other 'Two faces of Eve'.

Both the *Radio Times* of 5–11 September and the *Observer Magazine* for 6 September ran colour features. The *Radio Times* devoted its cover to a photo of Becky, Rawdon, and George, with the accompanying article stressing the contemporary relevance of the story:

Vanity Fair is a story for the 1980s. It's about the thrusting ambitions of a privileged class: opportunist and frivolous, concerned with the tiny social circle in which they weave their self-seeking games. Thackeray's characters were the yuppies of a century and a half ago.

The *Observer Magazine* also stressed the contemporary parallels:

In Vanity Fair, materialism is its own reward, and only the fittest, fastest, and cleverest survive. If Thackeray inveighed against any sin in particular, it was snobbery – a vice which has gained ground in Thatcherite Britain, with the increased appetite for titles, conspicuous wealth, and designer gewgaws.

The *Daily Mirror* featured full-page profiles of three of the younger actresses in the serial, Eve Matheson (Becky) on 17 December, Rebecca Saire (Amelia) on 21 September, and Vicky Licorish (Miss Swartz) on 5 October. Readers were able to discover that Eve Matheson's favourite perfume is White Musk from The Body Shop, that Rebecca Saire is 5ft 5in. tall, and turned down a university place to become an actress, and that Vicky Licorish's favourite music is Motown, and her ambition 'to keep moving'!

Less bland, and certainly less welcome publicity came in the form of newspaper reports that the production team had slaughtered horses to produce a more realistic Battle of Waterloo, and that several actors had 'recoiled in horror'. In fact, as Terrance Dicks, the producer, tried to point out, they had 'hired' horse carcases from a local abattoir for the day, returning them after filming was complete.

Episode 1 of the serial was transmitted at 5.50 p.m. on Sunday, 6 September 1987 on BBC-1, with subsequent episodes each Sunday until 20 December. There were high hopes within the production team that audience figures would be excellent: the Sunday teatime Classic Serial slot was well-established; the newspaper previews and publicity features had been promising; and virtually everyone

Table 8.1   Average viewing figures for Sunday Classic Serials

1985	*Oliver Twist*	8.3 million
1986	*Brat Farrar*	7.6 million
1986	*Alice in Wonderland*	5.9 million
1986	*David Copperfield*	6.3 million
1987	*The Diary of Anne Frank*	8.3 million

Table 8.2   Average viewing figures (in millions) for *Vanity Fair*, by episode

1	6 September	6.1
2	13 September	3.9
3	20 September	3.6
4	27 September	3.6
5	4 October	4.5
6	11 October	4.8
7	18 October	5.0
8	25 October	6.1
9	1 November	5.8
10	8 November	3.5
11	15 November	5.6
12	22 November	5.5
13	29 November	4.9
14	6 December	5.4
15	13 December	5.4
16	20 December	5.4
	Average viewing figure	5.0

within the BBC who had viewed the tapes before transmission had been highly complimentary.

Recent average viewing figures for Sunday Classic Serials had been those shown in Table 8.1. The *Vanity Fair* viewing figures for each episode were as shown in Table 8.2 Though quite respectable, these figures were nevertheless somewhat disappointing. While some weekly variation in a long serial is to be expected, caused in this case by occasional bright, warm Sunday evenings of early Autumn, and live coverage of the concluding stages of a golf tournament on another channel, the weekly average of 5 million viewers was still the lowest of recent Classic Serials. There seem to be two major reasons. First, there had arisen a false expectation that the Sunday teatime slot was somehow a cosy Dickens feature – not an angry political Dickens, but a sentimental, melodramatic one. Clearly, *Vanity Fair* with its cynicism and sexual innuendo, would not suit all Sunday teatime family audiences. The other problem seemed to have been the 16 half-hour episodes. A 16-episode serial requires considerable viewer commitment and staying power, and many criticized the half-hour episode as too short.

Wiser with hindsight, the BBC is, at the time of writing, well-advanced with plans to re-edit the serial into ten fifty-minute episodes, restoring some of the material which had to be deleted during the initial edit for thirty-minute episodes; and now the intention is to transmit the serial later on a weekday evening, recognizing that an adult audience rather than a family audience will appreciate better the subtleties of the plot.

There are clearly some problems with this re-edit, since, for example, the endings of revised episodes will obviously not coincide with the originally transmitted version. However, the estimated costs in repeat artists' fees is approximately a quarter of a million pounds, which makes the revised eight-hour serial comparatively cheap in terms of peak-time drama.

The generally very favourable reviews for the first transmission of the serial would certainly seem to justify the revised repeat: 'perfectly cast, and entertainingly adapted' (*Stage and Television Today*, 3 September); 'A frilly cut above most serialisations' (*City Limits* 2–9 September); 'Teatime on BBC-1 for the next 15 Sundays will be sheer bliss' (*Daily Mail*, 7 September); 'Beautifully designed, exquisitely dressed, and ably acted' (*Punch*, 16 September); 'In Eve Matheson, Becky has found her perfect embodiment' (*Listener*, 10 September). The *Daily Telegraph* for 7 September described the serial as 'standard BBC highly professional costume drama'. On the other hand, *The Times* for 26 October commented: 'The serial has succeeded handsomely in reducing Thackeray to a weekly slice of rich fruitcake', while the *Guardian* on 19 December compared it to a restored country house:

The television dramatisation of classic novels has much in common with the restoration of dilapidated country houses. Both achieve the same superficial verisimilitude – the same characters, the same facades – but also the same utter transformation into something else whose information is ordered in a different way.

The serial was also reviewed on Radio 4's *Kaleidoscope* on 17 September, in which the critic Anne Karpf was wholly complimentary about all aspects of the production: 'It's part of the BBC's role as a kind of cultural broker to the nation, and yet this is such a lively powerful production, that it doesn't seem at all dated. Long may they go on.'

The *Listener* for 17–24 December informed its readers that *Vanity Fair* was chosen by the Home Secretary, Douglas Hurd, as his 'programme of the year', and the *Daily Mirror* on 9 January 1988, that the Prime Minister, Mrs Thatcher, had asked the BBC to send her video cassettes of all 16 episodes for her Christmas viewing. As Anne Karpf said on *Kaleidoscope*:

Of course, in some ways, it's a very appropriate message for an era where a grocer's daughter from Grantham has made good. I mean in some sense, Becky Sharp is the bespoke heroine for the 1980s.

The transmission of *Vanity Fair* also produced the usual crop of letters from viewers, both to the Production Office, and to the *Radio Times*. Most were highly complimentary; others enquired about details in the production:

My interest here is in the oval pictures which appeared on the walls of the Sedley home. I have a complete set of stipple engravings of these pictures. . . .

Whilst others drew attention to supposed anachronisms in the production:

'A thing of beauty is a joy forever', called out the autioneer in Vanity Fair (4 October) selling the belongings of Mr Sedley who had lost everything following Napoleon's escape from Elba in 1815. John Keats wasn't published until 1818. Never mind – I've enjoyed the serial. [(Mrs) S. M. Fry, Gainsborough, Lincolnshire]

Congratulations on the 'few minutes of credible nastiness' in Vanity Fair (25th October). What was unfortunately not credible, as usual, was the non-recoiling artillery. Old guns produce lots of smoke as shown, then a violent recoil, either backwards or upwards. When filming, a similar effect could be produced by an idle extra with an out of shop piece of rope. . . . [Ian Sinclair, Norwich]

Moustaches in the British Army of 1814! No Sir! The majority of British troops during the Napoleonic Wars were clean-shaven and it was also a regulation that side whiskers were not permitted to extend below the bottom of the ear. The only regiments of the army allowed moustaches were the Second (Royal North British) Dragoons, all regiments of Hussars (8th, 10th, 11th and 18th) and officers of the Rifle Brigade. Moustaches only came into general wear in the British Army during the Crimean War, some 40 years after the period shown in BBC1's otherwise excellent serial. [(Mr) R. J. White]

Captain Rawdon Crawley should have worn his cartouche belt across his left shoulder and not his right as he was wont to do. The portrait of him on the staircase at the family residence was correct and complies with dress regulations. [G.M. Payne, Clevedon, Avon]

Many other viewers, resisting the urge to write to the producer, bought or borrowed the book. Joanna Webb of Pan Books (see the interview with her in Chapter 6) has described the massive increase in sales of the paperback edition to coincide with the transmission. We conducted a sample survey of all the major lending libraries in one representative area of England – Dorset and West Hampshire. In every case library staff reported noticeable increases in borrowings and requests for books dramatized on television, with a lesser response for cinema dramatizations. *Brideshead Revisited* and *The Thorn Birds* were both mentioned several times as dramatizations which had provoked considerable response; the serialization of *Vanity Fair* produced a steady stream of requests and borrowings at most of the libraries surveyed, with as one respondent summarized it: 'Much new interest in a neglected masterpiece, previously languishing on our shelves!'

BBC Enterprises are responsible for marketing, selling, and distributing BBC programmes to overseas broadcasting companies, and to other commercial organizations. In the past, for example, they have released video cassettes of BBC Classic Serials such as *Sense and Sensibility* for domestic hire and sales. Because of the length of *Vanity Fair*, at eight hours, there are no plans to issue it as domestic video cassettes. However, there are high hopes that it will achieve good sales abroad and thus recoup some of the investment which BBC Enterprises made in the production. Previous Classic Serials have achieved impressive sales figures. For example, *Sense and Sensibility*, transmitted on BBC-1 in 1981, has been sold to Caribbean Broadcasting Corporation, Cyprus Broadcasting Corporation, Dubai Radio and Colour TV, Arab Republic of Egypt TV, Radio Telefis Eirean, Gibraltar Broadcasting Corporation, Israel Instructional TV, Jamaica Broadcasting Corporation, Jordan Television, Mauritius Broadcasting Corporation, Television New Zealand, Nigerian Television Authority, Norsk Rikskringkasting (Norway), Pakistan Television Corporation, Qatar Television, Singapore Broadcasting Corporation, Swaziland TV Broadcasting Corporation, and Taiwan Government Information Office.

In the United States, Masterpiece Theatre transmits many of the BBC's Classic Serials, earning in excess of 2 million dollars for the BBC in 1987. John Reynolds of BBC Enterprises Co-Productions has commented:

It's a big glossy slot with which its funder, Mobil Oil, wishes to be associated; they need to be assured that very strong and expensive-looking production values are on the screen; they are also extremely concerned that it is suitable for a family audience.[1]

He is highly optimistic about sales abroad for *Vanity Fair*:

I have a feeling that this is going to be one of the top sellers because of its sheer lavishness, and the popularity of the title. I think we may be talking of up to 70 countries worldwide; and we're talking of several hundred million viewers over the years – because these serials do have a long life.

And certainly *Vanity Fair*, after its re-editing into longer episodes, and the consequent restructuring of artists' contracts, will be extensively promoted by BBC Enterprises at Showcase, its annual sales forum for overseas television buyers.

The *Independent* on February 1988 reported that Niu Zu Yin, vice

Director-General of the television station serving Guandon Province in China, with 50 million viewers, had said: 'Our station has already shown BBC productions of literary classics and would like to buy another, Vanity Fair, but its price is too high.'

Thackeray would no doubt have appreciated that his mid-nineteenth-century novel of English society was in the late twentieth century entertaining Chinese audiences, albeit in a dubbed television serialization.

Note

1. John Reynolds, *The Media Show*, Channel 4 TV, May 1987.

Index